"Julie Rowe r............................................ biological warfare & it's as exhilarating as ever."
—*Night Owl Romance*, Top Pick, 5 stars, on *Viral Justice*

"*Viral Justice* was an awesome read. I'll definitely be picking up the first two books in this series."
—*The Romance Reviews*, 5 stars

"*Deadly Strain* is a gripping, terrifying hybrid that combines suspense with romance without compromising either aspect of the story."
—*RT Book Reviews*, 4.5 stars

"Danger and desire mix in the perfect balance that kept me glued to my ereader all night.... I'm hooked and I believe you will be too."
—*Night Owl Reviews*, Top Pick, 4.5 stars, on *Lethal Game*

"Julie Rowe writes with a fast-paced, engaging style full of emotional honesty. Her three-dimensional characters are sure to tug at your heartstrings."
—*New York Times* and *USA TODAY* bestselling author Lori Wilde

"Julie Rowe blends the perfect cocktail of action and romance."
—*New York Times* bestselling author Brenda Novak on *Icebound*

# JULIE ROWE

# VIRAL JUSTICE

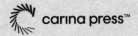

carina press™

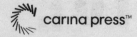 carina press™

ISBN-13: 978-0-373-00477-5

Recycling programs
for this product may
not exist in your area.

Viral Justice

Copyright © 2016 by Julie Rowe

www.CarinaPress.com

**Printed in U.S.A.**

To my daughter Megan—
for your help and inspiration.

# VIRAL JUSTICE

There are very few monsters who warrant the fear we have of them.

~ Andre Gide

# ONE

"THEY'RE NOT GOING to agree with your plan, Colonel," Alicia muttered as she stared at the group of military doctors standing several feet away.

Colonel Robert Maximillian, head of the US Army Biological Response Team, bent closer to the tiny, curvy Sergeant Alicia Stone and had to clear his throat before asking, "What makes you say that?"

"Look at their body language," she continued in that almost subvocal whisper. "They've closed ranks and you're on the outside."

He had to consciously hold himself still as he studied the group of men. Military doctors from five different countries. They were positioned in a tight circle, two with their backs to him, talking quietly. All of them stood at just a hair under attention. The faces he could see were set, eyes serious. Understandable. These were dangerous times, and their mutual enemy could be anyone, even someone in your own army.

Stone shifted and her shoulder brushed his arm.

His attraction to the sergeant was irrational and impossible. He wasn't a fan of either.

"They're having a simple conversation, Sergeant, nothing more."

"I've been on the receiving end of that kind of conversation," Stone said, her voice filled with enough acid to melt steel. "If they wanted to include you, they'd have left a space for you to step into, but they didn't. They've already decided and they know you're not going to like their decision."

"That's ridiculous." He knew every man in the group and had earned their respect. "They're professionals and they know I have new information for them."

"It isn't going to matter. Their minds are made up." Stone's voice was so sharp he stopped to really look at her.

"What happened?" he asked her.

"It's not what happened, but what's *not* going to happen that's the problem, sir."

"No." He waved away the reference to the meeting they were about to attend. "I mean, with you. I don't think I've ever seen you this angry before."

"Me, angry?" she said with wide eyes that did nothing to hide the displeasure on the rest of her face. "I'm *grateful*, sir, to be the only female combat trainer for the Special Forces." Her tone made it clear she was anything but grateful.

"Did you break another officer's arm?" Four months ago, an asshole who'd thought he was some kind of martial arts expert had tried to intimidate Stone during a training session. She'd put him on the mats twice before he got angry and attacked for real, thinking she couldn't handle an actual fight. She'd not only broken his arm, but two fingers of the opposite hand, as well.

The incident hadn't ended there. The officer had accused her of assault, but with so many witnesses the charges against Stone had been thrown out, and *he'd* been charged with assault. Since then, however, at least two other officers had lodged formal complaints against her.

The old boys' club, closing ranks.

"Nothing that would show up on an X-ray." Her voice sounded bland. Something had gone very wrong.

If someone hurt her, he was going to find out and make their life miserable. "Is there anything I can do to help?"

She jerked, as if the question startled her. "Don't argue with me if I tell you to do something."

"Arguing with one's bodyguard would be stupid. I try not to be an idiot more than twice a day. I reached my quota an hour ago." Yet, he always seemed to butt heads with her whenever they were involved in the same operation, even if it was just a meeting. Having her as a bodyguard for any great length of time would be uncomfortable at best.

She blinked.

He consulted his watch as several light armored vehicles pulled up nearby. "Gentlemen, I appreciate your early arrival," he called out to the five men. "The summit is scheduled to begin in an hour. Several more countries than expected have sent representatives. As a result the meeting has been moved to a larger venue." He gestured at the waiting vehicles. "If you would? We'll travel together."

Their cluster broke apart and they got into vehicles.

When he glanced back, Stone was staring after him with a profoundly confused expression on her face.

Max rode with Franz Meyer, chief medical officer for the German Army, while Stone got into the vehicle behind his with his British counterpart.

"Militants invaded another Kurdish village in Northern Iraq today." Franz sounded tired. "At least seventy-five dead and an unknown number of women and girls taken." He shook his head. "Last night a group of refugees attempted to cross the border between Bulgaria and Hungary. At least thirty died in a series of fires started by Molotov cocktails they threw themselves."

*Stupid.* Human beings had a great capacity for stupidity. "The unrest isn't making any of our jobs easier. Which is why we need countries around the world, not just in Europe or the Middle East, to agree to implement a global vaccination plan."

"But, do you understand the pressure we're all under?" Franz turned to him, suddenly intent. "We can't fight a war against an enemy we can't see. Your proposal is simply too expensive."

"We're facing a new era of biological weapons." Max made direct eye contact with him. "Weapons that are in the hands of people who can and will use them against any target they choose."

"We can't arbitrarily begin a counteroffensive against an enemy we aren't aware of yet," Franz replied. "We have to have more information, more proof than two isolated incidents."

Had he *read* the reports? "Akbar isn't an incident. He's a mass murderer who's just getting started. Treating the sick after the fact is what'll be expensive. You can't just ignore the problem because no one is sure how to pay for it."

"What I'm saying is, where do we start?" Franz spread his hands in a conciliatory gesture that didn't fool Max for a second. "Which do you feel is more important, training existing medical staff, or increasing staff numbers in both military and civilian medical aid groups in Africa and the Middle East? We can't afford to do both."

He held on to his temper with both hands. Stone was right. Franz had already made up his mind.

He had maybe ten more minutes to make his case before they arrived at their destination. Once there, he'd have to repeat his arguments to healthcare leaders from all over Europe, Africa, the Middle East and Asia. Franz had probably thought he was going to catch Max by surprise by asking the question now, but Max had been considering solutions to the problem of worldwide infectious disease control for a long time. Ten minutes might just be enough time to change the German's thinking.

There were other delegates in the vehicles in front and behind them, along with a military escort to keep trouble at bay. The decisions about to be made at this meeting would have a long reach, and there were many groups, extremists of one sort or another, who would do their best to disrupt and destroy any agreements or resolutions.

Max answered without hesitation. "Both." He met his German counterpart's gaze squarely. "If Akbar and Ebola have taught us anything, it's that no one country, or even a few countries, can handle a large outbreak alone. There will be a domino effect and the resulting chaos will take even more lives. When the Spanish flu circulated the world one hundred years ago, it took a year and a half to make the trip. Now, it might take a week." Max shook his head. "We can't afford to do the minimum, Franz. There's no time to build the support system *after* the next deadly outbreak occurs."

"But the cost…"

"The current cost of Ebola is estimated to be two point two billion dollars. That's just monetary. We lost a lot of doctors, nurses and other healthcare workers too. It's going to take years for Guinea, Liberia and Sierra Leone to replace those people. If they get hit by a second wave, or a new infection, they've got no more than a skeleton crew to handle it. Which means it won't be handled. It'll be chaos." Max shook his head. "With the Middle East hemorrhaging refugees into Europe, no one is in a position to help without a lot of prep time."

"We can't afford the plan you propose—" Franz began.

Max cut him off with a diagonal slash of his hand. "Then help me find another way."

The German sighed. "I agree with you on principle, but without an imminent threat, my government won't agree to spend that much time and money on an event that might never happen."

Their vehicle slowed and the soldier driving it yelled back to them, "We've got an accident in front of us, sirs. I'll have to take another route."

"That's fine, Corporal." Max turned to Franz, determined to see the German's not-quite-no as an almost-yes. "We start with a framework, an infrastructure—"

Shots and yelling from outside the vehicle cut him off. Their driver stomped on the brakes.

"What's going on?" Max demanded.

The young soldier never had the chance to answer.

The vehicle in front of them exploded.

For a long moment, the world disintegrated into white noise.

Slowly, his vision and hearing returned. But nothing made sense. Smoke obscured everything, and there was such an uproar of shouting and sirens, he wasn't even sure where he was.

Another, much smaller explosion farther away pulled him back into focus. Their vehicle was damaged—how badly wasn't clear—and the way ahead was impassable.

He turned to ask Franz if he was all right and found the German slumped against the seat, blood dripping from his head.

*Blood doesn't flow when you're dead.*

He put his fingers on Franz's carotid pulse and found it strong and steady.

*Thank God.*

Flames from the front of their vehicle caught his attention. They weren't safe yet.

He kicked his door open, then dragged Franz out and back down the street several feet. He went back for the driver, but the young man's head was all but disarticulated from his body by a piece of twisted metal.

*Son of a bitch.*

Max looked at the remains of the lead vehicle, but what was left was little more than a chassis covered in bent metal and melted plastic. No one could have survived that.

*Stone.*

Fear sank an ice pick into his gut. He whipped around to look at the vehicle behind his and saw her running with the men from her vehicle, returning to the base.

Relief burned away the cold, allowing him to breathe again.

Good, the survivors needed to evacuate in case of a follow-up attack.

Shouts from the other side of the flames grabbed his attention, but no one appeared. He turned to check Franz and discovered Ali running toward him, her rifle in her hands. "Max?" she yelled.

"What are you doing here?" he demanded. "I thought you were escorting the others to safety."

"They're in good hands." She glanced at Franz and the blood on Max's uniform. "You're the one who needs backup."

He couldn't argue the point. That didn't mean he liked it.

"Are you okay?" He put his hands on her shoulders, sliding them down and over her body to check for injuries.

"I'm good," she said, wiggling away from him to inspect him instead. "Are you? Is this your blood?"

"No, it's Franz's blood. Head wounds often bleed profusely."

"Help is on its way. Did you see what happened?"

"No."

She stared at the remains of the lead vehicle with narrowed eyes. "If we were anywhere else, I'd say that was the result of an IED."

"It could have been," Max said. "The Boston bombing was a homemade device." He looked around. "Any injuries in your vehicle?"

"Nothing besides a few bumps and bruises."

Another explosion had both of them ducking and stepping back from the flames and smoke.

A bullet struck the mess of debris where he'd been standing a moment ago. A second later, Stone took him by the arm and yanked him behind the wreck of his vehicle.

Stone snapped her rifle into position and fired back, but the bullets kept coming. "Get to cover," she yelled at him.

Not without her. "You too!"

"Max," she barked. "What did I say about arguing? Get the *fuck* out of here, before *I* kick your ass."

She was right. He could be an idiot later.

Max ducked and found himself using the smoking wreckage to hide from more bullets coming in short bursts all around him. He managed to get back to Franz and move the unconscious man into a sheltered doorway, but he still couldn't determine where the shooter was. There was probably more than one.

Goddamn it, he didn't have time to be assassinated. He had too much to do.

Movement from beyond the remains of the lead vehicle caught his attention, and a man—no, a boy, barely a teenager—walked slowly and calmly through the rubble and ruined vehicles. A bulky package was strapped to his chest and his gaze searched for someone or something.

The boy saw Alicia, but he didn't do anything threatening. In fact, he backed away from her, hugged the wall of the building behind him and kept moving.

That retreat from her, from blowing himself up, was probably the only thing that stopped Alicia from shooting him.

Who the hell would use a child as a suicide bomber?

Extremists, fanatics, madmen. It didn't matter what anyone called them, they were dead men if Max got his hands on them.

He'd taken a vow to preserve life, but the kind of animals who could plan and execute this terrible act of horror, with a *child* as a weapon, could not be allowed to continue breathing.

That wasn't going to improve his immediate situation. The boy was still walking forward and appeared to be looking for something. A target? In a moment, Max and Franz were going to be visible.

He sucked in a deep breath and prepared to leave the relative safety of the doorway. Perhaps he could talk the boy into surrendering. Franz and Alicia would have no doubt argued with him about that plan, but the German was still out cold and Alicia too far away.

He stood and walked toward the teen.

The young man saw him and took a second to stare at Max. An expression of recognition and fear flashed across the boy's face, and Max knew he was in trouble.

Someone had sent a child to kill him.

If he walked away, would the kid follow? How close did the bomber want to get before detonating the explosives? If there were no eyes on the boy, could he be convinced to abandon his mission?

Max sidestepped away from the doorway, then walked backward. "You don't have to do this," he called to the boy. "We can help you, keep you safe."

The boy followed, picking up his pace to close the distance between them. "They said they will kill my sister and brother if I don't," the boy said, his voice bleak and hopeless.

Max was about to turn and run when the young man jerked once, and pitched forward to land on his hands.

Someone had shot the would-be bomber, wounded him.

Shots pinged off the stone wall of the building behind Max and peppered the area around the child bomber. At least one of them hit the boy and he crumpled. Max ducked and ran back to the relative safety of the doorway where he'd left Franz.

Return fire halted the rain of bullets. Max waited for more, but none materialized.

Had Stone taken out the shooter? Or was he being lured out into the open?

He glanced back at Franz. A sizable blood pool had formed around the man's head. His head wound might be worse than Max had first thought.

Since no one had fired any shots at him for nearly half a minute, he took a chance and rushed back to their vehicle and pulled a first aid kit from the rear seat. It looked completely intact. He ran back to Franz, put on a pair of gloves and began searching for the source of the bleeding. It didn't take long to find a deep five- or six-inch long cut along the back of the German's head.

He pulled out a roll of gauze and a large non-stick pad, and proceeded to carefully stanch the bleeding.

The sound of several pairs of booted feet running toward his hiding place had him glancing up.

A contingent of soldiers in US Army uniforms surfaced out of the smoke.

"I need a medical team here now." Max didn't wait for a reply, but concentrated on getting the bleeding under control.

American soldiers filtered through the area, some to look for more bodies, others to investigate, while some stood watch. He ignored them until he had Franz ready to transport. By that time a group of combat medics had arrived and they were able to take the German soldier away to a nearby hospital.

Max searched the wreckage for more injured, but everyone still alive had been identified by the medics, and was in various stages of being removed from the area.

"What the hell are you still doing here?" Stone demanded.

He turned and stared at her and the rifle she carried, a sick feeling churning his gut. "Did you shoot the suicide bomber?"

"I wounded him. The sniper who was trying to nail your ass from the roof over there finished the kid off." She stepped up to him and poked his chest with a finger. "You're lucky I shot that asshole before he shot you. I also saw you step away from cover and allow that bomber to ID you." She paused, then asked with heavily laden sarcasm, "Do you have a death wish, Colonel?"

If he did, he wasn't alone. "You're the one who stayed out in the open to play shooter."

# TWO

ALICIA WANTED TO strangle him. She settled for yelling. "I wasn't the target."

"Our vehicles were full of targets, including you." He looked at her like he wanted to strip her naked and inspect her for bruises. "We can't know if the bomber was supposed to eliminate any one person or just as many as possible."

"Why didn't you leave when I told you to?"

"Franz was bleeding out."

"Saving others at the cost of your own safety is stupid."

He looked at her like she was crazy. "That's my job."

"Throwing your life away isn't part of your job." She poked him in the chest again. "I think you were the target. Everything else was collateral damage."

"We have no proof of that."

She gritted her teeth. "I'm sure we'll find it."

"Why does that matter?"

The man wasn't stubborn, he was willfully blind to threats to his safety. "Akbar isn't just looking for any target. He's fixed his sights on you."

Max pressed his lips together. "Don't get ahead of the facts. We don't know that he's behind this."

"Don't dismiss me, damn it. I know about the body with the message written to you on it." A gruesome find, discovered at the scene of a bombing, a massacre of civilians in Afghanistan a week ago. It warned that the wrath of God was coming, and had been addressed to Colonel Maximillian, US Army. That kind of death threat could derail even the most pragmatic man.

His gaze softened and he put a hand on her arm to guide her away from the carnage. "While I appreciate your concern, I won't avoid doing my duty because it's dangerous, or because someone attempts to kill me. I'll be careful and I won't do anything without making sure I'm performing that task as safely as possible." He stopped and smiled ruefully at her. "I'm a soldier. Danger comes with the job."

This from a man with few to no combat skills. "Max," she said, crossing her arms over her chest. "Planning for an attack only gets you as far as the first contact with the enemy. After that, no plan can keep up with the changing conditions. I've seen your shooting scores and I've faced you on the mats. You couldn't fight your way out of a paper bag. You're important. *General* Stone says that you've got one of the toughest and most important jobs in the army right now. He can't afford to lose you."

He sighed. "Blunt, but true." He shrugged, but didn't say anything else for several seconds.

His face was blank as he stared into space, and she could almost hear the cacophony of thoughts racing around in his head. Would he ignore her concerns, or take them seriously?

Finally he asked, "What do you suggest?"

"You need more training and a permanent bodyguard." What he really needed was head-to-toe body armor.

He snorted and stepped away from her. "I don't have

time for more training or a tag-along. I need several clones just to get my current workload done and still sleep once every few days."

She followed. "I guarantee the person assigned to you would slide into your team without any trouble."

He gave her a sour look. "You? I thought you swore never to leave your current position? Something about the rest of the army being too pansy ass for you."

"What can I say?" she said with a toothy grin. "I like a challenge."

"Lovely." His tightly pressed lips told her he wasn't happy with the situation at all. Would he argue against it?

"You need me, Max," she said, dropping the smile to show she was serious. "Don't fight me on this."

"According to you, I can't fight at all."

Alicia ran one hand over her face. "We can change that." If only she could do something about her own problems.

Max watched her with a frown on his face. "What am I missing? According to everyone, you love your job with the Special Forces. Why are you even considering this?"

He deserved the truth.

"I've gotten myself into some trouble in the past few months." She was going to have to explain it. *Fuck*.

"What kind of trouble?" Max asked slowly.

"Butting heads with a couple of officers." She sighed. "Complaints have been made."

"*Official* complaints?"

"Yes."

"And your father is…"

"General Stone does not practice favoritism."

"Bullshit."

Alicia turned to stare at Max. He seldom swore. "He's done as much as he can, but when I screw up, I really screw up. And now, today—"

"Today, you saved my life and Franz's life." Max's voice was filled with righteous indignation.

"And I did it by disobeying an order from the British Army's chief medical officer. It's one more nail in my coffin."

Max stared at her for a moment then muttered something under his breath. She only caught a couple of words, *stubborn* and *idiots*, but it was more than anyone else had said. He seemed to think about it for several moments, then looked at her and said, "I'll make the request for your training skills. Try to stay out of trouble."

"Yes, sir. Though trouble seems to have no problem finding me."

A MONTH LATER, Max hunkered down in the dirt, tucked his rifle into the hollow of his shoulder and waited for his target to show himself. The conditions were good, visibility excellent and no wind. Max had only to wait.

The enemy popped up. Max released a breath, then squeezed out three quick shots.

"You missed," a woman said from behind him. "All three shots."

Max's gut tightened at the sound of her voice. He looked over his shoulder at his personal peanut gallery. Sergeant Alicia Stone.

"I expected you three weeks ago," he said loud enough to be heard despite the hearing protection they were both wearing. "What took you so long?"

Her mouth tightened. "I was unexpectedly delayed, sir."

That was word for word what General Stone said when Max had asked him why his daughter was going to be weeks late in joining Max's team.

Word for word meant the answer had been carefully chosen. Chosen responses were used in three situations in the army: As a non-answer to a question that shouldn't have been asked in the first place. As a calculated response regarding a political or public relations messy event. Or as avoidance of a harmful incident. Which one was this?

Stone excelled in her role as a trainer for the Special Forces combatives program, but she had one major failing. She never hesitated to call anyone she was training on their mistakes, regardless of rank.

She was about to stomp all over him thanks to his.

He *was* a lousy shot.

He secured his weapon, then removed his ear protection.

"I knew you were a terrible shot, but this is beyond my lowest expectations." She looked at him like he was some kind of insect. "How did you qualify to carry your sidearm with aim like that?"

"A great deal of practice." He glanced at the rifle he held. "This is not my preferred weapon."

"You actually have one you like?"

She was pushing it.

He stood and looked at her, altogether enjoying how far back she had to tilt her head to maintain eye contact with him. This woman was a force of nature with a personality to match. To allow her to see weakness was foolhardy at best.

"My tongue," he said, staring at her mouth. "Weren't you the one who said I could flay a private alive with it?"

The corners of her lips twitched. "I don't know many extremists who'll take the time to sit down and have a conversation with one of us."

She'd said *us*. The flash of humor soothed something tense inside him. "Well, I've got one of them sending me letters. That's a start." He'd received six, filled with rhetoric and raving about a holy war. That wasn't counting the threats addressed to him, written on dead bodies left where they were sure to be found.

"No, someone is attempting to create fear by including flour inside the envelope to make you think they're sending anthrax," she said with concern.

He shrugged that away. "We know how to handle anthrax. It's the dead bodies that have me worried."

"The point I'm trying to make is that you need to be prepared to defend yourself, which is impossible with aim like that." She gestured at the target he'd missed a whole lot more than three times. "I knew you had terrible aim, but this is so bad, I have serious doubts about your ability to defend yourself in any situation." For the first time since she arrived, she didn't sound like she was accusing him of anything.

She did have a point. "I'm open to suggestions."

"It'll have to keep. We're expected by the general in his office in ten minutes." She came to attention and stared at his Adam's apple as any good soldier would do when addressing a senior officer.

"Very good, thank you, Sergeant."

She saluted and he saluted back.

Max exited the range with Stone behind him, then they went their separate ways.

He returned to his very drab and banal-looking building that contained his office and lab. The inside was anything but drab and banal. He had a fully equipped level-four containment lab, allowing him to work with some of the most deadly bacteria and viruses in the world.

He stowed his weapon in the locker in his office, cleaned up, and stopped to talk with his assistant, Private Eugene Walsh, who was just hanging up the phone. "I'll be busy for the next couple of hours with General Stone."

"Sir," Eugene said. "That was General Stone on the phone. He's on his way over here for your meeting."

"Ah. Excellent, thank you."

Max sat down at his desk and retrieved the latest email from Dr. Sophia Perry, a physician on his biological response team. She and her partner, Special Forces Weapons Sergeant Connor Button, were currently training medical teams from Afghanistan to respond to disease outbreaks. That was their official mission. Unofficially, they were attempting to track the movements of a very dangerous extremist—a chemist who'd lost his family in an American air strike on known terrorists in Syria.

No one had known Akbar's family was in the same hotel.

Since then, Akbar had attempted to deploy biological weapons twice. Once with weaponized anthrax and a second time with a modified rabies virus. His known body count now approaches two thousand dead. In his last attempt, he'd tried to kidnap Dr. Perry and force her to modify his rabies virus, but she'd blown up her lab to prevent that from happening. Unfortunately Akbar had escaped with relatively minor injuries.

There was a brief knock at the door. Eugene opened it and said, "General Stone and Sergeant Stone to see you, sir."

"Very good, Private."

Eugene disappeared and the two Stones came in and closed the door.

General Stone glanced at the two chairs in front of Max's desk and raised his eyebrows before grunting his appreciation.

Why such surprise?

Observing the two of them as they sat and looked at him made it clear. They were both astonished an officer of Max's rank would show a woman of her rank any deference.

"Sir, Sergeant." Max greeted them both with a nod. "I've been expecting you for a few weeks."

"I apologize for the length of time it took to get Sergeant Stone to you," the general said. "I hadn't anticipated the difficulty in arranging for replacements for her in the Special Operations training program. There was also some unanticipated red tape to getting her properly transferred."

"No apology necessary, sir." Max nodded at her. "I'd been warned by Demolitions Sergeant Smoke that it might be longer than initially thought. Sergeant Stone is highly respected."

The Stone in question blinked in surprise.

"It's good to know that boy can do more than grunt," the general said.

"Have you had time to read Dr. Perry's latest report?" Max asked, examining Alicia's expression. Something about her reactions was bothering him.

"Slippery bastard," General Stone muttered. "No clue as to what disease he's planning to use as his next weapon?"

"Not so far, no. I'm afraid that there are too many possibilities. He's proven to be adept at manipulating very complex organisms, though he's had no formal training in how to handle them. He's taking a lot of risks, not the least of which is accidently releasing a biological weapon in a highly populated area."

"How probable is that threat?" Sergeant Stone asked.

"If you're looking for a number, I can't give you one, but if it happens I won't be surprised."

"He's insane," she said almost to herself.

"Yes." Max thought the same. "A very dangerous sort of insanity. He's highly intelligent and without a conscience. It's not a matter of *if* he'll attack again, it's *where* and *when*." He paused, then added, "I think it will be soon."

"We're starting to see small outbreaks of cholera in some of the refugee camps in various places in the Middle East. The CIA has intel saying these camps are prime targets for the same extremists we think are supporting Akbar," General Stone said. "The problem is, we can't send in troops. These are countries who haven't asked for military assistance."

"Unless they start dying by the hundreds." Max was unable to hide the rough edge that eventuality put into his voice. "Then they'll call us, but it will be too late."

The general turned to his daughter. "Are you clear on your assignment?" There was a note of reprimand in the general's voice. What the hell was going on?

"Bodyguard and liaison for Colonel Maximillian with Special Forces," she replied, her back as flexible as a steel rod.

"Yes, and see if you can get him to shoot straight. I'd hate to lose him because he can't hit what he's aiming at."

"Why don't you just shoot me?" Max suggested sarcastically.

"No," General Stone said with an oddly flat expression. "I like you just the way you are. Alive."

"Has there been a specific threat against me made?"

"Dead bodies with your name on them not enough?" The general stood. "The sergeant will fill you in on the latest. Keep in touch." General Stone exited the office, closing the door behind him.

Max turned to her. "The latest?"

Sergeant Stone nodded. "The general has friends in the CIA. Your name keeps coming up in connection with several dangerous people."

"I suspected, but had hoped I was just being paranoid."

"Be all the paranoid you want. It might help keep you alive."

"You're full of happy thoughts today," Max said, examining her expression. "What happened?"

"Nothing good." She closed her mouth after those two words and pressed her lips together.

Fine. She didn't want to talk.

He wasn't the only stubborn one.

"Come on, I'll introduce you to my aide." He gestured at the door and she got to her feet. "We're a tight group, on a first name basis unless we're out in the general base population. How would you prefer to be addressed?"

She relaxed. It was subtle, mostly in her shoulders, but still noticeable. "Not Super Bitch."

Max couldn't keep his eyebrows from rising. "Someone called you that to your face?"

She laughed. It lasted only a moment, but the change in her demeanor was astonishing, as if she'd removed a layer of plain brown paper to reveal the hidden work of art beneath. "Not anymore." Before his eyes, she pulled the wrappings back around her, hiding the warm woman behind the uniform again. "Stick with Stone."

Max took in a breath, filed the incident away into a special section of his mind labeled *Alicia Stone*, and said with a nod, "Good, Stone." He led the way out of his office and stopped at Eugene's desk. "Private Walsh is my personal assistant."

Stone shook his hand.

"Call me Eugene or Gene," he said.

"Stone," she told him.

"Eugene always knows where to find me," Max explained. "Not sure how he does it, but…" He shrugged.

"Good to know there's a GPS for you, sir," Stone said.

"Max." He permitted a grin before he said, "Eugene, I'm taking Stone on a tour of the lab. I have my phone if you need me."

"Very good, sir," Eugene said, reclaiming his seat.

She leaned slightly toward him and said, "He called you 'sir.'"

Max leaned toward her and replied in the same quiet voice, "He's only got one or two bad habits. Calling me sir every once in a while is one of them."

"I was raised to be polite to my elders." Eugene said it without a trace of humor.

Stone laughed, while Max gave him a sour look.

Max set off toward the lab with Stone at his side. "So," he said casually, "what *didn't* the general tell me?"

A rueful smile came and went across her face. "Remember that suicide bomber I shot in Germany? It turns out there's a bounty on you. A big one. You're on the hit list of every mercenary and warlord in this part of the world."

# THREE

"How expensive am I?" Colonel Maximillian asked, one corner of his mouth crooking upward.

His smile melted something cold and hard inside Alicia. She couldn't relax her guard around many people, but Max was different. It frustrated the hell out of her sometimes, but he was honest with her. He didn't play games or tell her what he thought she wanted to hear. She'd had enough of *that* to last her a lifetime.

It didn't hurt that he radiated confidence and intelligence. Unless he was in the shooting range or in combat training. There he looked like a duck out of water, ungainly and awkward.

The contrast was jarring. Max was an irresistible puzzle, one she was determined to solve.

"More than what I'd pay for you, that's for sure."

"Sometimes I'm not sure you like me at all," he said with a glance her way.

She had to work to keep a smile off her face. "Of course I like you—you're a US Army asset."

"Nothing is ever going to be simple with you, is it?"

The question seemed mostly rhetorical, but she answered anyway. "People appreciate the things they work for," she told him, using the same tone her grandmother had used when she told Alicia the same thing during her first year in the army.

"Will our entire conversation be in fortune cookie—sized sound bites?" he complained.

Her façade cracked and she laughed. "God, I hope not."

His sense of humor surprised her, always had. He looked so buttoned up and stuffy, but he wasn't either. He was smart, funny and wasn't afraid of suggestions from lower ranks. She'd been impressed by his ability to focus on multiple goals, and achieve them. He was relentless when hunting a disease or containing an outbreak, and frequently got his hands dirty with jobs other men in his position would have given to an underling.

Max didn't assign tasks to anyone else that he wouldn't do himself, and he didn't waste his people or their time on meaningless work.

His inability to defend himself worried her. He was so competent at everything else, she suspected his personal life had something to do with it.

The shit his ex-wife put him through would have turned a saint into a killer. Alicia had witnessed exactly one meeting between them. They were outside a restaurant where Max and Alicia's father were meeting for a meal and a chance to talk away from the base. It was the first time she'd met Max, and his ex was screaming at him about money and shoving him. He said something low and calm, and she punched him in the face.

Twice.

Alicia had run toward the pair, intent on stopping the raging woman, but Max had waved her off, so she got her phone out and hit Record.

He didn't do a damn thing to defend himself, other than attempt to talk to his ex. The woman finally left when Alicia had shouted at her to stop. The cops showed up ready to arrest him for assault an hour later, until she showed them her video recording. They urged him to see a lawyer, but she was pretty sure he hadn't.

Now, he led her through a set of closed double doors. They walked about five feet down a hallway until they reached a row of internal windows. On the other side of the glass was a laboratory. She recognized microscopes, but not much else.

There were four people working inside the room, all of them in space suit—style outfits with hoses extending from the back of their helmets up to the ceiling.

"They have their own air supply?" she asked.

"Yes. The room's air supply is also filtered—scrubbed, really—to ensure that no pathogens get out."

What was in that room was as dangerous as any other weapon. "Do you work in there?"

"Sometimes. I have a fair amount of administrative work that cuts into my lab time."

"How many different pathogens do you have in there?"

"It varies." He was in his comfort zone here, relaxed and self-assured.

The best time to ask a tough question. With a bounty on his head, she needed all the intel she could get.

"Why don't you like guns?"

"Because I…" His voice trailed off. "I became a doctor to save people, not put holes in them." His voice sounded calm and controlled, yet she could see a hint of something that was neither in his eyes.

He turned away to stare through the glass again. "I don't like violence in any of its forms."

"Why did you join the army, then?"

He grinned at her as if everything was normal. As if he hadn't been in the grip of some negative emotion only moments ago. "It does seem counterintuitive, doesn't it?" He extended his hand toward the lab. "This is where real work is being done. Not in the research labs at the Center for Disease Control. We're on the front line of any attack using biological weapons. We can respond faster, diagnose and begin treating in hours. Not days. *Hours.*"

She took a moment to process that. He saw identifying and treating disease as battle? Disease as the enemy? "Your weapons are antibiotics and antiviral drugs?"

His whole face lit up. "Yes." He patted one of her shoulders and gave it an excited shake. "That's it exactly." He stared at her for a long moment, then seemed to remember he had his hand on her and abruptly let go.

For a long time she had thought Max wasn't a warrior, that he didn't have the skills or stomach for combat. She'd been wrong. His field of combat was simply different than hers.

Her mistake.

One she'd fix, starting now.

She glanced around and noted discreetly placed security cameras. "What security precautions are in place for the lab?"

"Good question. Eugene can give you the particulars and have an ID badge made for you so you can move throughout the lab."

"Those doors we came through are locked?"

"At all times."

She nodded. "Good. If you don't mind, I'll familiarize myself with lab security and provide anything else you or your assistant need from me to have me integrated with your group. I'd like to evaluate your hand-to-hand skills later today or tonight."

"They're no better than the last time you wiped the floor with me," he said with a sigh.

"I wasn't in charge of your training the last time. I need more information so I can create a program for you."

"You mean, you're not going to embarrass me in front of a couple dozen soldiers once, but daily?"

"Any soldier who laughs, comments or smiles too wide will get his own chance for embarrassment. After the first week, no one will bother watching anymore."

He winced. "I'm going to be all over the internet, and that crap never disappears."

"No photos allowed. Anyone taking them will face severe penalties." She stopped to frown at him. "You know that."

He pursed his lips like he tasted something awful. "Doesn't help. You know how clumsy I am."

She'd thought his reluctance stemmed from a desire to maintain his dignity in public, but there was something else in his voice. Maybe this wasn't all about his ego. "I've trained people who've never held a gun in their life to become expert snipers. You're smart and you know how to use your hands. By the time I'm done with you, you'll be able to hit your target and defend yourself as well as any soldier."

He stopped and turned to face her, his expression cold. "Have you ever considered the possibility that a man might not *want* to acquire some of those skills? Might find them at odds with his personal beliefs?" He strode off before she could respond.

She followed and ended up at Eugene's desk. Max had retreated into his own office with the door closed.

"Your boss is very good at shutting people down when he's not happy," she said, staring at that closed door.

"He can be intimidating," Eugene agreed. "But he's also the best man I've ever worked for, in or out of the military. He's had my back in a couple of tricky situations."

"Who has his back?"

"Your da…" He cleared his throat. "General Stone."

"Has Max needed the general's help often?" Most people who were good at their job pissed someone off somewhere along the way.

Eugene froze for a second before swallowing and saying, "A few times. Some regular army types. Not everyone agrees with how Colonel Maximillian runs the team. There's been some grumbling since Akbar started his personal war on us. Somehow information has leaked out and we don't know who's doing it or how. But it keeps happening."

"Let's work on that." She liked this kid. He was a good bridge between the team and the rest of the army. "I need to see all the info on the security for this building. I'd like to find out from you if you think there are any holes in it or if any of the staff who work here have mentioned any deficiencies."

Eugene's eyebrows rose. "Okay."

She smiled at him. "My job is to protect Colonel Maximillian. Not just the man, but everything he's accomplished. This team is important. I want to be proactive rather than reactive. Make sense?"

The kid sat up a little straighter. "Yes, ma'am, I mean, Stone."

"Good. So, tell me something I don't know."


COLONEL MAXIMILLIAN WAS CLUMSY, awkward and ungainly.

They'd been sparring for about fifteen minutes and he seemed two seconds behind every move she made.

No matter how hard she put him down, he didn't get angry or the least bit frustrated. It was almost like he wanted to lose. Wanted to have bruises all over his body from getting thrown, tripped and tossed to the mats. She'd never worked with anyone this hesitant, like he was doing it on purpose, and it was starting to piss her off.

She flipped him onto his back, then stepped back to give him room to regain his feet. "Attack me," she ordered.

He froze and frowned. "I've been attacking you for over an hour now."

*Like hell.*

"No. Really attack me."

He shrugged helplessly. "Do you want me to say it in another language?" Then he said it to her in French.

Her hold on her patience slipped and she stepped forward. He responded by moving a pace backward, but she changed her direction with her next move.

He hesitated, his body jerking one way then another as he tried to change direction also, but it was too late. She swept his feet out from under him, then grabbed one arm as she pounced, forcing him onto his back. A twist of his arm and he was under her control.

They stared at each other for a couple of seconds, then she got up. "Is it because I'm a woman?" If it was, she'd misjudged him.

"Pit me against anyone here, the result will be the same," he told her in a low tone. "I can't attack anyone."

"Can't or won't?"

He ran both hands through his short hair in a jerky motion. "Both."

Was he serious? She wanted to shake him, order him

to pull his head out of his ass. She tripped him, trapping him on his belly with an arm twisted behind his back. She leaned down to ask in his ear, "Why the hell did you join the army?"

"I told you before, this is where the work I want to do is being done," he said coldly.

She got off him and allowed him up. "You're an adult and this isn't the Boy Scouts. You knew you'd have to defend yourself, possibly even kill, yet you still chose the army. Why?" She crossed her arms over her chest and glared at him. "And don't give me a verbal runaround. I want to know the real reason."

"Defending other people, keeping them safe, stopping harm before it can happen is why I joined. I just happen to do all that without using my fists or a gun."

He meant it. She could see it on his face, and that certainty of purpose cooled her anger into something close to respect. "Even knights in armor had to do more than just stand in the way of an adversary. They had to fight too. You have a price on your head and Akbar is gunning for you. You need to learn this."

He closed his eyes and breathed deep for a moment. When he opened his eyes, his expression was composed. "I'm trying, I really am. Maybe I just need more time, more practice before this kind of fighting—" he gestured at the room at large "—feels more natural to me."

"That might work," she said slowly, reviewing their conversation in her head. Something he said niggled at her. "You said *can't* and *won't* attack anyone. I get *won't*, the whole Hippocratic Oath thing, but *why* can't you attack me?" she asked, tilting her head to one side.

He stood there, looking at her like she'd asked him an

impossible question. "Have you completed your assessment?" he asked instead of answering. "Or would you like to beat me up some more." He was breathing harder now than when she was beating the crap out of him.

*Holy shit*. She should have asked him *why* a long time ago.

"I'm done," she said, managing to maintain her even tone by the skin of her teeth. Then she watched him walk away.

Could it be that his problem lay in the words *beat me*? At some point in his life, had someone hurt this man and he'd decided it was his fault?

If she was going to get anywhere with Max, she had to find out.

The first place she went to was her father's office. He was busy and she had exactly two minutes to talk to him. She didn't waste any of it.

"Sir, I think I may know why Colonel Maximillian has such a problem performing his combat skills."

"Already? That didn't take long."

Fixing the issue was going to take a lot longer. "Was he abused as a child?"

Her father stared at her, frozen for two seconds. "Fuck."

"Is that a yes or no?"

"It's an *I don't know*." He sat back in his chair. "But that would explain a lot. What leads you to think he was abused?"

"I just tossed the man around the mats for an hour. He can't make himself attack me, or anyone else for that matter. It's not just an abhorrence of violence. He can't make himself do it. I think he'd be physically sick if he accidently did knock me down. I thought it was because I'm a woman, but now I don't think that's it."

"Talk to him."

"I plan to, but I thought I would start with you to see if you were aware of anything that might contribute to his behavior."

Her father sat back, his expression contemplative. "His ex said he beat her. There wasn't any evidence to support her claims, but even an accusation of that can damage a man's reputation. I think he gave her every-thing she wanted just to shut her up."

"I remember. I'll dig a bit more into that." Alicia left her father's office and after getting permission from base security, logged in to a computer and checked to see if Max or his ex-wife had any sort of criminal re-cord. Both of them were clean. Except... Max had a sealed family court record with an odd flag on it. Some-thing had happened when he was a kid.

Getting those opened was damned near impossible, but that didn't stop her from being curious.

When she put in a call to a lawyer friend and asked about the flag, she was told they meant a major case crime, like kidnappings, armed robberies, or murders. The child was somehow involved, almost always as a victim. The files were sealed to protect the identity of the child.

Alicia ended the call and headed to her quarters, picking through everything she knew about the colonel.

What the hell had happened to Max?

# FOUR

MAX STEPPED OUT of the shower and toweled dry, hissing as the abused muscles of his back burned with every movement. He glanced in the mirror over his bathroom sink and winced at the bruises on his shoulders. Alicia hadn't pulled her punches. She'd tossed him all over the place and every time she came at him he wanted to surrender, spread his arms wide.

She thought he was weak.

He'd chosen to be a doctor because he wanted to heal people and take away pain whenever he could. He'd joined the army to stop biological weapons. Human beings were very good at killing each other with weapons, from knives to artillery, and adding microscopic organisms that could easily spread outside the combat zone and kill off civilian populations was unacceptable.

Unfortunately, there were plenty of psychopaths out there with Akbar's skills, backed by money from extremist groups. If the human race wasn't very careful, biological weapons were going to wipe them out.

He pulled on a pair of briefs and crawled onto his bed. He didn't bother with the sheet or blanket, just lay down on his stomach and stuffed the pillow halfway under his torso. No doubt Alicia would have an entire day of painful training prepared for him tomorrow. The woman was relentless.

He didn't want to fight her. *Couldn't* fight her.

He respected her, respected her skills, but that didn't change how his hindbrain reacted to her.

Fuck, he'd known this was going to be difficult, retaining his objectivity where she was concerned, but the reality was even harder than expected. She was tougher than any of the male instructors who'd attempted to teach him the basics of self-defense.

He liked how she interacted with his staff. He liked her, more than he should. The physical attraction was part of it. Her size, her shape, her soft gold skin. The force of her personality was tangible and she never agreed to something unless she was all in. She was highly intelligent and had a sarcastic sense of humor that made him laugh.

Not that he was laughing tonight. Too many bruises for that.

He was afraid, terribly afraid she'd see his attraction to her. Nothing could come of it anyway. Nothing that wouldn't damage both their careers.

CLICK.

*Scratch.*

*Scratch.*

Max glanced at his clock. 0100. He hadn't been asleep longer than an hour.

Someone was outside his door doing something illegal.

Another kidnapping attempt? Akbar had tried to get Dr. Perry a few months ago.

*Click.*

*Click.*

The door opened a crack.

*Oh no you don't.* Anger chased all other emotions

from him. He wasn't going to let these terrorists commit any more atrocities. Not against his people.

Max rose from the bed and silently lowered himself to the floor next to it.

A figure slipped through the doorway and slowly, quietly closed it again. The hallway had some lighting, but inside his room the darkness was almost absolute. The intruder would have to wait for his eyes to adjust before they moved again.

Max didn't.

He pushed off the floor, coming in low and grabbing the front of the intruder's shirt. The other man moved to block, but it was too late. Max was moving too fast.

He twisted his body as Alicia had taught him, flipped the intruder and slammed the man down on his bed and put him in a choke hold. The intruder tried to suck in air, but Max's grip was too tight.

"Keep struggling," Max whispered in his ear, "and I'll put you out."

His captive went limp.

Could be a ruse to get Max to loosen up on his hold. Max waited for several seconds, then asked, "Who do you work for?"

A sensual voice said, "You."

It took a moment for the word to register, it was so unexpected. When it did, he dropped his captive and sprang off the bed. He fumbled along the wall until he found the light switch, then flipped it.

Alicia Stone lay on his bed, her hand rubbing her throat, her gaze flamethrower hot.

His hands were shaking. Her neck was red and bruised.

*What had he done?*

It took him back thirty years. His hands around his father's throat, the old man's face turning red, someone screaming in the background, a blow to his head and then darkness.

This is what happened when he let his emotions rule him, let *any* of his anger determine his course of action.

Max blinked and focused on Alicia. Her face was red all right, but not from lack of air. No, she looked ready to tear him apart with her bare hands.

He should let her.

Max took a step toward the bed, to apologize, to assure her that he would never touch her again, but she bared her teeth at him. "You've been holding out on me." She got to her feet and glided toward him.

Not good.

"You've been fucking holding out on everyone," she hissed.

He closed his eyes. She was going to kill him now. He knew it. He deserved it.

He'd help.

He opened his eyes as a whisper of breath caressed his collarbone. She stood in front of him, staring at him intently, with only a couple of inches between them. "Explain that."

"I apologize for putting my hands on your…you," he said, attempting to sound professional. "I thought you were an intruder. I will report this to General Stone first thing in the morning, resign my position and—"

"Shut the fuck up." She glared at him for another second or two, then poked him very precisely in the center of his chest. "I came here to show you how easy it would be for someone to enter your room and subdue you. Explain to me where the klutz I beat up earlier

warrior who dan...

the time she got to the...

...rds we sharp enough to cut

"You ...was the wrong answer. "You

...ke me and I realized

...room. All I could

...ap or kill me,

him ...room."

He win... ...ow."

Her face told ...

owe me the truth."

He did. "A strange noise wo... ...someone was trying to get into my r... think was someone was trying to kidn... I got angry like they tried with Sophia. I didn't think— and just moved."

The fury in her face didn't leave, but it was tempered with other emotions now. She pointed at the bed. "Sit. We're going to talk about this."

Max sat. He didn't want her inside his head, didn't want to talk about things that still hurt as much today as they had thirty years ago.

She watched him for a few moments, then sat next to him, so that her leg was nearly touching his. "Someone did a real number on you."

He couldn't stop looking at the bruises on her neck.

"Yes, someone did." That's all he got out before his own body threatened to choke him. Fuck. This couldn't be happening to him in front of her. He tried to cough, but that just made it worse. He opened and closed his fists and focused on getting his breath back.

It was as if his father had his hands around Max's throat again.

Choking him.

Killing him.

A small hand settled on the nape of his neck, then rubbed up and down his back. "You've done nothing wrong, Max." She p... ...nd kept ...y. Eventu-...athe again. At

...lly his throat opened...

...rubbing. Her shamp...

...Her sham...

least

...little.

"You,

"Alicia said ... ...ghtful tone, one he'd

never heard from her ... "could defend yourself

against a faceless en... ...n the dark, but not one you

can see in the li... ...en if it's a paper target."

He'd never ...ught about it that way, but she was

right. The d...k had never bothered him. He could

cloak himself in it and hide from all kinds of danger-

ous things, ...most of which lived in his memories.

The tightness sitting like a thousand-pound weight
in the space between his collarbones shifted and shed
more of its bulk. Her warm weight comforted him more
than he wanted to admit. This fuzzy pajama-clad Alicia was more dangerous to him than any woman in a
long time. If he didn't distract her soon, she was going
to discover just how arousing he found her.

She lifted her head to look at him. "For most people
it's the opposite." She sounded almost…excited.

*Oh no.*

"What are you planning, to teach me hand-to-hand
combat while I wear a blindfold?" He was just as
shocked as she was at his question.

He could breathe freely.

Her wicked grin made him even more uncomfortable. "That is an excellent idea."

He rubbed his face with both hands. "That's not
going to work."

"Why not?"

"I tried it. More than once. All I ended up with was
bruises." And nothing else.

She pursed her lips. "I'm not going to give up on this," she said. "I promised my dad I'd have you able to defend yourself at least."

"I promised him the same, so no giving up here. But what about just now? I *hurt* you."

"You took me down, then let go as soon as I made my identity clear. No harm, no foul."

"No harm?" Not when she was sitting right next to him, her neck red everywhere he'd applied pressure. "I'm lucky I didn't do any permanent damage to your neck."

"Max," she said, slanting him a look. "Small injuries happen. It's an occupational hazard."

He was shaking his head before she finished speaking. "No. This—" he waved his hand around to indicate their current situation "—can't go unpunished."

Whatever else he might have said was cut off when she took his face in both her hands and kissed him.

She might as well have stuck his finger in a light socket. The sensation of her lips wrecked any hope of keeping his attraction to himself. He pulled her close, the soft warmth of her pajama-clad body a pleasure he couldn't resist.

Damn it, he needed to resist. They couldn't do this. He didn't want to lose the respect and friendship he was slowly developing with her.

There had to be fifty reasons why this was a lousy idea.

She pulled back. "Stop thinking so hard." She kissed him again.

*Shit*.

"This is not a good idea." If she'd stop touching him he might be able to think of a reason why.

One of her hands landed on his knee and trailed an invisible path from mid-thigh up to the edge of his briefs.

There was no missing his erection. His underwear barely contained it.

She stared at it, then looked at him through her lashes and said, "I disagree."

He nearly came right then and there. "It would be completely inappropriate for us to…" He was terrified that if he named what he wanted to do with her he'd lose control again and start something they'd both regret.

He wanted no regrets between them.

If only she'd stop drawing little circles on his thigh. It was driving him crazy.

"Have sex?"

He met her gaze. "Yes."

She leaned a little closer. "I've been hot for you for a long time, Max, and I think we both might need this."

*We?* Why would she need him? "What about—"

She kissed him again. It was a quick slide of her lips across his, but he was already addicted to her taste.

He took her shoulders in a firm grip and pulled away. "It's been more than two years. I don't think I can do slow or gentle."

She grinned. "I can't wait."

He couldn't either.

Tomorrow was going to be a bitch.

*Fuck it.*

He yanked her close and kissed her hard, his tongue in her mouth, the softness of her lips under his.

She shifted, stood, then straddled him without breaking contact. Her heated skin scalded him as she wiggled closer until his cock was trapped between them.

Holy fuck, he was going to come in his shorts if she kept it up.

"Lift up your top. Show me your breasts," he ordered.

She stared at him, her breathing becoming choppier as she complied.

Her breasts were the perfect handful. He nuzzled the sensitive skin below one nipple then took it between his teeth and nipped her.

She gasped, shuddered and held his head to her.

Alicia liked it a little rough. *Yes.*

She rubbed herself over his cock and he thrust up against her. Then he treated her other breast to the same attention as the first.

She dropped her head back and groaned.

He sucked. Hard.

She bucked and made incoherent noises in the back of her throat. The strongest woman he knew was getting off on giving him control.

She was close and he was going to push her over.

Clamping her body close with one arm behind her back, he sent his other hand down the front of her soft sleep pants and inside her panties. He stroked one finger down the seam of her and flicked her clitoris, then shoved two fingers into her at the same time as he gave her breast another nip.

She exploded and hid her face against his neck to muffle her cries.

He stroked her through her orgasm, bringing her down gently even though he was still rock hard and shaking like an addict staring at his fix.

She opened her eyes and looked at him with such satisfaction that he got, impossibly, harder. "Your next order, sir?"

# FIVE

MAX WAS STARING at her like a tiger does when it has sighted prey.

Total focus.

Bottomless hunger.

Sexiest thing ever.

"I want you naked," he ordered.

She shimmied off him and slid her pajama pants off. Panties too.

His gaze dropped to caress her skin. She'd thought he looked feral before, but that had just been the appetizer. If she didn't feed him something quick, he was going to pounce.

She was tempted to let him, but what she'd just learned about him told her it would be better if she made it completely clear she wanted sex.

She didn't want him castigating himself tomorrow. Or the day after that, or next week. If he decided he didn't want to sleep with her again, so be it, but she wanted tonight more than she wanted to make general. She didn't want him angry with himself for having sex with her. Hell, she wanted him to want it for a while.

Alicia took two steps toward him, her hips swaying. He reached out and grabbed her, putting her flat on her back on the bed.

He crawled over her, straddling her, and leaned down to whisper in her ear, "You can say no if you want."

Her hands came up to slide over his shoulders. "Impossible."

He leaned down and kissed her, coming over her, settling his chest against hers. She arched into him and he flicked her nipples.

"I could kiss you for hours," she whispered against his lips.

"Maybe next time," he said, his voice a low rumble. "I'm much too hungry to linger."

One of his hands slipped around to stroke her back, and down, down to the base of her spine where he circled a spot below her tailbone. Every movement, every touch sent shots of adrenaline mixed with need through her body. Her hips couldn't hold still and she rocked herself against the long hard length of his erection.

Something was in the way, damn it. "Take your underwear off."

"Are you sure?" he asked, nipping at her neck and pressing his finger a little harder against the spot he was using to drive her out of her mind.

She barely recognized her own voice when she snarled, "Fuck me."

He lunged up and took over her mouth while he did something to remove the cloth between her and his cock.

As soon as it was free, she palmed it, humming in delight at the thick length of him. "Do you have a license for this concealed weapon?"

"Expired." A slow smile lit up his face. "Do I need another one?"

Oh, she *liked* this sexy side of Max.

"How about I give your license—" she gave his cock a squeeze "—a little mouth-to-mouth resuscitation?"

He kissed her, sliding his hands with slow deliberation over every dip and curve of her body, and said against her lips, "I think you've already revived it."

"Condom?"

He leaned back to open the drawer on the small nightstand next to his bed and pulled out an unopened box of them.

As soon as he got one out, she took it from him. "I want to put it on you."

He gave it to her and lay back to watch as she opened the packet, then rolled the condom over him.

She watched his face from beneath her lashes as she sank down on him without warning.

He groaned and gripped her hips, but didn't do anything to slow her down.

She hissed. He was big and she hadn't had sex in a few months, but she didn't stop rising and falling over him until he was all the way in. She rode him slow and easy, thinking to tease him, but one of his fingers found that spot at the top of her ass and she stopped thinking altogether.

He was whispering something in her ear, but she couldn't process the words, not when her entire existence depended on finding orgasm.

It built inside her, wound tighter than anything she'd ever experienced before. She was afraid it had the power to disarm her completely, but she didn't care. She needed it.

She needed it now.

He thrust up into her, hard and fast, and the crest broke, white-hot pleasure searing through her. She was still riding the high when he grabbed her hips and held her still so he could hammer in for one, two, three strokes.

He grunted and his thrusts turned into short digs that stroked something needy deep inside her.

*Holy fuck.* They'd just wrecked each other and she was ready to go again.

He held her tight, her body plastered to his, while they both caught their breath.

"Goddamn, Max," she said, still out of breath. "That was unreal."

"Hmm." He opened his mouth over her neck and sucked, his tongue flicking her skin.

She wiggled and found his cock was half-hard already. "What did you do, take a Mr. Happy pill?"

He chuckled. "No, I'm…hungry." His fingers found that spot at the base of her spine and she jerked in his hold.

"Oh God in heaven, please fuck me again."

"Need a new condom." He pulled out, flipped her onto her back and dove down to suck one of her nipples in his mouth. "You're so polite I hardly recognize you."

"I've wanted you for a long time," she said as she clutched at his head and lifted her chest to beg for more. "I figured I'd better be on my best behavior."

He took the old condom off, threw it in a trash can in the corner and opened a new one. She watched, entranced, as the staid physician and colonel stroked himself a few times before rolling another condom on.

So *hot.*

He took his cock and teased the entrance to her body with it, rubbing the head around in tight circles. "What do you want again?"

He was driving her crazy. "I want you inside me."

He thrust into her, fast and deep, and the shocking pleasure of it made her diaphragm stutter.

He didn't stop, kept up the insane pace and penetration and shoved her into another orgasm that caught her completely unaware.

It was blinding, even stronger than the last, and she thought she might pass out.

A couple of minutes later, Max pulled out and got off the bed. He disappeared into the bathroom and came back with a warm cloth. He cleaned her, and she didn't bother putting up even a token resistance.

She drifted off into sleep as he came back to bed, gathered her up and pulled a blanket over them both.

ALICIA WOKE WRAPPED in warm, muscular arms.

Max.

Had she known he was going to burn her up between the sheets, she'd have attacked him in the dark months ago. The man blew her mind.

She slid her hands over his chest and down over his abs, loving the dip and flow of his skin and muscles. Her fingers encountered a rough puckered area over his ribs and she stopped to explore it more completely. A bullet wound?

Max stirred and she pulled her hand away. The scar was old, probably some scrap he'd gotten into when he was a kid.

On the nightstand a small digital clock told her it was 0400. A good time to get back to her room—this part of the base should be deserted.

A few months ago, the Navy Hotel had housed many American personnel, but it had been burned to the ground by extremists trying to kidnap one of Max's people, Sophia Perry. Compact trailers had been moved in to form temporary camp-style accommodations within the base proper.

Which is where it should have been in the first place. She'd never liked the base's use of the off-site hotel and had said so on more than one occasion. She was careful, however, not to say *I told you so* to her father.

Being a general's daughter only got you headaches, not leeway.

Alicia slipped out of bed with the stealth of a ninja, but Max woke despite her smooth moves.

"What's wrong?" He looked like a sleepy bear, all growly and ready for action, and she almost said fuck it to propriety and got back into bed with him.

Another woman probably would have gotten away with it.

She could never forget, not for one moment, no matter how sexy or how into her a man seemed, she was General Stone's daughter. She was held to a higher standard, and could never let her guard down.

"Bathroom," she whispered to him, and headed in that direction. When she glanced over her shoulder as she reached the bathroom door, he'd gone back to sleep.

She pulled on her clothes and left Max's room. This time, he didn't wake up.

MAX'S ALARM WENT off at the same time it always did, 0600.

He lifted his head and came face to face with a pair of thong panties, ruby red in color.

That was different.

The memory of his unexpected guest flooded his brain.

A shadow picking his lock and sneaking into his room. Grabbing the intruder and slamming them down on the bed. Alicia, wearing a soft pair of pajamas and an *I got you* smile. The feel of her lips on his as she kissed him. Her breasts in his mouth, his cock in her as deep as he could go. He still wasn't satisfied.

He wanted her again, hot, wet and demanding, but she wasn't here.

He was naked in bed and alone. Not a good combination.

What if he'd hurt her?

What if she'd left so she didn't have to deal with a morning-after moment?

He snorted at his own ridiculousness. This was Sergeant Stone, combatives program instructor for the Special Forces. She didn't do awkward morning-after shit.

So, why had she left before they could have a conversation about what happened? Most women like to talk about their feelings, and sex was important. His ex-wife had used the after-sex high to ask for things he'd already refused.

*Can I go to Mexico for the weekend?*

*It's a girls' only shopping trip.*

*How about for a couple of days in Vegas?*

Stone had just disappeared, and he found he didn't like it. He felt awkward and uncomfortable, and he didn't know if last night would affect their working relationship or not. He needed to talk to her, get her feelings on it, before he could decide what to do next.

Max showered, dressed and grabbed a coffee and a quick breakfast at the food court before heading to his office.

Eugene was already there, glaring at his double screen computer.

"Trouble?" Max asked him.

"Yes, sir. There's a cholera outbreak in Sierra Leone. It seems to be the worst in the areas hit hardest by Ebola."

"Have they requested assistance?"

"No, but they lost so many of their infectious disease leadership that whoever is in charge might not know when or how to call for help in a situation like this."

"I know a couple of doctors who might be able to give us a clearer picture of the situation. Next?"

Eugene glanced over Max's shoulder, and since Max hadn't heard anyone walk in, it had to be Stone.

"A hospital pharmacy in Kabul was broken into last night and most of the contents stolen. It looks like whoever did it took everything they could get their hands on."

*Son of a bitch.*

"That's the second one this week. Someone is stocking up."

Eugene nodded, but continued on with his report. "Four people reported to the medical clinic here on base with flu-like symptoms last night." He clicked something on his screen. "Fever, nausea and vomiting."

"Keep an eye on that, Eugene. What departments did those people work in?"

"All four were in the receiving department."

"Have the cleaning staff disinfect every surface in the department. The last thing we need is the flu making the rounds on base."

"Yes, sir." He gave Max's shadow another glance, then went to work, typing impossibly fast.

"Come along, Stone," Max said without looking behind him as he strode into his office.

"Eugene gave it away?" she asked as he sat down behind his desk and she took the chair in front of it.

"Partially. I don't know any other soundless soldiers besides you." He gave her a bland look and turned on his computer.

She angled her head back at Eugene. "He looks for anything that might be an infectious disease?"

"We try to track everything we can. Africa has been particularly difficult to get timely information from since Ebola wiped out so many of their top infectious disease people. It could easily take off again." He continued with his boring lecture voice, "Would you mind closing the door? I have a couple of delicate issues to discuss."

"Yes, sir." She closed the door, then stood at parade rest, her gaze riveted to a spot on the wall behind him.

Like that was it.

He got up and came around the desk so he could talk to her without anything between them. "Was there something wrong with my bed?" he asked her in what he hoped was an even tone.

"No."

Her face told him nothing. "Did I hurt you?"

"No."

"Did I do or say something to make you angry?"

"No."

"Then why," he demanded, "did you leave in the middle of the night?"

She kept her eyes on the wall. "My apologies, sir. I woke at zero four hundred and thought I'd let you sleep. It was a good time to return to my room unseen."

He stared at her for a moment, irritation chafing at him like sandpaper. It sounded reasonable, considerate even, but her saying it while addressing him as a superior officer and not meeting his gaze was intolerable.

"Alicia, look at me."

She glanced at him, but didn't hold his gaze.

"What," he asked, enunciating each word carefully, "did I do wrong?"

Her head jerked up and she looked at him with wide eyes. "Nothing."

"Bullshit." He took another step closer to her and had to clench his fists to stop himself from taking her by the shoulders. She'd have him on his back in two seconds flat. "You snuck out of my room without a word and now you're standing here treating me like a stranger."

Halfway through his sentence her jaw had fallen open. She snapped it closed, took in a deep breath and smiled. A real smile, one that caused the tight tangle of emotion deep in his gut to loosen.

"I didn't wake you," she said, her voice the husky tone she'd used while she straddled him in the dark, "because you looked so damn sexy and cuddly I wanted to stay, but I knew if I didn't go back to my room then, it would be hard to go there without being seen by some big-mouth grunt." She smiled and tilted her head. "I knew if I woke you, you'd have no trouble convincing me to stay, and I like this assignment."

"Oh." *Jesus, it's hot in here.* He swallowed and watched that smile of hers turn naughty. "Your precipitous departure robbed me of something."

"What?"

"A good-morning kiss." He took the final step to reach her, slipped a hand behind her head and claimed her mouth. He took his time tasting her, showing her what she could have had before she'd tiptoed back to her room.

Her arms wound around his neck and she moaned low in her throat.

He ended the kiss very, very slowly, waiting for her eyes to open while he stared down into her flushed face.

"I," she said, opening her eyes to treat him to a heated look, "will never sneak out of your room while you're sleeping again."

No regrets, plans for more. *Mission accomplished.* He released her and went to sit down behind his desk, because if he didn't, he would *have* her on his desk. "Excellent."

Her relaxed posture went back to military straight. "I will continue to treat you with the respect your rank demands in public, Max."

"Just now, you treated me like you'd never met me before, when you've beaten me up numerous times and have a habit of needling me with it. In public. If you stop, people are going to wonder about that too."

She nodded. "I overcompensated. I'm sorry. Speaking of hand-to-hand, we need to talk about how well you took me down last night and why you otherwise can't."

He froze, ice spreading through his chest like a deep, hard frost. "We've already discussed it, and I agreed to continue practicing with you."

"That's not what I mean." She leaned forward, studying his face with eyes he feared saw too much. "You look like a deer caught in headlights. What happened to you?"

Faces flashed through his head. He locked the memories down. To give them a voice would be the same as issuing an invitation to anarchy to take over the world. It was a lie he'd spoken a hundred times to as many people. He took a deep breath, then looked into Alicia's eyes and told it one more time.

"Nothing."

# SIX

Alicia watched Max's expression change from a reflection of old hurts, to a closed book. He wasn't going to tell her anything.

Stubborn fool.

She was stubborn too, but she'd let it go…for now. Let him think she'd retreated, when all she was doing was holding her advance until the right moment. She'd just found a man who accepted all of her without hesitation. She wanted the chance to explore what was between them.

"Fine." She sighed. "I'd like to talk about that report Eugene just gave you."

He raised an eyebrow. "What about it?"

"I had no idea you kept track of outbreaks in such a wide area."

"Wide area? We track them worldwide."

"Why?"

"Because they're so damned dangerous. If people knew how easy it is to create and spread a biological weapon in a populated area, they'd be afraid to leave their homes."

"Even the military?"

"Yes. Nothing about the weapons we fight is tangible. It's an invisible war. Most people don't even know they're fighting it until they're already the walking dead."

She held his gaze for a moment longer, then asked, "May I sit?"

He gestured at the chair in front of his desk.

"I'm surprised the fallout from the anthrax attack at Forward Operating Base Bostick didn't making things more difficult for you."

"The details of that incident have been kept as quiet as possible." He rubbed his face with both hands. "Akbar came very close to killing a large number of our men, your father included. That's news we don't want every extremist out there to know."

"News is exactly what I mean. I listened to Eugene's situation report this morning. Couldn't you send out information that could help and not hurt your team?"

"We're not a bunch of journalists. We're lab techs, doctors and medical scientists who deal with disease and death on a daily basis. Eugene gives me that report twice per day, minimum, because I need to know what's going on a lot farther away than just a country or two. What happens in Africa affects Asia and the Middle East and vice versa. From an infectious disease stand-point, the world is a very small place."

She stared at the top of his desk for a long moment. "What do you think Akbar will do?"

"It's hard to predict—he's not rational—but I can try." He swiveled his chair and got up to face a map encompassing the Middle East, most of Asia and the northern half of Africa.

"Akbar is from Afghanistan." He pointed at a red tack stuck in the map. "After his family was killed, he disappeared for a couple of months. We all thought nothing of it. I would have done the same thing if my family had been wiped out. When he came back, he'd lost ten or twenty pounds and was subdued. His siasm for diplomacy was gone. Again, no surprise th He gave the impression he wanted to keep himself bus with work. He told me he wanted the deaths of his wife and children to count for something. For peace."

"He told you?" Stone asked, leaning forward. "You know him?"

"I know him. At least I thought I did. He did a lot of good things for his country at one time." Max shook his head. "What I didn't know, what none of us knew, was that he'd decided to enact revenge on the United States military through terror. By releasing the one thing he'd always said was the most cowardly of weapons. Biological weapons."

"Losing his family must have broken him," she said quietly.

Max sighed. "I don't know if he made the decision himself or if he reached it through the encouragement of other extremists. It doesn't really matter now."

"I think it does matter," Alicia said, leaning forward. "Knowing if he was influenced by a particular group might help us narrow down his possible targets."

"There's been no pattern to his targets. The first one made sense, sort of. He targeted a remote forward operating base in Afghanistan. You must know some of this—you mentioned Bostick. He tested his weaponized anthrax on a small village while poisoning the ear of the base commander. He convinced the base commander to disregard the advice and opinions of one of my doctors, who was embedded with a Special Forces team on a training mission. General Stone had to go there and take over in order to figure out what was going on. He was the real target, and Akbar's plan would have worked except he wasn't able to eliminate my doctor and all of her Special Forces escort. They took out Akbar's delivery system."

"I read the report. Do you think he's fixated on the general?"

Max shrugged. "The second target had nothing to do with General Stone. He poisoned the water supply of a refugee camp with some kind of souped-up rabies virus. He wasn't finished tinkering with it and decided to try to force Dr. Sophia Perry to find a way to make the virus easily transmissible from person to person." Max shook his head. "Your father would have never gone there."

They were both silent for several seconds, then Alicia asked, "What do you think he'll do next?"

"He seems fixated on creating the perfect biological weapon. I don't expect that to change."

"So, his goal is to create a bacteria or virus that can kill a lot of people?"

"I think he wants to create a pathogen that will wipe out as many people as possible. His own life is worthless to him. All he cares about is killing in great numbers."

"If he's supported by other terrorists, do they know they're just as much of a target as we are?"

"Probably not. Akbar is an educated and charming man and he's good at putting things in their best light. He knows how to tell people what they want to hear."

"Perhaps that's the message we should send," she said diffidently. "Plant a few seeds of doubt."

"I don't think that will work. These are people with their minds made up, and they've decided we're the bad guys."

"We could still try, couldn't we?"

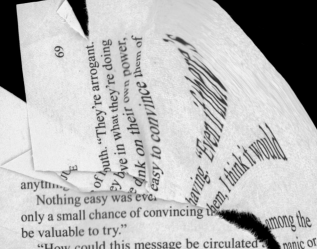

anyth...

Nothing easy was eve...

only a small chance of convincing t...

be valuable to try."

"How could this message be circulated... panic or right people? We don't want to spark massive... whatworse, anarchy. That could kill more people tha... ever pathogen he's planning to unleash."

She smiled, putting as much violence into it as she could. "We use our covert community to spread the word at the grassroots level."

"As soon as you do that, you lose control of the information. Terrorists will spin it any way they want to, blaming the United States and its allies for the problem. We're back to panic and anarchy."

Couldn't he at least try to see her point of view?

"I still want to try it." It had the potential to change public perception, and that played a huge part in influencing who'd show up to the battle.

"Even if we had time to try to leak the kind of information we want, we don't have the contacts to leak the information to."

He might not have the right kind of people to pass the information to, but she knew people who did. "But if we did?"

"We're back to the bad guy thing again. They're not going to accept anything we say, even if it's intercepted and supposedly secret."

"But—"

"Ali," he inter...

bate. The work we...

military machine...

no more." He smile...

just made her ma...

...or de- ...e rest of the ...ey need to and ...n his words, but that ...ber of people whose opin- ion I care abou...mall." He sat back in his chair and waved a...d at large. "The rest can fuck off." ...d, could they? "May I speak plainly,

Oh, the...

sir?"

He frowned, but nodded.

"I think you're making a mistake."

He stared at her, his expression unchanging. "I'm sorry you feel that way, but the subject is closed."

It was like last night had never happened.

"How am I supposed to help you if you won't even entertain my suggestions?" she demanded. The time for tact was done. "Your security is my number-one concern."

"What's that got to do with starting rumors?"

"It's one way to make you safe." She leaned forward. "People have no idea what a dangerous man you are. They think you're this…this uncoordinated moron who couldn't find his asshole with a map and a flashlight."

"Seeing as how it's behind me," he drawled with a half smile, "they'd be right."

She smacked her face with one hand as disappointment burned a hole in her gut. He wasn't taking this seriously at all. An insidious thought occurred to her.

"Is this because the general is my father?"

He snorted. "Your father could be the president of the United States and it wouldn't change my opinion, or my decision."

"Thank God for small favors," she muttered under

her breath. Just the thought of him treating her differently because of her family connections made her want to spit fire. "Tying my hands behind my back with a gag order so I can't fight effectively for you is stupid. Your safety is determined by a lot of factors, and you're only making my job harder."

"I thought your job was keeping me safe?"

"I'm also supposed to advise you on ways to do that."

He just shook his head.

She watched his face for any sign that he was willing to compromise, but his expression was closed.

"Permission to leave, sir?" she asked, getting to her feet.

"Granted, Sergeant," he said as if tired.

She shut the door, rather proud of the fact that she didn't slam it.

MAX WAITED THREE SECONDS, then got up and went to the door himself. "Eugene, find out if General Stone is in his office."

There was only one man he could consult with on the subject of Sergeant Stone and how to get through the woman's thick, stubborn skull.

"Yes, sir," Eugene called out from his desk.

A few seconds later, Max's phone rang.

He picked it up and barked, "Maximillian."

There was silence for a moment, then General Stone said, "Who died?"

"No one yet," Max said, wincing. "I apologize for my tone, sir. I've just had a frustrating conversation with my self-defense trainer and wanted to ask your advice." He hoped to God doing it wasn't a mistake.

Silence again. "I see."

When the general didn't say anything else, Max continued. "She proposed a course of action I couldn't condone. Unfortunately, even after I explained my decision, she refused to back down. Given her precipitous departure of my office, I can only assume that she's very pissed off. Any advice for me on how I might affect a change in her attitude?"

"Patience."

The general didn't add anything else.

"That's it? I was hoping for something constructive I could do or say."

"My daughter has a stubborn streak wider than the Grand Canyon. The best way to convince her of anything is to give her time to think. Stand firm on your decision and she'll come around eventually. Unless you're wrong, and then she'll never give up."

"I'll settle in for a long wait, then. She was very angry with me when she left."

"Angry is fine, insubordinate is another." The general's tone was questioning.

Why would he be asking, even adroitly, if his daughter had been insubordinate? "Angry, sir."

The general grunted and asked, "Anything else?"

"No, sir."

The line clicked dead.

Max punched in Eugene's number.

As soon as the young man answered, Max said, "Eugene, come to my office please."

Eugene was at the door two seconds later. "Yes, sir?"

"Shut the door and come in."

Eugene carefully approached the desk and came to attention.

"Take a seat," Max said. "Anyone not lab personnel outside my door or in your area this morning?"

"There was as Sergeant Stone left—a couple of people from Supply with our daily order, but they left… uh…after you asked for General Stone."

Supply? "Do the same people deliver our order every day?"

"Yes, sir."

"Do they drop the supplies and go or stay to chat?"

"Both. They make small talk while they're dropping things off and getting the paperwork signed."

Normal behavior. Alicia had him seeing conspiracies where there were none. "I'd like you to look into Sergeant Stone's military file. Check for charges brought against her or warnings."

"Yes, sir." Eugene blinked a couple of times, but otherwise managed to hide his surprise.

As much as Max hated to ask this, he couldn't ignore any sources of information. "What does the rumor mill say about Stone?"

"Well, sir," Eugene said, then cleared his throat. "There's a few things going around. The main one is that she's tough but usually fair on those she's training. I've seen her sparring and her reflexes are unbelievably fast."

Max nodded at him to keep talking.

"There's also a story going around that says she was late coming to the team because she was brought up on insubordination charges. Charges that are still under investigation."

"Do you know who brought those charges forward?"

"No, sir, but I'll try to find out."

"Anything else?"

"There's a general feeling she's gone as far as she's going to go in her current role. People are taking bets on if she'll leave the military or transfer out."

"Is staying with the team included in this transfer scenario?"

"No, sir. Most people think we're just a regular medical lab and she's here to try to get you, uh, straightened out."

Max shook his head and smiled ruefully. "It sounds like she's gotten herself into a shit storm. Don't mention this conversation to anyone. Understand?"

"Yes, sir. I've been doing that all along." The private nodded and left Max's office.

"That boy needs a raise," Max muttered to himself. "Or a promotion."

Putting his assistant and his bodyguard out of his mind, he went to work, sifting through the detailed reports of the current outbreaks Eugene had mentioned in his morning summary.

Akbar was there. Somewhere.

The rumble of his stomach had him checking his watch. Lunch. Well, he'd better get a move on and get to the food court.

Eugene had already gone. Max locked his office and left. He nodded at a few people he recognized from the clinic and other departments. When he got to the food court, he took a seat with Eugene and Jones. The two were in a clandestine relationship that his assistant refused to admit was happening. It frustrated the hell out of several other officers, but he'd decided to overlook it until the two did something overt in front of him. Which they never would, since they were smarter than ninety percent of the people on the base.

As he dug into his food, someone sat next to him.

"Hand-to-hand training this afternoon," Stone said in a cold voice. "Fourteen hundred. Two hours."

Wow, she was pissed. He kept eating. "Last time I checked, a colonel outranked a sergeant."

"On the training ground, the sergeant outranks everyone," she replied.

The conversation around them died down to nothing.

What the hell was she doing?

"Is this how you get your jollies, Sergeant? Beating people up?"

"No, sir. My job is to make sure you're able to defend yourself and your unit to the best of your ability and to a standard set for every soldier in the United States military. A standard you can't seem to meet."

Was she *asking* to be charged with insubordination?

She appeared in complete control of her emotions. There was no shaking of her hands, her breathing appeared slow and even, and she wasn't tense.

Was this her way of getting around his decision not to use rumor as a weapon? Start one herself? Did she think he wouldn't figure it out?

"This venue is hardly appropriate for this discussion," he said after a couple of moments.

"You can say whatever you want wherever you want, it won't change anything." She got to her feet. "See you at fourteen hundred."

Max managed to keep his eyes on his food and not on Stone as she walked out. He was going to spank her ass the next time he got her alone.

# SEVEN

ALICIA STRODE THROUGH the base like she owned it. She'd been called a lot of different names over the years. The cast-iron bitch, man-eater and ballbuster were a few. This was the first time she figured she actually earned any of them.

Word of the fight between her and Max was going to spread like a Texas grassfire on a windy day. She wanted to tell her father what was going on before he had a stroke.

His office wasn't grand, tucked in behind the chaplain's office, with not a lot of space for more than the desk and two chairs. He said that since he was there only part of the time, he needed only part of an office.

She walked in while he was on the phone, closed the door and sat down.

He glared at her, his death glare, and she knew she hadn't walked fast enough.

He finished his call without saying anything and stared at her.

"It's not what you think," she told him without preamble.

Her father didn't move for a moment, then asked, "Are you telling me you didn't challenge Colonel Maximillian's authority in full view of anyone who happened to be eating lunch in the food court?"

"No, sir. I did, in fact, do that."

"Give me one good reason why I shouldn't arrest you right now."

"I am attempting to show Colonel Maximillian how effective a rumor can be in sharing specific information. He refuses to consider it a legitimate way to influence what Akbar might do or what his supporters might do."

The general blinked, then let out a sigh. "Damn it, Ali, you're the one thinking wrong."

"Excuse me?"

"You can't look at a problem and decide you know best, when you don't have all the information."

"But—"

"And you sure as hell can't keep bending or breaking regulations to do it."

*What.*

*The.*

*Fuck.*

"When have I *ever* broken a regulation?"

He stared at her. "The incident in Germany isn't going to go away. You disobeyed an order from an officer. The judge advocate general is considering charges."

"The officer who gave me those orders wasn't a member of the United States military. Those orders would have compromised the safety of Max and the wounded German officer."

"Those distinctions may or may not matter in the long run."

The long run.

What was her long run? She'd been in the military for eight years. She'd graduated from Brown with a degree in Psychology and Cognitive Science, thinking she would concentrate on dealing with cultures and languages in some capacity. It turned out her martial

arts training, begun as a child, ended up being even
more valuable.

It had started by accident during Basic. An instructor
called upon her to demonstrate how to resist a takedown
technique, only she did too good a job. She'd put the
instructor on his back and when he continued to come
at her, she put him down twice more. He asked what
training she had, so she told him. Black belt in Brazil-
ian jujitsu, expert in Krav Maga and some Muay Thai.

He'd asked her if she'd killed anyone.

She'd told him the truth. Yes, but it was in self-
defense.

The next day, she'd been told not to participate, only
observe the training sessions. Which she was fine to
do, until the instructor demonstrated a technique completely wrong. She'd walked forward then, begged the
instructor's indulgence, and demonstrated the technique
correctly as an alternative. The instructor proved he
wasn't an idiot by naming another technique and having her demonstrate it. Then she offered slight correc-
tions based on size of attacker and defender.

That evening, the instructor asked her to train him
after hours. Four other instructors showed up for training three days later.

Two weeks after that, her father came to see her. Her
skills in combat and instruction were more valuable to
the army than her university degree.

She'd looked on it as a challenge. Before long she
was training the military elite and teaching them that
women aren't weak.

Eight years of combat training.

She'd made enemies during that time. Twice she'd
fought off men who thought she needed to be brought

down a peg or two through rape. Others had tried to remove her using other means, but her skill and the support of the majority of the men she trained had thwarted
their efforts.

What was her *long run*?

She'd helped to train some exceptional soldiers. Some
of them had the skills and enthusiasm to take over her
training role for the Special Forces. They could carry
on, should she decide on a different path for her career.

Max's group was doing important work. Work that
would become only more important in the future.

"I agree," she said to the man who was her commander as well as her father. "*If* I were to stay in my
training role."

He sat back, as was his habit, to consider what she
said and didn't say. "Are you thinking of a permanent
transfer to Max's team?"

"They need me. Special Forces doesn't. There are a
half-dozen men just as qualified to teach hand-to-hand
combat as I am."

"Most of them you trained yourself."

She smiled. "Exactly. I know how good they are."

Her father pursed his lips like he'd taken a big bite of
a lemon. "Max needs you. He can't shoot and couldn't
fight his way out of a kindergarten class."

"True."

The general drummed his fingers on his desk for a
moment, then leaned forward and said, "He's not someone you can fix, Ali."

"I don't want to fix him, Dad. I want to help him
fix himself."

"You don't know what's wrong with him."

"Do you?"

"Not entirely."

"I thought he was an arrogant ass for a long time, but I've changed my mind. He's not arrogant, he's focused. So much so that he doesn't always know what to say and who to say it with. He's almost too honest. He needs someone like me to bridge the gap between his people and the rest of the army."

General Stone grunted. "So, tell me again how having an argument in public is going to help the situation with Akbar."

"I want to see if we can send inaccurate information by way of the grapevine to Akbar. Fool him into thinking Max's people aren't all on the same page. Convince him we're divided on a number of issues and any response we might make will take longer or go in the wrong direction. I also want to plant doubt in the minds of the men supporting Akbar, help them see that he's as much a danger to them as we are."

"Baiting a man like Akbar is dangerous, Ali." Concern creased her father's face, and for him to show it meant he was scared.

"It's our best chance at catching him." She did her best to project confidence. If she didn't find a way to reassure her father, he could put a stop to the whole thing. "Before he's ready with whatever plague he comes up with next."

"Akbar isn't playing a game, he's lost his moral compass. That makes him dangerous and he's not going to be easy to predict."

"He's an extremely intelligent, angry, vengeful man," she said to her father. "I think predicting his actions will be the least of our worries."

"How many people he's going to kill…" the general began.

"…is the bigger one," his daughter finished for him. "We need to keep him off his game. If his allies start asking questions or begin to doubt his stated agenda, we win."

He sat back and stared off into space for a long while.

Her father was not a man to waffle on a decision, but he did take other opinions into account, if those opinions were based in facts, sound strategy and good tactics.

"No, Sergeant, I can't condone this social experiment of yours. The situation is too volatile."

*Well, shit.*

"Understood, sir." She stood and saluted.

Her father returned her salute, then ordered, "Keep the verbal sparring down to a dull roar or you might find yourself facing those charges."

Alicia left the general's office and marched toward the lab.

Max was going to be happy to have the general on his side. She, on the other hand…

*Son of a bitch.*

No matter how mad she was, she was going to have to keep it tucked away where no one could even get a whiff of it. For her father to mention those possible charges meant it wasn't an idle threat. He didn't do that.

She didn't have time for legal stupidity. Max needed her.

Needed her in a way no one had for a couple of years.

In many ways Max was the perfect soldier. Built to protect at the cost of his own life, he took his fear and used it to fuel his brain. He was one of those guys who

thought of his own safety last. If someone threw a grenade into a crowded room, he'd throw himself on it.

The problem was, he wasn't disposable. There were
only a few people who could step into his role and all
of them were busy running their own organizations.

She made her way back to her quarters and made
a couple of phone calls to the men who had stepped
into her role as a combat instructor. Just in case those
charges stuck.

They reported no issues and seemed enthusiastic
about the work. If she ended up on trial or decided to
transfer permanently, the program would be in good
hands.

A few seconds after she hung up, her phone went off.

"Stone," she said.

"This is Private Walsh," Eugene said to her, his voice
high with stress. "Colonel Maximillian would like to
see you in his office."

"I'll be there in a few minutes." She hung up. For Eugene to sound so strung out, Max had to be pissed off.

When she entered the lab building, Eugene was on
his computer, but his hunched shoulders told her he
wasn't a happy camper.

A female soldier was standing to one side by several
boxes, writing on a tablet.

Alicia met Eugene's gaze.

The private's expression didn't change.

"Is he in?" she asked.

"Yes, Sergeant." The private swallowed hard, but
nodded. "Go right in."

"Thanks." She gave him a nod, then opened the door
and stepped inside Max's office. The snick of the door
closing sounded louder than usual.

"You asked for me, sir?" she asked from her spot just inside the door.

Max stared at her, then said, "I just got a call from General Stone."

She didn't reply, except to shrug.

"Then I got a call from the Judge Advocate General's office."

He watched her body go rigid.

"Do you know what they asked me?"

"Not specifically, sir."

"They asked me if I wanted to press charges against you for insubordination. It seems they'd heard of our slight disagreement at lunch."

She didn't reply.

"I told them it was a private matter. They informed me that they were considering insubordination charges related to another incident with a different officer."

She remained silent.

"So I explained our unique situation to them, how horrible my shooting and unarmed combat skills are, and how, when it comes to training, you're in charge regardless of your student's rank. I also told them that sometimes, officers who've been in a position of authority for a long time forgot that."

She made eye contact with him then, surprise relaxing her face a tiny bit. "Thank you, sir."

"No thanks needed. It's the truth. It's also the truth when I say going over my head to your father isn't going to change anything. This is my team, and when we're not training, I'm in charge. Are we clear on that, Sergeant?"

"Yes, sir."

"Good, you're dismissed."

"Don't forget our sparring session, sir."

"I'm unlikely to forget," he said wryly. "I've been offered condolences for my upcoming ass whooping."

Her jaw dropped. "Really?"

"Ever since our conversation at lunch, people appear convinced that you're going to pound me into the mats. I haven't had anyone point and laugh at me yet, but it might be just a matter of time."

"No one would laugh at an officer of your rank."

"Maybe not where *I* can see them." He shrugged. "But it may make things awkward for my staff to have the whole base gossiping about us."

"I told you before," she said. "Anyone I find gawking or making fun will have to face me on the mat instead. See you at fourteen hundred, sir."

She left the office, wondering how she could make this situation work. When she looked up, she found herself the subject of Eugene's gaze.

"He's all yours, Eugene."

"Um, thanks?" the private said, uncertainty making the statement a question.

THE SPARRING ROOM was unusually busy that afternoon, yet Alicia found herself in a wide circle of open space. She glared at the men who were working hard at not looking at her while she waited for Max to arrive.

She'd shown up five minutes early to give herself time to claim adequate space. That didn't look like it was going to be a problem.

A couple of minutes later Max arrived and joined her on the mat. He looked around sourly and fixed her with an accusatory stare. "Are you going to beat up everyone in the room?"

She smiled, but it didn't reach her eyes. "Let me start with you first."

He sighed in resignation, but came toward her.

She started by demonstrating a simple judo throw used against an attacker coming at a person directly. She went through the motions, landing Max on the mats quite gently three times. Then it was his turn to throw her.

She came at him slowly, allowing him to grab her shirt just like he was supposed to. Instead of pulling her forward and twisting his torso like he should have, he tripped over his own feet, fell to the mat on his back and yanked her on top of him.

A couple of people chuckled and she untangled herself from Max as she identified the ones who had laughed.

She called both men over and told them to attack. They decided to double team her, but she didn't hesitate to take them both down. One of them rolled to his feet to attack her from behind.

Did he think she couldn't handle that? Of course, knowing a woman trains Special Forces in hand-to-hand and discovering she can beat your ass at the same time as beating another guy were two different things.

She put him on his back again. And again.

When he got up a fourth time, Max stepped in. "You're done and you're cutting into my training time."

The soldier sneered at Max and took two swaggering steps toward him.

Max just looked at him for a couple more seconds.

"Permission to leave, sir?" the guy asked, all the bravado wiped off his face.

Max nodded once and the moron took off. His buddy picked himself up off the mats and followed him out.

"Now," Max said, turning back to her. "Where were we?"

Alicia sighed. "Two left feet, that's where we were."

"If it makes you feel any better I can't dance either."

"Not really." She considered him for a moment, then shook herself and continued with the lesson.

She put Max on the mats in every position imaginable—front, back, sides and practically standing on his head. She didn't say much beyond "Up." And "Again."

Max didn't say anything at all.

The men sparring around them moved slower than usual, obviously watching with increasing amazement as she, half the size of the colonel, threw him around. She moved from judo to the other martial arts she was an expert in, careful to pull her punches, kicks and strikes, or she'd have knocked Max cold a dozen times or more.

He tried to stay out of reach, tried to defend himself, but she moved with speed and confidence.

Near the end of their sparring session she began to see the expressions of the soldiers watching them, clandestinely or she would have called them on it, shift into extreme respect for her and sympathy for him.

It wasn't the rumor she'd wanted, but it might do. For now.

One man cleared his throat after Max was pinned to the mat by a move she was sure he hadn't even seen coming.

"Excuse me, Sergeant," the soldier said with respect. "Could I ask which martial art you just demonstrated to the colonel? I've never seen that takedown before."

"Krav Maga," she responded.

The soldier's eyes widened. "Any chance I could sign up for lessons?"

"At the moment my plate is full." She glanced at Max, whose expression could only be described as patient. "But if things change," she continued, "I'll post a sign-up sheet near the gym doors."

"Thanks, Sergeant," the soldier said to her, then he nodded at Max and went back to his own sparring partner.

Stone glanced at her watch. "That's enough for now, Colonel."

"Thank you, Sergeant." He walked out of the training area.

How did he do it, maintain his calm demeanor? He wasn't emotionless or cold, just inhumanly composed.

She quickly washed up, changed into a clean uniform and went to his office.

They needed to have a little chat.

She knocked on his door.

"Come," he said.

Alicia walked in. He was buttoning his uniform shirt. She raised an eyebrow at his not quite dressed state, and closed the door.

"Quite a performance," he said to her. "Have you had to do that before?"

If she hadn't been intrigued by his behavior before, that question alone would have sparked her interest. Instead of calling her on her shitty attitude, disciplining her for her lack of respect or getting plain mad because she wasn't entirely cooperating with him in the way he wanted, he showed concern and curiosity.

What would it take to make him lose it?

She looked at him. "Unfortunately, several times. The guy who asked for lessons is just about the best-case scenario I can expect. It means no one else is going to test me." She tilted her head to one side, studying him.

He caught her expression. "What?"

"You're calm. After a very difficult training session, you look like you've done nothing more strenuous than going for a stroll."

"Officers are supposed to retain their ability to think and divorce themselves from strong emotion during an attack. It's the only way to ensure your decisions are the right ones. Anyone who allows emotion to cloud their thinking or dictate their actions is a dangerous liability."

"Yeah, but officers are human beings too. I just realized I've never seen you angry. The way you reacted to that asshole I tossed around was the closest thing to anger I've ever seen from you, but you weren't really angry, more…annoyed."

"He forgot who I was." Max shrugged. "I reminded him."

She nodded and pressed her lips together. "What would make you angry?"

"You want to motivate me to fight with emotion?"

At least he didn't pretend to misunderstand. "Yes."

"Not going to happen."

She blinked, genuinely confused. "Why not?"

"Because," he told her, "that's one thing no man of moral character ever does."

For a moment she stared at him as one of the pieces of Max's puzzle finally became visible.

He'd been hurt. Badly.

This was a man with bruises on his soul, bruises so deep it was going to take a lifetime to heal them.

How could she train a man whose immediate and unconscious response to violence, even controlled violence, was to avoid it completely? How could she keep him safe?

If something happened to him, she'd never forgive herself.

# EIGHT

ALICIA TURNED TO leave the office, then stopped with her hand on the doorknob. "What if you looked at what you're doing in a different light?" she finally asked after several seconds.

"Such as?"

She glanced at him over her shoulder. "Think of it like this—you're not attacking anyone, you're getting them out of the way, removing them from the possibility of coming to harm."

Now it was his turn to blink. "How do you mean?" Max stared at her, trying to comprehend her idea.

"I mean, you're not attacking me, you're saving me from attack."

For a moment Alicia's face was overlaid by his mother's. Screaming echoed from the dark hole where he'd buried those memories. Then the screaming stopped and all he saw was his mother's death mask.

He had to work to control the urge to grab Alicia and run. Where didn't matter, he *had* to get her away from the monster about to kill them.

"Max?" Alicia's voice cleared the fog of memory from his sight.

He cleared his throat and attempted to breathe normally. He had to fight his own body to do it. "An interesting idea. Can I think on it? Possibly discuss it later? The rest of my afternoon is already busy."

"Of course." She fixed him with a look that told him she wasn't going to let the topic slide. She opened the door and left.

Max collapsed into his chair and stared at his shaking hands. He'd had two flashbacks in as many days. That hadn't happened to him in years.

A knock at the door gave him two seconds to compose himself, then Eugene came in with a note from Medical about an outbreak of what might be a flu in the supply department.

"Check your email, sir," Eugene said.

Max read with some concern that half of the staff in the supply department were now showing flu-like symptoms.

Max stopped in the medical clinic and suggested the sick be encouraged to either isolate themselves in their quarters or be partially quarantined in the clinic's overnight ward.

Flu was a concern because of its ease of infection and transference from person to person. Unchecked, it could have a third—or more—of the base personnel down at one time.

Max left Eugene in charge of the outer office while he went to the supply room where he had his portable lab stored. All his specialists had their own version of a portable lab. Some of the equipment was the same: microscopes, rapid test analyzers and the special media needed to grow bacteria and viruses. Each specialist, however, added their own equipment depending on what they might need. Max specialized in emergency care and infectious diseases, which meant he tended to have more first aid supplies tucked away in several of the bags that made up his lab-on-the-run.

He checked his supplies often. It was mandated for once a week, but he often added or removed items based on what he was seeing as hot diseases or pathogens out in the world. Today he was adding an additional back-pack filled with IV sets and bags of saline.

Stone walked in while he was adjusting the check-list of supplies.

Memory of hands on him, the sexy growl her voice became during sex, punched him the gut. His dick got so hard he had to adjust more than the damn checklist.

One of the techs, Jones, was giving Stone a more in-depth tour, explaining equipment and how it was used.

Alicia stared at the bags lined up against the wall and asked incredulously, "You've got a complete diagnostic lab in those bags?"

He managed to get control of himself and answer in a professional tone. "Yes. With its own specially designed tent and ultra-compact, ultra-energy-efficient batteries. I can run the lab for forty-eight hours before I need to recharge."

"How do you do that?"

Smart questions apparently turned him on. He cleared his throat. "Multiple ways. On base, I can plug them into the wall plugs and recharge off the base's electricity. Off base, the preferred method is solar panels." He showed her the panels, which were flexible and could be rolled up for storage.

"This is impressive," she said, looking at all the bags and the checklists of contents on the wall above each bag.

"Feel free to examine the contents," Max said. "Now's the time, before we're on the ground at an outbreak."

"Tomorrow," she said, nodding at him. "I'd like to find out how to set up those panels." She and Jones left, already discussing a time to meet to go through the bags.

Max blew out a relieved breath, then finished up, put the room to rights and headed to the food court for a little dinner. He ate quickly and retreated to his room to write in his journal. A lot had happened today. Most of it good, some of it surprising, with the odd moment of terror thrown in for fun.

Alicia had somehow opened up the black hole full of horror he thought he'd locked shut in the base of his brain a long time ago.

She kept pushing and pushing, and he was afraid, *terrified*, she wasn't going to stop until she had him all laid out before her.

What she didn't know, what he didn't want anyone to know, was that parts of him were broken. Some of them beyond repair. He hadn't had this problem with his ex. She'd never asked, but he had the feeling Ali wasn't going to leave it alone.

He never wanted that part of his life to touch her.

Mulling over it all wasn't going to help. He shut his journal after writing what he deemed was safe to commit to paper, then took a shower. He stepped out, dried off and wrapped a towel around his waist before leaving the bathroom.

His bed was occupied.

Heat flashed through him. Fuck, he loved seeing her waiting for him wearing those soft pajamas.

"Is my lock that easy to pick?" he asked Stone. She sat on the bed with her feet tucked underneath her.

"Yup."

If she was trying to get under his skin, she was succeeding.

"Did we have something else to discuss?" he asked, because he wasn't going to assume she was here for a repeat of last night. He really, *really* hoped she was, but he'd learned long ago that it was never safe to assume anything.

She smiled at him.

"Drop the towel, Colonel."

As much as he wanted to drown himself in her, it was also dangerous. He swallowed. "This is highly inappropriate, not to mention against regulations. We should've discussed it last night."

The selfish part of him wanted to take what she was offering with both hands. He could numb the pain of his broken pieces with pleasure.

"No one saw me," she said in a husky tone that turned his cock to stone.

She looked so damned innocent in her pajamas, the same pair she'd worn last night. Then she bit her lip and stared at the tent his cock had pitched with the towel around his waist. "Come here," she whispered.

"Your father is going to shoot me himself," Max said, his voice gone to gravel as he came to stand in front of her.

"No, he won't." She pulled the towel away and dropped it on the floor. "He likes you."

"Enough to look the other way if we get cau…" His brain short-circuited as she went down on him. Her mouth was hot, wet and tight around his cock, and when she pulled back and sucked, *hard*, he lost his mind.

Somehow his hands were tangled in her short hair, guiding her to take him a little slower than she would have. "That's it, Ali," he said as she lifted her head, her tongue doing illegal things to his cock. "*Holy fuck*, don't rush, let it build." He looked down and met her gaze, her face flushed and hot, and there he was on the edge of an orgasm he knew would wreck him. "Ali, stop. I'm going to—"

She did the opposite, taking him even deeper than before, one hand stroking his balls while she watched him from beneath her lashes.

His brain hazed over as he came.

She pulled her mouth off him and finished him with her hands.

When he recovered enough to make sense of what just happened, he shook a finger at her. "That was naughty."

Ali laughed, and the sound of it, relaxed and happy, gave him another buzz of pleasure. He'd made her feel that way.

He wanted to keep that smile on her face for as long as possible. "Stay right where you are."

She tilted her head to one side as he backed away into the bathroom, then came out only seconds later with a wet cloth to clean them both.

Her quizzically amused expression didn't change as she asked, "What are your orders, sir?"

"I," he said, throwing the cloth into the bathroom then returning to the bed, "want to return the favor." He put his hands on her hips and slid them up, pulling her top up and over her head. Then he knelt in front of her and did the reverse, taking her pants off.

He sat her on the edge of the bed, slipped his fingers into the waistband of her panties and slowly pulled them down her legs. His mouth followed his trajectory, kissing her belly and sucking on the tender skin over the point where her thigh and pelvis met.

Alicia gasped and her legs came around his shoulders. "I had no idea that was an erogenous zone."

"Hmm, I'm making it my mission to find them all."

"No argument here."

At least in the bedroom they agreed on things.

He moved closer and closer to her sex until he had her clitoris under his tongue and lips.

Her breathing became deep yet choppy and he knew she was close. "Give it to me, Ali," he whispered. "I want all of you."

She stared at him with pleasure-glazed eyes, and when he stroked two fingers into her without warning, she went off like Fourth of July fireworks.

He brought her down slowly, petting her until she groaned and flopped back on the bed. A quick trip to the bathroom to clean up and he went back to the bed, anticipating sleeping with her, but she was pulling on her clothes.

She smiled at him and walked over to kiss him. "I'll see you tomorrow."

"You could stay," he said, rubbing his hands up and down her back.

"No." She kissed him again. "I'd better slip back to my room now." She stepped lightly to the door, peeked outside and was gone.

Max stared after her, standing naked and alone, the scent of sex in the air.

He felt like he'd been kicked in the gut.

Alicia had gotten under his skin and now that he'd touched her, made love to her, he only wanted more. A lot more.

More than she was willing to give?

He could understand not wanting to get caught sneaking out of an officer's room, but this felt different. Had he done something wrong? She seemed happy, so why the quick dash as soon as they were done?

He wanted more than a fuck buddy. He wanted all of her—her devious brain, insolent mouth and deadly body. Without getting caught.

MAX ARRIVED AT his office a few minutes early, before Eugene and the rest of his staff. He turned on his computer and discovered a couple of reports from two of his teams in the field.

He was writing a reply to a request for supplies and additional personnel when Eugene knocked.

"Sir?"

"Come in, Eugene," Max said without looking up from his computer.

"Sir, I have an update on the flu here on the base." Eugene's voice was much too calm. "No more new cases, but three of the people who reported feeling sick yesterday are now showing symptoms of pneumonia."

Max stopped typing to look at him.

"All three were admitted to the clinic ward last night."

"How many are sick in total?"

"Twelve, sir."

Not reassuring numbers. A flu with a 25 percent rate of serious secondary infection could be ridiculously deadly.

"I'll head over to the clinic shortly to review their charts."

Eugene nodded. "Another hospital pharmacy was

broken into and all of its contents stolen last night. This time it was in Kirkuk, Iraq."

"Do you have any good news for me, Eugene?"

"I'm afraid not, sir. We also have a report of an outbreak of flu in a refugee camp in Northern Iraq near the Turkish border. The numbers coming out of there are mixed. One person says only a dozen people are sick, while another says hundreds. What is clear is that the fatality rate among the infected is high, 25 percent."

"Was that the only consistent thing to come out of the camp?"

"Yes, sir. That and a rather desperate request for help. Two doctors who were working there for the World Health Organization have already died."

"What was the timeline?"

Eugene consulted his report. "The two men first showed signs of the illness, fever and intense vomiting approximately thirty hours before they died."

"Was the cause of death dehydration?"

"No, sir, the report says viral pneumonia."

"Thirty hours? That's fast."

"Yes, sir. I think they're scared."

"I would be too." Max pulled up his master spreadsheet of all his specialists, where they were today and what they were dealing with.

Everyone was dealing with a medical crisis that they couldn't just up and leave. That left only one person able to respond to this outbreak.

Him.

# NINE

ALICIA WALKED INTO the lab building expecting to meet with Max regarding the training schedule for his people. A perfectly normal, professional conversation. If only she could convince her brain to get with the program.

Her head kept replaying his expression when she'd gone down on him. Maintaining a professional distance was going to be a problem, but she couldn't dredge up a speck of regret either. Last night had been amazing. She'd never felt as connected to another human being as she did to Max.

That was some kind of scary shit.

It all took the backseat when she walked into the lab office and found Eugene talking into two different phones at the same time. Max's portable lab bags were on the floor next to Eugene's desk and Max was pacing outside his office talking on the phone.

Eugene saw her, but didn't do much more than angle his chin toward his boss's office.

Max saw her a moment later and waved her over. He indicated she should go into his office. He pointed at his computer, so she sat down in his chair and read the report open on the screen.

Some kind of flu had killed three people in a small village in Iraq that had swelled in size due to an influx of refugees from nearby parts of the country recently taken over by extremists. Three out of the dozen infected people dead. She didn't need a medical degree to know that was bad.

Max ended his call. "I've just arranged coverage for me from the chief medical officer on the base. I'm heading to the outbreak myself. He's going to monitor the flu that seems to have knocked half of Supply on its ass."

"Is there a connection?"

"I hope not, but we'll find out."

"Who's going with you?"

"You are."

Thank God she didn't have to argue her way onto the team. She waited for him to list more people, but he didn't. He just walked around her and headed toward the supply room. Two names wasn't enough. "Just us?"

He didn't even slow down. "I want this to be an in-and-out mission. We arrive unobtrusively, identify the pathogen for the World Health Organization and leave. Short and quick."

That was *it*? "Who treats the sick?"

He walked into the supply room like he was on a one-way mission. "The WHO will assign a team once we know which flu we're dealing with."

"You make it sound like it's going to be a cakewalk." If he didn't stop to listen to her soon, three seconds soon, she was going to make him stop the hard way. He'd look good tied to her bed.

He stopped and looked at her. Well, *finally*.

"It won't be," he said. "But the fewer people we bring, the easier it'll be to do our job and get out without ruffling any feathers."

"Ruffling feathers? You sound like my grandmother." Could she strangle him, just a little? "What you really mean is to do the job without pissing anyone off or pissing on their territory."

He winced like he was in actual pain. "Your use of colorful language isn't necessary is it?"

She laughed. "*Piss* is not a swear word. In fact, I don't think it's even on the soldier's checklist of stress-reducing bad language."

He glanced at her. "It's a pedestrian word, and you're smarter than that."

"What are you, Greek now?"

"*Audentes fortuna iuvat,*" he said absently.

"What?"

"Fortune favors the bold."

Now he was quoting military mottos. "I thought you didn't speak fortune cookie?"

He huffed and glared at her. "I was saving it for a special occasion."

He was getting mad. Good. Maybe he'd stop and think for a minute. "Really? What are we celebrating?"

"Wednesday."

She couldn't help herself. It just tumbled out of her mouth. "Shouldn't we be naked?"

All activity within twenty feet stopped.

She shrugged. "Since we're, you know, celebrating hump day."

Max frowned at her. "Are you drunk?"

She rolled her eyes. "No, I'm somewhat bemused at all the frenetic activity. If this isn't going to be danger-ous, you wouldn't be so wound up. So, tell me again why we're not bringing any backup?"

"You're not going to let this go, are you?"

"I'm the security expert."

"Right, dumb question." He squared his shoulders as

if preparing for bad news. "How many people do you think we should have?"

"Total of four. Two extra to help lug your stuff around and watch our backs."

Max stared at her like he wasn't sure he understood what language she was speaking.

She smiled sweetly at him. "You thought I was going to demand an entire twelve-man team, right?"

"I did."

"You want in and out, that's what you're going to get. Fourteen people are going to make an impression. Four, not so much." She glanced around. People were back to the busy rushing about. "When do we leave?"

"In two hours."

No regrets. That was Alicia's usual motto. Today, she wanted more time spent with Max the man, not the colonel. She wasn't going to get it.

"I'm going to grab our escort and load up on weapons and ammunition. If that meets with your approval, Colonel?"

He raised a brow, then nodded.

Alicia left the building, hiding her bemusement. Max had thought she would argue with him, and she would, but she also knew how to pick her battles. She'd been managing powerful men most of her life. Her father and grandfather, her own officers, and officers from other branches of the military. They all said they wanted to be trained by the best, but very few ever went without challenging her skills or right to teach hand-to-hand combat to men twice her size.

Max was a pussycat compared to some of the assholes she'd had to deal with.

She headed straight for her father's office and found him about to leave.

"Sir? A moment, please?"

"What is it, Sergeant?"

"Sir, Colonel Maximillian is heading to a village in Northern Iraq to identify a possible flu virus that's killed four people. I'd like to take a couple of Special Forces soldiers as escort."

He looked at her for a moment, searching her face. "Approved. I'll give the order on my way out."

"Thank you, sir."

"Don't forget your backup weapon."

She stood a little taller. "I won't, sir." She saluted and headed out of the administration building. Once outside she jogged to the firing range, where the on-base Special Forces soldiers were scheduled to be. At the moment only one team was in residence. A dozen soldiers who were trained by the best to be the best.

At the range she talked to their unit commander, Sergeant Miles Hamston, and asked him who he recommended for this short mission.

Ham, as everyone called him, stood with one hip cocked forward and crossed his arms over his chest. "Don't ask me a bullshit question like that. I know you have two guys in mind, so just tell me who the fuck you want."

She loved working with men who didn't bother with chitchat. "I want Bullard and Irving."

"They're yours. Give me twenty seconds to get them."

It wasn't even that long. Fifteen seconds after he left, he was back with two men. "Try to return them in one piece."

"Will do." She turned to her new recruits. "Get your gear. We're going into a medical hot zone. Possible flu, and it's killing people. Your job will be to watch Colonel Maximillian's back while he does his thing to identify the bug. Prep for three days and don't dress fancy."

She glanced at her watch. "You have fifteen minutes to gear up and meet me at the helipad. Go."

They went.

Alicia jogged to her own quarters, grabbed her go-bag and jammed as much extra ammunition, water and food into it as she could. She added an ankle holster on her right leg with her back up Beretta. Her primary Beretta rode in a leg holster on her right thigh. She tucked four extra clips into the pouches on her belt made specifically for that purpose.

Her primary weapon, an MK 16 Mod 0 SCAR-L, fired forty five-mm rounds and used thirty-round magazines. By the time she was done stashing extra magazines in all the places she could, she looked like a Christmas tree.

Her backpack was filled with survival gear, high energy protein bars, a couple of additional canteens of water and more ammunition.

At the helipad, Max was talking to Eugene when she walked up. The colonel took one look at her and said, "We're going for two days. *Two days*. To identify a pathogen, not rescue hostages." He waved his hand up and down in front of her. "You look like you're going to siege an entire city for a month."

She saluted. *"Leo in deterius expectabit."*

"Plan for the worst, hope for the best?" Max shook his head. "Is that your motto?"

"It is today." She turned and gestured at the two soldiers who'd appeared next to her. "This is Weapons Sergeant Bill Bullard and Medical Sergeant Tom Irving."

Max shook their hands. "It's just the four of us on this trip, so call me Max. My goal is to fly under the radar, so no ranks, sirs or salutes."

"Call me Bull."

"I'm Tom to most people most of the time," the medic said. "Unless shit's going down, then I'm Tomahawk."

"Let's get moving," Max said to them. "I'll brief you in the air."

They got on the bird and a few minutes later, they took off.

Max gave everyone a headset and began explaining to the two Special Forces soldiers the parameters of the mission.

"We're going to a village in Northern Iraq. It was overrun by extremists last month, and approximately forty to fifty people were killed during the takeover. A week later, the extremists pulled out of the village to take over a larger one forty kilometers away. Quite a few of those people escaped and some of them landed in the first village because they had family members or friends there. Two weeks ago a few people came down with high fevers and other flu-like symptoms. More people reported the same symptoms in the following days. Last night, a lot more people reported getting sick, enough to ask for help. Four of them died of what appears to be breathing difficulties. Our job is to get in, identify the pathogen, report the results to the WHO and our own command, then get out without injury."

"Sir, is this going to be like the mission in Northern Lebanon, when your doctor ran into Akbar?" Bull asked.

"Unlikely. My doctor went into that camp not knowing what the pathogen was and worked on the assumption it could be anything. This time, I'm reasonably sure it's an influenza virus, I just need to verify it and determine which one."

"What if it isn't?" Irving asked.

Max shrugged. "The mission will change."

"And Akbar?"

"Is unlikely to be involved in this. He's trying to create the next great plague. While the flu can be deadly, and has been in the past, there are easier pathogens to use as biological weapons than influenza. It's just too... unpredictable."

"Sounds like my last girlfriend," Bull said.

Max looked confused. "You're comparing your last girlfriend to the flu?"

"Yeah, when you put it that way," Bull said, "it does sound kind of bad. But trust me, that bitch made me feel every flu symptom there is."

Stone ignored him. "How many people live in this village?"

"Numbers seem in contention, but approximately six hundred. Two or three hundred are new."

"Who got sick? The residents, the newcomers, or a bit of both?"

"Unknown, but those are good questions. We'll have to ascertain all that when we get there."

He unzipped the duffel bag nearest to him, took out a medium-sized bag and pulled out a fancy-looking medical mask, showing it to everyone. "This is a surgical mask designed to fit snugly on the face and create a seal so no air droplets can get in from the sides. They come in a bunch of sizes, so go through the bag and try them out until you find one that fits. Once you find the right size take an extra mask and keep it with you." He handed Stone the bag.

Max went back to the duffel bag, grabbed a small box and pulled several pairs of gloves out of it. "Take several pairs of gloves, as well."

"Do we have a contact on the ground?" Stone asked.

"Yes, the UN has a couple of different groups with people in the village, an international aid group based out of France has a couple of people in the area, and the World Health Organization has a small emergency clinic set up. They're the ones who contacted me about the flu. Officially, we're not there. We're not going to be there, and no matter what anyone says, we were never there."

"Unofficially?"

"We're coming in to support the WHO. Once we have a diagnosis, we leave. The army's only official act in regards to the village will be a supply drop if needed of emergency food and/or medical supplies."

Alicia studied Max's face as he finished speaking. His shoulders were raised, and that along with clenched hands told her there was more on his mind than he was saying. "In the interests of proper planning," she began, and received instant attention from all three men. "What kind of worst-case scenarios could we see in this village?"

Max's mouth tightened and she knew she'd read him correctly. He was worried about something. "Unfortunately, there're several. When one group of extremists takes over a village they'll usually kill a large number of the men and often boys. Sometimes they kidnap women and children. Sometimes they kill indiscriminately. Sometimes they target specific religious or ethnic groups. The Kurds have been hard hit in the area. So have Christians, as well as any Muslims who don't follow the teachings of the specific extremist group."

He hunched over a little, almost as if he were praying. "Then, another extremist group or the relatives of the displaced might retake the village. They perform the same atrocities as the first extremists in revenge or retribution."

"A vicious cycle," Stone said in a tone that sounded tired already, even to herself.

"One that doesn't end quickly or well." Max shook his head. "We're going into a volatile environment. The aid group workers are in almost as much danger as we are, but the American military is everyone's preferred target, so be cautious."

He pointed at a duffel bag attached to the fuselage of the helicopter. "There are some poncho-like coats that are common in this part of the world in the winter. Where we're going gets pretty cold at night, so no one is going to think twice if they see you wearing one. There're also some scarves to camouflage your helmets and face masks."

He made eye contact with Alicia. "Do you want to go in wearing female or male clothing?"

"I'd rather not advertise I'm a woman."

"Fair enough." He glanced at the two male soldiers to include them. "Who speaks Arabic or Dari?"

He put his own hand up. Alicia put up hers, so did Bull and Tom.

"Excellent. One last thing. We're landing a couple of miles away from the village and walking in. Getting dropped off by an American military helicopter would be enlarging the target that's already on our backs."

"Already?" Bull asked.

"We're outsiders, so by definition, we're suspect."

"Of what?" Tom asked.

Max shrugged. "Everything."

# TEN

THE HELICOPTER HOVERED only long enough for the four of them to grab all the equipment bags before it took off as rapidly as it had descended.

Everyone had to carry their personal pack and weapons in addition to one duffel bag. Max worried that Alicia would be overloaded, but she made no complaint as she hoisted the duffel she'd grabbed over her shoulder.

The Green Berets and Alicia had their MK 16s strapped on under their ponchos, partially hiding them from sight, but still easily accessible.

Max didn't carry one. He had two weapons, besides his brain. A 9mm Beretta and a knife he kept strapped to his right calf under his clothes. It was one of those survival knives that had a hollow hilt filled with a flint, wire and fishhook. He couldn't fight his way out of a cardboard box with it, but having the minimal survival gear attached to his body always gave him an extra degree of confidence.

They'd been dropped off next to a rutted road. The terrain was rocky, and with the temperature only a few degrees above freezing, the only vegetation around was winter brown.

Alicia talked with Bull for a moment, then started off in the point position. The two Special Forces soldiers nodded at Max to follow, putting him in the protected position as they brought up the rear.

They headed perpendicular from the road until they got about one hundred feet away, then they paralleled it to avoid highwaymen, robbers or other armed bandits.

Alicia set a good pace. Her head constantly moved from side to side as she looked for threats.

How did she define a threat? Was it anyone who saw them, or anyone with a weapon who saw them? One person or more than one?

He sometimes got the impression that she saw everyone as a threat, until you proved you weren't. Until then, your continued existence was in question and your ability to keep breathing in doubt.

Was he a threat? Was that why she didn't stay, sleep with him?

Alicia suddenly stopped moving and crouched, giving a hand signal for him, Bull and Tom to do the same.

Max tried to find what she was looking at. There it was. A boy sat on a rock about twenty feet away. A dog crouched near him, along with seven or eight goats.

The boy watched them graze with an unmoving face, like he couldn't see them at all.

Tom rose and ambled over. He sat down near him and offered the child something. The boy accepted whatever it was, said a few words, then Tom got up and came back.

"Shepherd," he reported. "His family lives in the village. What's left of his family, anyway. His father and four brothers were killed when the first group came through. He's the oldest man in his household now. His mother is sick and at the makeshift hospital in the village. I told him we had a doctor, so he's going to tell anyone who might come this way he's never seen us."

The continued blankness on his young face said the boy had already seen far too much.

They marched on. The terrain got rockier and Max found himself following without really looking too far ahead. He was busy watching where he stepped and trying to avoid twisting his ankle.

Alicia slowed, then came to a stop.

The village was in sight, but it wasn't what he was expecting. Stone-and-wood houses dotted the opposite side of a small valley, and seemed to be organized mostly in a circle, perhaps surrounding a well. Most of the buildings and houses appeared intact, but a few looked damaged and others burned out.

It was the couple hundred or so tents set up around the buildings, extending down into the valley, that were the surprise. He'd been told there might be one or two hundred refugees from the neighboring town. This was no one or two hundred. If each tent represented one family, they were looking at several hundred extra people.

Alicia glanced at him. "In and out, huh?"

"It appears my information was incomplete," Max intoned as if he was James Bond.

Bull snickered.

"Very fucking funny," Alicia said in the voice all women used when frustrated by a man acting like an idiot.

Suddenly, he felt very, very tired. "This doesn't change anything. It might even make it easier for us to get our job done without the wrong people being the wiser."

Alicia didn't respond to that, just sighed and said, "Let's go."

The walk down into the valley took longer than he thought it would. Alicia and the Special Forces soldiers adapted their pattern of walking from efficient and alert to tired and unobtrusive. Like four men who didn't want anyone to pay too much attention to them because they didn't have anything interesting.

Except they all had duffel bags slung over their backs.

As they came upon the first tent, a couple of men casually blocked their way.

Bull moved forward to look at them. All he did was stare.

Max wasn't sure what the living roadblocks saw on Bull's face, but they got out of the way within seconds.

No one else seemed interested in making it difficult for them after that.

Max looked for his contacts. Most of the aid groups that helped in these kinds of high volatility situations had interesting people on the ground. People who were quite capable of defending themselves, but were even better at blending in.

They cleared the tents and entered the village itself. Shortly after that a man came toward them. He looked like a local—bronzed skin, dark hair with a full beard—except for one major difference. He smiled and made direct eye contact. Something no local would do.

"Welcome, *cousin*," he said in Arabic to Max. He spread his arms and Max went along with the triple cheek kiss that was the way men greeted their relatives in this part of the world.

"I'm sorry it took so long to get here," Max replied in the same language.

"No, no, don't apologize. The world is a crazy place,

yes?" He put a hand on Max's back and guided him
and his three shadows to a house near the outskirts of
the village proper. A tent had been attached to it, dou-
bling its size.

Max's cousin opened a flap and waved the four of
them in.

The tent had been added to the front of the house.
The front door stood open and a sort of clay potbelly
stove sat in the middle of the canvas room. All around
it were people on cots and pallets. People who were
coughing.

Max immediately pulled his mask and gloves out his
pocket and put them on.

Alicia, Bull and Tom followed suit.

Max's cousin pulled one up out of the scarves around
his neck and hooked it around his ears.

There were fourteen people that he could see on the
cots and pallets.

"Are there more sick inside the house?"

"Yes, cousin." The man's voice was sad. "Many
more. All day the sick have been coming to see grandmother, but she died an hour ago and we have no more
medicine. Did you bring any with you?"

Not enough for all these people. "Is there somewhere
I can show you?" Max glanced at the other bags.

"Yes, yes. Come." Cousin led them into the house
and to what might have been a bedroom, but it was
mostly empty. Two dirty and stained windows filtered
the winter sun, turning the room a hazy grayish brown.

Max put his duffel down and nodded at Alicia, Bull
and Tom to do the same. He stepped close to his cousin
and said in English, "Are we safe?"

Cousin replied in kind. "No. My name is Jonah Cornett. I'm with ACT, a French disaster relief organization. Dr. Amanda Beaulieu from the WHO contacted you... Dr. Maximillian?" For the first time the man sounded uncertain.

"Yes, Colonel Maximillian with the US Army's Biological Response Team. Dr. Beaulieu asked for an infectious disease specialist to come and identify the pathogen making all those people sick." Max glanced back through the doorway into the house full of sick people. "Where is Dr. Beaulieu?"

"We thought we had an influenza," Cornett said absently. He shook himself like a wet dog trying to dislodge water, and continued in a stronger tone. "But half the people who were sick last night have died."

"How many is that?"

"Thirty."

"Where are the dead? I didn't see any bodies as we came in."

"The locals have a place up in the hills where they bury their dead. I don't know if they're all in the ground, but most of the bodies were taken away."

A cold rock formed in Max's gut. "Thirty, that's eighteen more sick and twenty-six more dead than I knew about."

"In the past four hours, a dozen people have stumbled into this house, three of them are already dead."

*Holy fuck.*

"Of what?"

Cornett shrugged. "Pneumonia?"

"What symptoms did they present with when they arrived?"

"A high fever, vomiting, dehydration and a wet, racking cough."

*Pneumonia?* Sudden onset of fever and vomiting followed by dehydration, pneumonia and death. Pneumonia was a common secondary infection of flu, but it didn't usually happen so fast. Could this be a swine flu outbreak?

"It's the blood that's upsetting people."

Cornett's words took a moment to register. "Blood?"

"Come, let me show you."

Max stepped in his path. "Where is Dr. Beaulieu?" Behind him, he could feel Alicia and the boys tensing up, preparing for...anything.

Cornett's eyes looked sunken and black above his mask. "That's who I want you to see."

He led them to another room next door. This one was furnished with bedroom furniture, but the person on the bed was shrouded with a sheet. There were three other bodies stacked against the far wall, also wrapped in blankets and or sheets.

Cornett unwrapped the sheet from around the head of the body.

She appeared to be a woman in her early thirties. There were blood trails leading from the corners of her mouth and both nostrils. The skin of her face was unblemished.

"I need to see her arms and torso."

"Why?" Cornett asked.

"I'm looking for lesions or blisters."

Cornett unwrapped her upper body and Max helped him push her clothes aside so he could see her skin.

"No lesions," he reported aloud.

"Is that good or bad?" Tom asked.

"Since she's dead, it doesn't mean much," Max explained. "I need a sample of mucus from the nose or mouth of a person who's recently begun showing symptoms. Actually, I'd like to test samples from a half-dozen people." He looked at Cornett. "Will that be a problem?"

"No." Cornett's shoulders were hunched and his head hung like it was too heavy. "Everyone is frightened now and afraid they're going to die." He glanced at the body, then turned to Max and said, "You can start with me."

*"Fuck,"* Bull said behind him.

"Rewrap the body," Max told Cornett. "I'll have a swab ready when you're done." He walked back into the room where he'd left his bag and crouched down to open it. Alicia and the boys added their bags to his.

"What do you need?" Alicia asked in a voice only one decibel louder than a whisper.

"I need to set up my equipment and gather the samples. The first test is quite quick. Takes about fifteen minutes. That test isn't very specific, though, so if it's positive for flu, I'll have to do a second one that takes a little longer."

"What do you need from us?"

"Keep people from interrupting me."

She smiled—he could tell from the wrinkles dancing around her eyes. "We can do that. Bull is especially good at roadblocks."

"One of my favorite things to do," the soldier said with a nod.

"Just don't be a pain in the ass when you do it," Tom told him.

"Don't worry, Max," Alicia whispered loud enough for the two men to hear. "I've got you covered. I'll keep these two bozos from tripping you up."

They were making fun of the situation, a common

coping strategy among soldiers. Soldiers who had a bond with each other. Trust. And they'd invited him in. "I feel *so* much better knowing that." He glanced over his shoulder at Alicia, who crouched next to him, and the two men standing behind her. He gave them all a nod. "Carry on."

He began pulling out what he needed to get the samples. Given that there were a lot of people in the vicinity, he left the analyzer in the bag.

"Is Cornett close by?" Max asked Alicia.

She moved away, but was back in only a couple of seconds. "He's talking to someone in the hallway."

"As soon as he's finished, ask him to come in. I want to give him some of the extra medical supplies I managed to jam into these bags."

"Sure." She left the room.

Max pulled out six sterile swabs for collecting mucus and set them aside. He then went through all the bags and pulled out IV sets and bags of saline. Of all the symptoms the patients seemed to be experiencing, dehydration was the easiest to combat. A liter of fluid would go a long way to helping the sick survive long enough for the flu virus to run its course.

As long as there were enough trained people to set up the IVs.

If Dr. Beaulieu was dead, who was left to treat the sick?

Cornett came into the room and looked at all the stuff on the floor. He seemed only mildly curious.

"Do you have medical training?" Max asked him.

"Some," he replied. "But not enough to put one of those into someone's vein. I'm here to determine the needs of areas like this one. Food, shelter and other ne-

cessities. I've already told my people not to send anyone else here. Until you determine what's causing the
deaths, they're going to coordinate with the UN and the
WHO to make sure no one else sends in relief teams."

"Good. The last thing this place needs is more people. Any other doctors or nurses in the village?"

"A couple, but we're overrun." Cornett's face turned
bleak for a moment and he looked like he was about to
be sick. "There were more, but when I went looking for
them, I couldn't find them. Their tent, yes. Them, no."

Max sighed. "I didn't come here with the intention
of running a hospital."

"How could anyone plan for this?"

Max considered the situation. If these people didn't
get help now, a lot of them were going to die. He had
only a finite number of IV sets and when they were
gone, they were gone.

Tom was standing with Bull in the doorway.

"Tom," Max said.

The Special Forces soldier strode over and crouched
next to him. "Yeah?"

"You and I are going to triage the people in this
house. I need to collect samples and you're going to set
up IVs for as many as you can. Got it?"

Max turned to Cornett. "You're going to get a cot or
whatever set up in here for yourself and lie down. I need
someone in this room to keep an eye on the equipment
when I have to step out. Okay?"

"Yes, cousin," Cornett said in Arabic.

Max glanced out the door. A couple of men stood
there arguing with Bull about talking to a doctor. They
were staring at the IV sets and bags of saline.

Cornett walked over to them. "This is my cousin, a

doctor in a hospital in the city. He took some supplies with him when he left, but it wasn't enough. So many more people are sick today than yesterday."

One of the men said, "Give it to the children. To my son. He's twelve years old and strong, but now he lies on the ground breathing like a winded horse. His lips are blue."

Max paused. *Rapid breathing resulting in not enough oxygen?* He stood and joined them in the hallway. "Take me to your son."

# ELEVEN

ALICIA FOLLOWED MAX, Cornett and the man whose son was sick out of the house and down a stone street strewn with rocky debris from explosions and gunfire.

Bull and Tom stayed behind. Tom was already starting IVs for the sick while Bull guarded their gear and watched Tom's back.

She'd argued briefly with Max about the wisdom of making this house call. Briefly, but vehemently. His own mission parameters didn't include caring for the sick. Not an hour had gone by in the village and he was violating his own orders.

It was also damned near impossible to guard a body in motion. They weren't staying in the primary location—they were wandering through a village full of an unknown number of sick people, many of them armed with Russian-made rifles. Instead of the four of them together, they'd split up, making themselves far more vulnerable to attack.

Max had shut her down and told her the situation had changed. She disagreed. It hadn't changed that much, but Max refused to listen to any other complaints.

Fine. She'd ream him out when the mission was over. One of the reasons why she was assigned to him was to give him sound advice regarding security.

Checking out a sick child was the humane thing to do, but it sure as hell wasn't safe.

They entered another house, this one in poorer condition than the one they'd left. It had taken some hits from bullets and probably a grenade or two, leaving debris and rubble all around.

Two women backed themselves into a corner of what looked to be the kitchen while a parade of strange men went through their home. Well, mostly men. They probably thought she was a young man or teenage boy.

The rifle in her hands didn't look at all out of place.

The men ahead of her entered a small, dark room. There wasn't space for her, so she hovered in the doorway keeping an eye on them as well as the way out.

Max crouched next to the pallet on the floor with his stethoscope in his ears as he listened to a boy's chest. The boy's breathing was audible several feet away, sounding like popping bubbles as he struggled to take in air. His whole body looked involved in the effort, not just his diaphragm. She'd witnessed something like this during an advanced conditioning training event. One man had to drop out when he experienced one of the forms of altitude sickness where his lungs filled with fluid. Alicia had ended her training to help get him down the mountain and she'd never forgotten the sound of his breathing—wet popping of air mixing with the fluid in his lungs.

This boy sounded just like him.

Max swabbed the boy's nose and mouth, then pulled out a small handheld device, which he swiped across the kid's forehead.

"How long has he been sick?" Max asked the boy's father.

"Since yesterday. At first he had a fever, headache and a cough. A few hours later the cough got so bad he was bringing up blood, and no matter how fast he breathes, he feels like he's drowning."

"Your son has pneumonia and a high fever," Max said. "He needs to be in a hospital."

"We have no way to get to a hospital," the man exclaimed, putting his hand on the boy's shoulder. "Please help my son."

Max didn't say anything right away. He stared at the young man dying on the floor, then motioned for his father to follow him. "I don't have the medicine or equipment he needs," Max whispered urgently. "If you don't take him to a hospital, he will die here."

"Can you do anything to help him?" the man asked.

"I can give him fluids and some pain medicine, but that's all I have." Max shook his head. "I should have brought a pharmacy."

He knelt next to the boy, got an IV started and hung a bag of saline on a nail in the wall above the boy's head.

"This will help a little, but probably not enough," Max said to the father. "When the bag is empty, pull the needle out of his arm, understand?"

The man had lost all color in his face. He nodded after a moment, then Max strode out of the house like the damn thing was on fire.

She didn't blame him.

He'd come to this village thinking all he'd have to do was test for the pathogen. He forgot the first law of war.

*No plan of operation extends with certainty beyond the first encounter with the enemy.* Helmuth von Moltke the Elder may have died in 1891, but his basic understanding of war was timeless.

Alicia liked to put it this way: no matter what hell you've planned for, reality will be infinitely worse.

They reentered the hospital house and Max went directly to the room where his equipment was mostly still inside the duffel bags. Cornett came to a stop next to Alicia and watched him for a moment.

"We're all going to die," he said softly in English. "Aren't we?"

Alicia decided to answer him. "None of us gets out of life alive."

He seemed to think about that for a minute, then he stiffened and turned to examine her face. "You're a woman?"

She shook her head slowly. "I'm a weapon." She angled her chin toward Max. "His weapon." Then she decided to let Cornett in on another secret. "We weren't told that the illness was so widespread. We expected a couple dozen sick and a handful dead, not all this."

"So, we really are all going to die."

"Maybe," she said, a little frustrated with his defeatist attitude. "But you're still alive and so are we. As long as you're breathing you can make a difference."

"For a weapon, you sound awfully smart."

"Every soldier has to face their mortality at some point."

He straightened a little, walked into the room and said to Max in Arabic, "Can I offer you a sample?"

Max glanced at him and nodded. He pulled out more swabs and took one from Cornett's nose and one from his throat.

"Where's Tom?" he asked Bull in Arabic. Since anyone could be listening in, it was a smart choice.

"He's trying to figure out who gets the IVs and who doesn't."

"Ask him to come back here. I need him to get some more samples for me."

Bull headed off while Max pulled out a compact machine Ali'd seen but never used before. Max called it a Sandwich. It was some kind of analyzer that could identify a long list of bugs and viruses.

He did something with the swabs, turned the machine on, then pressed go.

"How long until you know?" Cornett asked.

"A few minutes. I haven't heard you coughing."

"No, but I had a fever last night."

"The illness seems to progress quickly, so perhaps you don't have it."

Tom came back and Max handed him a handful of swabs. "Try to get samples from the most recently sick. They're more likely to be contagious and have lots of whatever is making them sick in their mucus."

"Will do." Tom left.

"Stone," Max said quietly. "Would you mind having a look around to get an estimate of how many people there are in this village, both new and old residents?"

"Send Bull," she said.

Max turned to look right at her. "You're the better choice. You don't look like a walking tank."

"I can't guard a body I'm not with," she hissed at him under her breath.

"I'm not going anywhere," he muttered, glaring at her.

Cornett spoke up. "I'd estimate between one and two thousand people. I don't know how many sick, but a lot." He glanced at Alicia and added, "Your son should stay here. I'll go for a walk and see how many sick there are."

Max glanced at Alicia, who shrugged.

Max nodded his assent and Cornett left.

No one spoke as the Sandwich did its thing. The house was quiet, the only noise the sound of weak coughing from a variety of throats. Too few.

Tom came back in with some swabs and gave them to Max. "Half the people I checked are dead."

Max stared at him like Tom had spoken a language he didn't understand. "How many?"

"Fifteen."

The machine beeped.

Everyone either took a step toward it or leaned forward to see what the results were.

"Both samples are positive for influenza," Max reported. "No other infections."

"If this is the flu, why are people dying so fast of pneumonia? Is this some kind of bird flu?" Tom asked.

"It's possible. I have a piece of equipment here that will differentiate between specific flu variants, but it takes longer." He glanced around. "And even if I know which variant it is, people aren't dying of the flu specifically. They're dying of the body's response to the flu. It's called a cytokine storm, an overreaction by the body's immune system. We're seeing one of the ways the immune system reacts. Your lungs fill up with fluid and you drown."

"Can you stop it?"

"That is a matter of debate. Some physicians think you can prevent it if you know it's coming, but most of the time you get no advance warning. You get no warning at all. Once it's started, it's almost impossible to reverse. The body has to survive the storm and hang on until the storm has played itself out. Most people don't survive that long."

"Is it like the SARS outbreak a few years ago?"

"Yes. Very much like that. It can kill anyone, no matter how healthy they are before they get sick. In fact, the healthier you are, the stronger the immune response is. So the strongest often die faster than someone whose immune system isn't as healthy."

Holy shit, this stuff was worse than she'd imagined. "So, there's no way to help these people? No treatment?"

"If we had a vaccine for the specific flu strain, that would help prevent people from getting sick, but until we determine the exact variant, it's unlikely that any vaccine we try would work. It would be like shooting at a target in the dark."

"What's our next move?"

"We start the other test. In the meantime, Bull, you contact the base and arrange to have food and medical supplies dropped."

"Dropped?" Alicia asked. "Why not trucked in? We could evacuate some of the sick to hospitals."

"Until I know which flu we have here, I don't want a bunch more new people coming or leaving the community. If this is something new, which is likely because the flu mutates so rapidly it's almost always different than the last time you've seen it, I may be recommending a quarantine of the area."

"I'm on it," Bull said, stepping out of the room and pulling out his satellite-connected radio.

No escape route meant keeping Max safe just got a lot harder.

Max began pulling out items from one duffel bag, quickly putting them together into a narrow work table. On it, he set other items that looked like some of the stuff she'd seen through the glass when he showed her his level-four lab.

"Tom," Max said. "Were you finished putting IVs in?"

"No, I've got two people left."

"Go ahead and get those started, then check on the first ones to see if their condition has improved any."

"Okay. Can I have a few more pairs of gloves? These are my last ones."

"In the duffel closest to the door."

Tom stripped off his current pair, put a new pair on and took several more for his pockets.

"Son," Max said in Arabic, looking right at Alicia, "could you bring some water from the well?" He glanced at the Sandwich and she knew what he wanted to do.

Test the water from the well. If it was contaminated this was going to turn into one giant clusterfuck. She could understand why he asked her to do it—she looked less threatening than Bull or Tom—but could she leave Max and be reasonably sure he'd stay safe?

The house was solid. Tom was playing nurse and none of these sick people had the ability to attack anyone.

She said, "Okay, but under protest," in a suitably quiet tone, and walked to the kitchen. She found a bucket tucked into a nook in the wall.

She picked it up and left.

There were a number of people walking around, old men and women, at least a dozen children, and some men, but no healthy young adults.

With all these new people arriving suddenly and throwing up tents, were they hiding in their homes?

She hoped so, because it wasn't just the living that were making an appearance on the streets. There were bodies, wrapped in cloth, lying outside some of the houses.

Ali hurried past them, careful to keep her scarf up over her mask so no one realized she had medical supplies no one else in this place seemed to own.

The well wasn't far from the house where Max and her team worked, about a three minute walk. It was busy. Two women waited in a short line behind a third who was already using the well. Alicia got in line behind them.

They glanced at her, noted her rifle sticking out from under her poncho and stepped back. The woman using the well waved Alicia forward and instead of taking the water she'd scooped and hauled up, she put it in Alicia's bucket.

These women were used to putting men first, even young men. Was it the rifle that made them think she was a guy?

After a nod of thanks, she began her walk back to the house. There were only a few people out, a few kids, two women and an old man. Not very many for midday. Had the news spread about the sickness? Were people staying home, hoping to avoid the sick?

She was two thirds of the way back to their quasi hospital when gunfire erupted behind her.

It had come from the area around the well. She hesitated. This wasn't her fight, and she had a commitment to Max and her team. She'd taken a couple more steps when a man began yelling in Arabic, demanding to know where the Americans were.

Okay, maybe this was her fight.

A woman screamed, while another yelled back that they'd seen no Americans.

More shots echoed.

Extremists on the hunt for Americans were so not what they needed.

Alicia set her bucket on the ground against the outer wall of a house and walked stealthily back to the well.

She crouched down behind a crumbling stone wall that might have been a small pen for chickens at one time, to take a good look at what was going on.

Was it a small, disorganized group or a larger, disciplined one?

A half-dozen men in traditional garb stood over the bodies of two women prone on the ground and one woman who was kneeling.

One of the men yelled at the kneeling woman, again demanding she tell him where the Americans were, specifically the American doctor.

Max. *The bounty.*

The extremist screamed at the woman again and she fell on her face, crying. The son of a bitch was going to murder her too. Ali could see it in the way he'd shifted his body weight forward, as if he were about to attack her with his bare hands.

Alicia set the butt of her rifle into the hollow of her shoulder and settled into a kneeling shooting posture she could maintain for hours if she had to. She brought her head down and rested her chin on her knee.

The few people who had been between her and the well, blocking her shot, had disappeared. No one wanted to attract the attention of these men.

The woman wailed that she hadn't seen any Americans, but that there were so many new people in the village, in the tents, that there could be foreigners any-where.

The man punched the woman with a closed fist and she went down hard.

Alicia sighted down her rifle, a clear shot to the man's head.

Scuffing noises in the dirt behind her and a breath of warm air fanning over the back of her neck told her she wasn't alone. She turned just far enough to see two little boys, the oldest no more than six years old, hiding behind her watching the scene by the well with wide, frightened eyes.

*Holy shit.* She'd trained in every type of shooting condition but this one.

Could she kill a man with two little kids watching?

What was her escape plan?

Could she make it with two kids in tow?

# TWELVE

MOVEMENT IN THE street behind Alicia had her tucking the rifle out of sight between her and the wall of the house. She kept her head down as four or five men walked swiftly toward the six surrounding the well.

The two little boys shuffled closer to her, shaking and breathing hard. She wanted to look at them, find out if it was shock freezing them in place or if one of them was hurt, but she couldn't take her eyes off the action unfolding in front of her.

"Are you okay?" she asked them softly in Arabic.

They didn't answer. Fear held all their attention. Fear and the murdered women on the ground next to the well.

The newcomers to the party halted about twenty feet away from the gunmen, yelling questions and demands to leave.

"What are you doing here?"

"Why did you kill these women?"

"You don't belong here, go away."

"There is already enough death here, take your guns and go."

The leader of the gunmen shouted back, "We are looking for the Americans. The doctor. Give them to us and we'll leave."

"There are no Americans here. The French doctor is dead. She died last night. Killed by the same sickness that killed my son," one man replied. "Can't you see? This is a place of death now."

"The Americans came a few hours ago," the leader snarled. "We saw the helicopter. Where are they?"

"You are fools," the same local man replied. "None of the helicopters stop here. No one has come here to help us. We're all dying."

The leader of the gunmen lifted his rifle and shot the local spokesman.

A woman screamed and everyone started shooting at everyone else.

Alicia kept her gaze on the leader of the gunmen as he ducked behind the well for cover. He was the worst kind of coward, the kind that attacked the weak so he could feel powerful.

That one needed to die.

As shots and return fire turned the area into a scene that could have come straight out of a spaghetti Western, Alicia narrowed her focus on her target. The sounds, shouts and movement around her disappeared as she mentally placed herself into a pocket of calm resolve.

She assumed her crouched shooting position, aimed and, when her target lifted his head to shoot, she squeezed the trigger.

His head snapped back and he crumpled to the ground.

Target down, she released her mind to take in the scene entirely again.

A bullet hit the stone wall a few inches above her head, raining debris down on her. She eased back from the corner of the house.

When she bumped into the boys, she urged them to

back away as well. "We cannot stay here," she said in Arabic. "Go, quick, quick."

They just stared at her with wide and glassy eyes. Shock.

"Where is your mother?" she asked them.

The bigger one pointed at the well. "She's lying on the ground over there."

Shit, they'd probably witnessed their mother being murdered.

Several bullets hit the house, much too close to her and the kids.

Time to go.

"Come with me," she said to them. "We'll find somewhere safe." She urged them to move away from the fight.

They blinked a couple of times, then scrabbled away, crouching as they ran. She followed, covering their backs with her own body. They made it past the next house, but shouting voices from scene of the fight told her that they may not have gotten away cleanly.

Alicia kept the boys moving with one hand while the other kept hold of her weapon. One of them tripped and fell, and she dropped her weapon to dangle by its strap so that she could grab him. She carried him a few feet before putting him down so he could run on his own again.

She glanced up as she moved to grab her rifle hanging underneath her poncho, and saw a man coming around the house in front of them, his rifle pointed right at her.

The boys froze and put their hands in the air. She followed their example. There was no way for her to get her rifle up before he could shoot her or one of the kids.

The man was one of the six from the well. One of the six looking for the Americans, and she didn't think it was to ask for help.

"Who are you?" he asked in Arabic. "Answer me." His shoulders were tense as was his grip on the rifle. He wouldn't hesitate to shoot if he thought she was a threat.

"No one," she answered, trying for a tone that might fit a teenaged boy. She nudged the children behind her, but that way wasn't safe either. They had to get back to the hospital house to warn her team.

She moved toward him slowly. "Will you help us?" she asked, keeping the children pressed against her legs as she made to edge around him.

His shoulders relaxed the tiniest fraction and for a moment she thought he might let them go, but a second later, it was gone and the man's face lost all emotion.

Decision made, he raised his weapon.

For the first time in her life, Alicia fully released the protective warrior at her core. There could be no mercy for a man who'd murder children.

A shout to someone who wasn't there past his shoulder distracted him. He automatically glanced behind to evaluate the threat.

She launched herself toward the ground, rolling, grabbing a handful of dirt and throwing it at his face as he realized no threat existed and turned back to shoot her.

The dirt spoiled his aim and the shot went wide.

She came up inside his reach, thrusting the heel of her hand against his chin. Her blow knocked him back a step. She grabbed the rifle with one hand while the other hammered down on his wrist, breaking it.

She turned, elbowed him in the face and landed a

mule kick to his right knee. The crunch of his kneecap shattering sounded oddly loud.

Something hot and wet scored her side. She completed her turn to find he'd drawn a knife with his left hand. He must have landed a hit, but it didn't feel significant, so she ignored it.

She blocked his next thrust, and the next, then landed a hard punch against his temple.

He went down like a sack of rocks.

She turned and grabbed up the smallest boy with one arm while tugging on the hand of the larger one, and hurried down the street and away from the fight.

Five seconds passed, and no one shouted at them. A couple of men raced by them toward the well.

Ten seconds passed. The sounds of the battle receded and people peered out of doorways and windows to see what was going on.

Fifteen seconds passed. The hospital house was in sight.

A man called out and rushed toward her. Both boys wiggled out of her hold. She let them go and they ran toward the man, calling him father.

"Go, hide," she said to him. "There are men with guns near the well." She hurried on two houses further and into the hospital house to follow her own advice.

Except this was no place to hide. Everyone in the entire village knew where to take their sick. It was only a matter of minutes before the men at the well obtained that information and showed up.

Tom was observing the street through a gap in the canvas and his rifle's scope. "What the fuck?" he asked as soon as she was inside the tent entryway.

"Six armed men showed up at the well right after I

got my water. They shot two women, then beat another while asking where the Americans are."

"We're blown?"

"Completely. Watch for bogeys. We'll probably have some incoming sooner rather than later."

"Fuck."

She left Tom to his lookout position and found Max in the room he'd taken over for his lab.

"What's going on?" Max asked her. "I heard gunfire."

"There's an armed group looking for Americans. *You*. They shot a couple of women and some of the locals took exception to that. I killed a couple of the assholes looking for us, but there're more out there, so we're in trouble." She looked at the lab equipment he had set up. "We need to leave. Find somewhere defensible to hole up."

"If we leave now, I'll have to start all over."

"If we don't leave now, we're all going to die."

"Well, when you put it that way…" He sighed. "Damned inconvenient of these people to show up now."

"Should I ask them to reschedule for three days from now?"

He snorted. "I'd love to see the reactions to that question. Did you get some water?"

Not exactly. "I had to leave it behind to save a couple of kids."

"I'll accept that answer. Can you help me with this stuff?"

She grabbed his backpack and checked the contents. It looked like he hadn't taken anything out of it. Good. She put it along the wall a few feet from the door, where it could be grabbed on the run.

The Sandwich was still out, so she got it back into its padded bag and shoved it into one of the duffels. He was fussing with the rest of the equipment. She glanced around, certain there was something she should be doing.

What was she missing?

"Where's Bull?" she asked.

"He went out to call the base and arrange for a food and supply drop." Max's head came up and he paused in his packing. "Wait. He should be back by now."

"Be ready to run," Alicia told him calmly.

She trotted toward the front entry and met Tom coming in.

"We've got company," he said, voice low. "At least four, armed with Russian rifles. Older models, but they look like they shoot just fine."

"Shit. We need to go now." Alicia turned around and ran back to grab Max's backpack. "Max," she said sharply.

He looked at her. "What?"

"Catch." She threw the backpack at him, but he let it hit his chest.

"What the hell—"

"*Now*, Max," she growled at him.

Tom raced past them both and attacked one of the windows. He broke the latch on it and shoved it open.

He climbed out of the window, with Max right behind. Alicia slipped out just as gunfire erupted at the front of the house.

What were they doing? Shooting the sick? *Assholes*.

"Masks off," Alicia whispered to the two men in front of her. She whipped her own off and shoved it into a pants pocket.

They walked through the village and out into the tents, tying not to draw attention by hurrying. Max would have increased the pace, but Tom put his hand on Max's shoulder and held him back. They took a right, then found a fairly busy area and sat with their backs to a tent.

No one said anything for a few seconds.

"Where's Bull?" Tom asked quietly.

"He should have reported in a while ago," Max said.

The smell of smoke, present because of open cooking fires, became much stronger. A small explosion had them all on their feet, along with many other people who came out of tents to look in the direction of the noise.

They let the crowd of people surround and carry them toward the noise and commotion.

Black smoke billowed out of the house they'd left and flames devoured the canvas that had enlarged the amount of space for the sick. And the dead.

The heat shattered the glass in the windows, allowing screams to rise above the flames. There were people still alive in there?

Alicia took a step toward the building, but a heavy hand on her shoulder kept her from moving any farther. Max's eyes had gone hard and flat. It was the kind of expression an officer wore when he made a command decision between equally bad options.

Someone bumped into her and pain radiated out from her side, enough to make her gasp.

Max's hand tightened and he looked at her with his brows low over his eyes.

She shrugged.

He gave her a little yank and pushed at Tom to get him moving away from the burning house.

At least the screaming had stopped.

They retreated into the tents until they were standing with no one close enough to overhear.

Max examined her, bending down to get a good look at her. When he got to her left side, he touched her poncho and came away with blood on his fingers. "Why didn't you tell me you were injured?"

"Oh." She stared at the blood and tried to remember when she'd gotten hurt. Right, when she'd killed the asshole. "I forgot."

He gave her an *are you kidding?* expression.

"Sorry." She lifted her hands. "It was a knife. One of the men who killed the women at the well must have tracked me. He was about to shoot me and two little kids who had the bad luck of being near me when the shooting started."

"If he had a gun, why do you have a knife wound?" he asked as he lifted her poncho and bent closer to her.

"I was trying not to draw attention, so I didn't want to use my rifle again. I took his weapon away, but I guess he had a knife too."

"You killed him with your bare hands?" Max asked, rearing back to stare at her. "A man with a rifle *and* a knife?"

"Like I said." She was trying to be patient with him, but sometimes Max made it difficult when he kept asking her to repeat what she'd just told him. "I was trying to be quiet and quick."

"Your hands are quicker than a gun?"

"They're quieter," she said between clenched teeth, working hard to refrain from smacking him.

"I can't see how bad it is. You have too many layers of clothing in the way. How painful is it?"

They had bigger problems to deal with right now. "It's not bad."

"Right," Max drawled. "You forgot all about it."

"We can worry about it when we're out of danger."

"Speaking of which," Tom said softly, nodding behind them. "Here comes a little trouble."

Alicia turned.

The bigger of the two boys she'd gotten to safety stood only a few feet away.

# THIRTEEN

THE BOY WAS staring at Alicia's bloody clothing.

Max watched as the child came over to take her hand.

He patted it as if she needed someone to calm her. "Come, my father will help you."

Alicia opened her mouth, but Max interrupted whatever she was about to say by stepping forward and crouching next to the boy. "This is my friend, and I'm a doctor. Where is your father?"

"We have a house in the village. Come. Father said to bring him." The boy looked at Alicia.

"Can we come too?" Max asked him.

The boy shrugged and took Alicia's hand. He pulled her along with him while Max and Tom followed.

"Where are we going?" Tom asked, his voice pitched so it wouldn't carry.

Max grunted. "Down the yellow brick road."

"Not funny, Max." Tom kept up a constant visual sweep all around. "Bull is late, which means he's in trouble."

"I'm well aware." Losing one of the men under his command was an open wound that seemed to tear wider and wider with every passing moment. "The moment we're secure for more than five minutes, you're going to find him."

"Thank God."

"Did you think I was going to let him rot wherever he was?"

"No, I thought you'd want to send for reinforcements first."

"Why would you think that?"

"You're an officer."

"I think I've just been insulted, but I'll let it pass this once."

"No insult intended. Most officers don't know their right foot from their left."

"I feel so much…smarter now."

The boy took them around the crowd still watching the house burn and back into the village. The house he brought them to was small in comparison to some others, but it was clean on the inside. It had two rooms, one kitchen/living area and one bedroom.

A man stood in the kitchen with the smaller boy, who was hanging on to the man's pants.

Tom came in last and shut the door.

The man looked them all over, then stared at Alicia. "You saved my sons' lives."

Ali glanced at Max, so he stepped forward and smiled. "Children should always be cherished and protected." He gave the man a little bow. "We shouldn't stay." He gave Tom and Alicia a nod and they all turned back to the door.

The man's voice stopped them. "You're hurt."

Max said quietly, "We don't want to bring trouble to your home. We are going."

"You're the Americans those pigs are looking for," the man said. "They will find you if you don't stay out of sight."

Out of the corner of his eye Max could see Tom slowly reaching for his rifle under his poncho.

"I have a place to hide you." The man turned and walked to the large fireplace dominating one end of the room. The chimney looked like it was part of the wall, but there was a narrow gap between the stone and bricks of the fireplace. The opening was dark and there were some rough stairs leading down into the darkness.

"Thank you, my friend," Max said, then bowed and said, "My name is Max."

"Ferhat, and these are my sons, Berez—" he put his hand on the head of the youngest boy "—and Coban." He gestured at the older boy.

Alicia went first. She had to take off her pack, but slid through no problem after that. She came back after a couple of seconds and whispered, "All clear."

Max walked carefully down the steps into the darkness until Alicia turned on a small flashlight.

The room wasn't very big and the ceiling was low. Both he and Tom were going to have to be careful not to hit their heads on it.

A few sacks lay in one corner.

Alicia looked in them. "Vegetables."

"I need to check your wound." Max turned to Tom. "Can you find out what's happening? Where's Bull? Who started that fire? Do we need to call for a retrieval?"

Tom nodded. "I'm going to try to get up on a roof."

"Good." Max turned to Alicia. "This will be easier with a chair or something to sit on. I'll be right back."

She angled her head. "I'm not going anywhere."

Max went upstairs and asked if there was a stool or chair they could use.

Coban grabbed an ancient-looking chair that had lost its back at some point, leaving only the seat. The four legs were wobbly enough to make a drunk look sober.

Max thanked him, took the seat, then went back into the dark root cellar.

Alicia stood in the middle of the room, looking like she was waiting for nothing more serious than a haircut.

He paused.

"What?" she asked when he didn't move toward her.

"It's too dark down here."

She pressed her lips together. "They think I'm a boy," she whispered. "We need to keep it that way."

Damn it, she was right. "Can you hold a flashlight pointed where I need it?"

"Sure." The word was tossed out as if she needed stitches every other day. Here he was, angry at himself for sending her out on an errand resulting in her getting hurt, while she brushed it off.

He was going to have to stitch her up, hurt her again, and she didn't seem to care.

What was going to happen next time? She was good, but she wasn't Wonder Woman, didn't have super powers.

It made him want to turn her over his knee and spank her. Hard. "I know you're a soldier, but this cavalier attitude of yours toward injury is making me crazy." He glared at her. She really had no concept of how close she was walking the line between what he could accept and what he couldn't. "You need to stop it."

She studied his face. "You're worried."

It wasn't a question, but he answered it like it was one. "Yes. There's no situation where you getting injured is ever going to be acceptable. Yet, you act like it happens all the time."

"It doesn't," she said, taking off her poncho and the rifle underneath it. She set them both on the floor carefully and quietly. "Happen a lot, I mean." She removed the body armor, a thick shirt underneath that, and lifted the side of the tank top that was her last layer of clothing.

He wanted to take her out of this dark, dirty place and go somewhere safe, somewhere he could spend the time he wanted to explore her. Pleasure her. Tell her what was between them was more than just sex.

The bloody line that scored her skin an inch above her hip told him his fantasy was beyond reach.

First he had to knit her back together.

"The knife got you just below your body armor." He handed her the flashlight and she pointed it at the wound while he put on fresh gloves and gently palpated the area around the wound.

"It isn't as deep as I thought," he said grudgingly. "But it's still bleeding. I'm going to put a few stitches in, enough to keep it from getting worse if you have to move fast or fight again."

"Okay."

She was much too agreeable.

He took the flashlight from her and shone it to one side of her face, then the other. Her pupils reacted normally and she didn't seem to have any blood or bruises above her neck.

"What are you doing?"

"Making sure you haven't suffered a head wound you hadn't told me about."

"Why would you think I have a head wound?"

"Because you're cooperating without a word of complaint, and that's the opposite of normal for you."

Her frown turned into a scowl. "I'm trying not to be a pain in the ass." She leaned forward, then said with far too much enthusiasm, "But I can do that if you prefer."

"Well, shit." He tried smiling in apology. "I really screwed that pooch."

She snorted a laugh, then caught herself. "Stop that. Stop."

He handed her the flashlight and took off his backpack. Most of his equipment and supplies had been in the house that had gone up in flames, but he preferred keeping his first aid kit separately in his pack.

He pulled out a suture kit and opened it up. He gave Alicia a local anesthetic, cleaned the wound with iodine—call him old school, but he preferred it to other antiseptics—then closed the wound with six neat stitches.

He covered it with a self-adhesive bandage and took the flashlight from her so she could put her clothing back on.

"How do you feel?" he asked. "Light-headed, dizzy?"

"No," she answered, meeting his gaze with ease. "I'm good." She looked at the stairs leading up. "Check in with Tom?"

Max nodded and brought the radio to his mouth. "Tom?"

No answer.

"Tom?"

"Hi, Dad." Tom spoke in Arabic, his voice low and careful.

Relief loosened tight muscles along Max's shoulders. He was safe, but not alone. "How's the weather?"

A long pause, then a reply. "It's raining bullets all over the place. There are two separate firefights going on at opposite ends of the village. No sign of brother Bull."

"Is the fire out?"

"Mostly. It spread to another house, but a few people finally got a bucket brigade going and threw some water on it."

"What are the chances of leaving the village safely?"

"Not so good. I saw a couple of people try to leave. They were chased back into the village by some armed men who must be hiding in the hills around the village. That's not the only bad news." He paused for a moment. "There are a few bodies in the streets. Some of them are wrapped in sheets, but some are just lying outside doorways. Not all of them are the result of the weather."

"How many?" Max asked, despite knowing he wouldn't like the answer.

"I don't know, twenty maybe."

*That many?*

"Call me with another weather report in ten minutes." He ended the call and looked at Alicia.

"What's wrong?" she asked him, her gaze sharp.

"Leaving is out of the question. Tom said he watched a few people try to leave, but they were forced back by armed men. He also reported seeing dead people in the streets." He shook his head. "The number of dead *inside* people's homes has to be even greater."

"Holy shit," Alicia breathed.

"Nothing holy about this." He frowned. "I've never seen a flu infect so many people, then kill them so fast. Identifying it is my top priority."

"No argument here." She shrugged. "Order a supply drop."

"It would have to be unobserved and possibly snuck in by someone on the ground."

"Tonight?"

That was their only option. "I'll make the call."

He contacted the base, and after a couple of conversations was able to arrange for a modified supply drop. General Stone also insisted on four more Green Berets to help with operations on the ground.

More soldiers to worry about.

Max didn't want more people, but with Bull missing and the violence a huge barrier to getting anything worthwhile accomplished, no one was listening.

He ended his call and gave Alicia a sigh. "Company's coming."

"Sweet," she said. "How many?"

"Four of your favorite cousins."

"Sounds like a party."

"More like a disaster waiting to happen."

She fell silent, and Max wondered what she was thinking.

A lot of things had gone wrong since they had arrived. Discovering his contact was dead and the flu virus had a mortality rate far above the norm. The presence of armed fighters who seemed to know there were Americans in the village and were willing to kill to find them. Alicia becoming injured in a fight. Bull's disappearance. A fire that destroyed their equipment and killed several people. And lastly, currently hiding out in an old basement.

"We can't stay here," he said, breaking the silence.

"Why not?"

"We're putting this family in danger." His radio crackled in his ear. He held up a hand to Alicia then replied to the caller, "Hello."

"Dad, you need to come up here." Tom's voice was no louder than his last call, but it held an unmistakable note of fear and anger in it. Something had gone horribly wrong.

"How do we get to the roof?" Max asked.

"One of the kids will show you."

"Tom needs us on the roof," Max said to Alicia.

She preceded him out of the basement and when they got to the kitchen, the older boy was there to show them the ladder on hinges that took them up to the roof.

Alicia stayed low as she exited the hole, so Max followed her example.

Tom lay on his front, sighting down his scope at something some distance away, given the narrow incline of his rifle. Alicia took up the same position on Tom's left. Max did the same on his right.

Alicia had her own rifle out and was using her scope Max didn't have a rifle, but he carried a scope for just this purpose. He pulled it out of a pocket and sighted in the same direction as Tom.

No, his problem was with shooting people. Looking at them didn't hurt anything.

What he saw made his heart falter.

It was the well at the center of the village, the same place gunmen had killed two women and attacked Alicia. More gunmen had a crowd gathered, mostly of men and boys. They were standing in a rough circle around the well, giving several feet of open space for the gunmen to walk around, gesture with their weapons and yell.

To perform.

Near the well, kneeling and with their hands behind their backs, were two men. Behind them were gunmen with rifles pointed at the back of the kneeling men's heads.

A few of the words one was yelling were audible. The gunman screamed about Americans, safety, death and disease, and what the world would soon know as surely as they did.

Nowhere was safe.

The leader of the group suddenly lifted up the heads of the two kneeling men to show the crowd what an infidel looked like.

Cornett and Bull.

# FOURTEEN

THE FUCKERS HAD Bull and their French buddy Cornett. Had them and it looked like they were going to kill them. Bastards.

On the other side of Tom, Max turned the air blue around him. Ali hadn't realized he knew that many swear words. The situation called for every single one. Fury made her hands shake a little, because there was nothing she could do to stop what was about to happen. Max wanted to go unnoticed, had ordered them to make no unnecessary contact with anyone. She understood his orders, but it tied her hands, made it impossible to help Bull or Cornett.

Until Max changed the rules.

"Tactical evaluation," he said to her and Tom. "I want to hear any and all ideas that might get Bull and Cornett out of there alive."

"Sir," Tom said, his voice that of a man who has to deliver bad news. "We're not allowed to—"

"What?" Max asked. "Save a valued asset?"

"Sir, there're a dozen men armed with rifles and they all look like they know how to use them. If we try to extract Bull and the other guy, it will just get them killed."

"Is that your tactical evaluation of the situation?"

"Yes, sir."

"How many armed men are there?"

"At least ten," Tom said.

"I see fourteen," Alicia put in. "A couple are walking a circuit around the edges of the crowd." She studied the situation for another few seconds. "There's no way for us to pick off more than two each without them taking cover. There are too many places to hide and too many people to hide behind."

Max stared down his scope for a few seconds, then asked, "Can either of you tell if Bull and Cornett's legs are tied?"

"I think they're loose, but it's hard to tell," Tom answered.

"What if you hit just one man? The one doing all the talking," Max said.

"Or the one doing all the talking and one other. Someone aggressive…" Alicia's voice trailed off. "The one standing behind Bull. He seems steadier than the guy behind Cornett. Shooting those two will give our boys the best chance of getting away."

"Where are they going to run to?" Tom asked. "Tied like that, someone would have to meet up with them right away and get them out of there and out of sight quickly."

"Max, do you mind a suggestion?" Alicia asked. Did he really think of her as a soldier capable of doing her job, or a woman who needed to be protected?

"I would be grateful for one."

*Score.* "I play sniper and take out those two targets specifically. Max, you act as my spotter while Tom helps get them out of the danger zone."

Max didn't respond immediately, but she could almost see him running her idea through several mental simulations. After a few seconds he turned to Tom. "Your take?"

"The same. It's the only option I can see working."

"Let's do it. How long until we set this in motion?"

"Give me a couple of minutes to get down there and close enough to do some good before you start putting bullets into people," Tom said, already crawling backward toward the hatch in the roof.

"Okay," Max said, sliding closer to her. "What does a spotter do?"

"Normally, you'd have a special scope to determine wind speed, but the one you've got isn't bad. Use it to keep an eye on all the moving targets and anything else that might be a distraction."

"Got it."

Max settled in, his body relaxed in a way it never was when he was shooting at a target, be it a paper outline of a man or the real thing.

She almost pointed it out to him, but stopped herself. He didn't need to think about that now.

She followed his example instead, relaxing into her prone shooting position, following the target doing all the talking. He was moving around a lot, but he paused to pivot on one foot then turn to pace one way then the other. Those pivots would be the best time to take her shot.

She was so wrapped up in formulating her shooting strategy that she caught only the last of Max's whispered comment.

"...ave a couple of minutes."

*Shit.*

"What?"

"I don't think we have a couple of minutes. Look at the leader's body language," Max said, sounding worried. "He's working himself up to something. I think he's almost there. Can you take the shot without Tom in position?"

"I might get both men killed if I take it now."

A second later, the leader shouted and walked with purpose toward the two men kneeling on the ground. He raised his rifle and pointed it at the back of Cornett's head.

She found the center of the leader's head in her scope and tightened her finger on the trigger. Not enough to fire, but enough to keep her body poised on the edge of action.

All her choices had disappeared but one.

Would that one save either man or would it make no difference at all?

"Take the shot," Max ordered.

An evil smile spread across the leader's face.

Alicia squeezed the trigger.

She watched as a small dark hole appeared on the leader's forehead. He toppled over backward.

She found the forehead of the second man, the one with his weapon trained on Bull. "Second target acquired."

"Take the shot," Max ordered again.

She complied, then watched as this man also fell back bonelessly.

For a moment, the scene seemed frozen in time. Some of the gunmen stared blankly at the two dead men. Others hadn't yet seen what had happened.

A second later, people scattered, some screaming, some firing their weapons.

Bull jumped to his feet, and though his hands were tied behind his back, he launched a kick at the man

who'd had his rifle pointed at Cornett before the leader
had come along.

He was a fraction of a second too late.

There was a muzzle flash and Cornett slumped forward.

Bull's kick landed, sending Cornett's murderer to the
ground. He kicked the rifle out of the gunman's hands,
and would have stomped on his head, except that someone else tackled Bull.

He hit the ground hard.

Two men raised their weapons at him, but before either could fire, they were shot instead.

Tom raced toward Bull, shooting everyone who
pointed a weapon at him or Bull. He reached the soldier's side and a knife flashed as he cut the rope tying
Bull's hands together.

Bull grabbed the rifle of one of the dead men, then
he and Tom raced back into the maze of houses, where
they disappeared from sight.

"Where are they?" Max asked after a couple of seconds.

"They went to ground," she told him. "Which is what
they should do in a situation like this. They'll surface
when it's safe."

"I'd like confirmation that they're okay," Max said,
his voice hoarse as if he'd been yelling for hours. "Fuck,
Cornett is dead."

A bullet ricocheted off a rock near his head and they
both ducked down.

When a second shot in their direction didn't mate-
rialize, Alicia used her scope to scan the area, try to
find the shooter. Picking any one particular person was
going to be difficult. It was chaos down there.

People were running, yelling and there was some shooting still going on, but it didn't seem planned or deliberate, only reactionary.

Whoever was holding the reins to the men looking for the Americans was either dead or gone.

She and Max kept watch on the entire village, but no one stood out as either a threat or assistance.

Tom would likely wait an hour for dark to arrive before moving.

Darkness would bring more men and more supplies. She could only hope it didn't bring more bad guys with it too.

Next to her, Max seemed particularly interested in a specific house whose front door and windows faced them.

"What are you looking at?" she asked. The place appeared average in every way and there was no activity that she could see around it. There were a couple of dead bodies, still clad in their clothing, pushed up against the wall of the house. Their faces had been turned toward the wall, but they hadn't been wrapped in sheets or blankets.

"The dead," he replied. He was silent for a few seconds before he added, "And the living."

He pulled away from his scope to look at her. "I'm seeing a lot of sick people, Ali."

A cold shiver went through her body at his tone and expression. She'd never seen him looking so worried. "What does that tell you?"

"We could be looking at a new pandemic flu."

"You mean like that bird flu from a few years ago?"

"Sort of. That one didn't spread like we feared. Which is the reason why the human race is still here, because its mortality rate was horrific. We got very, very lucky with that one. This one looks worse, and all I see when I look at the unarmed, is the sick." His hands opened and closed like he was holding himself back from some action.

"You really need your equipment don't you?"

"Yes. If this virus gets out of this village, it'll be too late to do anything about it."

"Well," she said, turning her weapon and scope toward the edge of the tents surrounding the village. "No one is getting out at the moment." As she watched, armed men stopped a group of six and forced them to turn around and return to the tents.

Max shifted to observe them. "Are they afraid of getting sick or are they doing it because someone ordered them to?"

"I want to know who's looking for Americans," she said. "Is it extremists who want hostages to threaten on TV, or was someone expecting us?" She looked at him. "Does this feel like something Akbar would do?"

"Unfortunately, yes," Max said with a frustrated huff. "The problem is believing that he'd be using a flu virus."

"Why?" Alicia asked. "I mean, one virus isn't much different than another, right?"

"No." Max ran his hands through his hair, something he did only when he was worried. "Influenza viruses mutate extremely rapidly. They pick up bits of genetic code from other viruses they come in contact with inside carrier animals. Pigs, birds and bats are some of the animals that act almost as a mixing pot for influenza viruses."

"Could Akbar control the changes? Make a custom-ized flu?"

"It's been done in labs, but you need specialized equipment and supplies he just doesn't have access to. It would be dangerous to try to create something with-out a fully equipped lab. Even more dangerous than working with anthrax."

"From what I've seen, he doesn't care about danger." She'd read the reports, especially Dr. Sophia Perry's ac-count of her run-in with Akbar, when he'd tried to cre-ate a rabies virus that could be easily transmitted from human to human.

"I hope you're wrong," Max said.

Movement in the street below. Alicia turned her scope to see who was approaching.

"Tom and Bull are coming. That was fast."

"I'll go down and meet them," Max said. He crawled to the hatch and disappeared into it.

She watched the street for anyone following, but no one seemed particularly interested in what two men, one playing sick with a racking cough, were doing.

Just before they got too close to the house for her to keep watching, Tom looked up at her, his expression dark and worried.

So, not good news, then.

A woman's crying grabbed her attention. The door to a home a few houses down the street as opened and a man came out carrying a small bundle. He put it on the ground, but the woman moved to pick it up. He grabbed her by the arm and tried to pull her away.

She'd gotten a piece of it and the blanket-wrapped bundle unraveled.

A child.

The pale skin and absolute stillness of death made looking at the body harder than it should have been. She'd seen death before, but never like this. Never with the agony of the living right in front of her.

A whisper of sound behind her. Someone was coming out through the hatch.

Tom. He crawled over to her and said quietly, "Max wants you downstairs. I'll keep watch."

She nodded and made her way down into the house.

Max was examining Bull in the kitchen. The soldier was bare to the waist, while Max was standing behind him poking at one massive bruise on his back.

After what she just witnessed, she craved Max's lean, confident strength and warm hands on her skin. Strength that knew exactly how and where to touch to take away pain or bring pleasure.

"I don't think you have any broken ribs," Max said to Bull. "But I'm going to wrap them anyway. Broken or bruised, they'll still hurt."

"Thanks, Max."

"Any knife wounds, cuts or other damage?" Max asked as he pulled out a stretchy, self-adhesive bandage from his backpack and began wrapping it around Bull's rib cage.

"Nothing so specific. They beat the shit out of me, but it was all fists and feet. No weapons were used."

Max nodded. "You can put your clothes on. Please repeat your story for your youngest brother."

Bull pulled a T-shirt over his head, then carefully shrugged into his shirt while he said, "Cornett was CIA. He'd been in that French group for a couple of years. He tracked a rumor that Akbar was here, but found no evidence of the man. The goons who grabbed me acted like your standard extremist group. All holy jihad and destroying the infidel. The thing was, some of them whispered that they weren't supposed to shoot any of the Westerners they caught."

"How was Cornett's cover blown?"

"He didn't know, but someone gave the goons an accurate description of him and what his cover story was. They knew exactly where to find him."

"How did you get caught?"

"Pure, dumb, bad luck. I'd found him in one of the tents with a couple of other people from the aid group he was with. We got corralled together and no one asked us a thing until we were tied up."

"Were you questioned?"

Bull smiled, showing off split lips and two black eyes. His whole face was one giant bruise. "Yeah, I played dumb son looking for his mother and sisters."

"So, killing Cornett was a mistake?"

"Yeah. Some of those goons were afraid of what would happen if the nutcase leading them killed any of their captives. They're afraid of someone. Very afraid."

## FIFTEEN

"WHAT ABOUT THE other aid workers?" Max asked, his stomach tight. Cornett might have been CIA and aware of the risks he was taking, but the people he was using for his cover probably weren't.

"We were separated into two groups. The other three were taken somewhere else."

"Anyone trying to leave is being forced back into the village by armed men, so they've got to be here somewhere," Alicia said.

"We don't have enough people or weapons to liberate them," Max said, knowing he wasn't the only one to consider the idea. "And a firefight inside this village would result in too many civilian casualties."

"They're dying anyway," Bull grumbled. "Out in the tents, people are dropping like flies." He sucked in a breath and let it out slowly, testing his ribs and the bandage around them.

Max tilted his head to one side. "How many of the men who took you were sick?"

Bull shrugged, then winced. "At least half of them."

"Did you notice any bodies that could have been their dead?"

Bull stopped poking at his ribs. "Yeah, there was a pit they were throwing the dead into. When I looked in it, all I saw were men. No women or children."

"So," Alicia said in a businesslike way. "We have a

village and refugee camp full of extremists and a flu that's killing people in large numbers."

What a clusterfuck.

What was even worse, this had been planned. By someone else.

"This is not the situation I was told to expect," Max confessed. "The illness, yes. The extremists, no."

"Well," Alicia said. "This is the situation we've got." She looked at him and smiled. It was the kind of smile that reminded a man that not all women were sweetness and light. If you made her mad or hurt those she considered hers, she'd rip your guts out and thank you politely when she was finished. He'd never really considered the advantages of having a partner who could be ruthless in doing what she thought was right. He was starting to love that about her.

"Do we stay or go?" she asked him.

If they left, most of the people here would die.

If they stayed, they'd be fighting on two fronts. Against militants and against a virus whose exact identity was yet unknown.

The virus was the first priority. If it spread and maintained its current infection and mortality rate, thousands—no, millions—of people could die.

"We stay."

Bull and Alicia both straightened a little.

"Screw just four guys. I'm going to ask for a full Special Forces team and another portable lab."

"A supply drop," Alicia said, "would give our extremist friends something to chase while our guys infiltrate."

"These people need the help as well." Max nodded, then grinned. "Excellent suggestion, Sergeant." There was nothing sexier than a smart woman who knew how to play dirty.

Bull coughed and looked away.

Alicia bit her bottom lip and said. "Thank you, *Dad*."

Max sighed. "This cloak and dagger shit is a pain in the ass. I'm going up to the roof to make my *call*."

On the roof, Tom was watching a group of people at the edge of the tents.

"Are they coming or going?" Max asked him.

"Going, but I don't think they're going to get very far," Tom said quietly. "There are enough assholes with guns forcing them back. This is their third try and they're looking pretty desperate."

Max looked down his scope at the group. "They have women and children with them," he murmured, his stomach sinking.

"Yeah." Tom sounded as horrified as Max felt. "This is not going to end well."

As Max watched, one of the group trying to leave rushed a man with a rifle pointed at him. He managed to rip the weapon away, but another gunman took aim and fired.

The man trying to escape fell and the rest of the group seemed to fly apart. People scattered and the gunmen patrolling the edge of the tents began firing at anyone moving. Including the women and children.

*"Motherfuckers."* Tom looked ready to kill them with his bare hands.

"Who are those men?" Max asked.

"I want to know where they're camped so I can give them a taste of their own fucking medicine," Tom growled.

Max pulled his head away from the scope. "That is an excellent point. They can't be camped in the village or the refugee camp. It's got to be somewhere close, though." He glanced at Tom and noted his amazed expression. "What?"

More gunshots echoed and both men dove for their scopes to discover the gunmen shooting at a second group of people from the tents.

"Holy fuck," Tom said, his voice vibrating with fury. "Someone needs to kill those assholes."

"I might let you when our backup gets here."

Once again, Tom turned his head to look at him, surprise lifting his eyebrows. "You calling in the troops?"

"A full Special Forces team along with another lab. I'm also going to order a supply drop for cover when they're ready to come in."

Tom's grin was lethal. "Fuckin' A, Dad."

Again with the shock and awe. When he had ten minutes and no one was trying to kill them, he was going to ask why every fucking soldier on this mission thought he was an idiot.

Leaving Tom to his observations, Max pulled out his satellite phone and called General Stone direct.

After the issues with one of his other teams a few months earlier, Max had insisted on the lead physician having a more reliable way to communicate with their command than cellular phones or the same radio communication system that the rest of the team had. His doctor had had to resort to near suicidal actions in order to achieve her mission because someone used a cellular phone blocker in the area.

"Stone," the general answered. "You're still alive I take it, Max?"

"Yes, sir," he replied as quietly as he could in English. Being overheard by someone in one of the houses nearby would not bode well for the future of their mission. "We've run into some problems and need support."

"Problems?"

Max didn't have to ask for clarification. Stone wanted to know what had gone wrong.

"My contact was dead of the disease by the time we arrived. Another aid worker met us and took us to what they were using for a hospital. I was able to identify the virus as influenza, but a large group of armed men set fire to the house. We got out, but my equipment didn't. Bull and our aid worker friend dropped out of contact. The armed men had them and executed the aid worker before we could get him and Bull out of there."

"Bull?"

"He's fine. Some bruised ribs. He told us our aid worker friend was CIA. Do you know anything about that?"

"No." The word was spoken like the general was spitting it through clenched teeth. "I'll look into it, but I want you and your team out of there."

"Sir, this influenza virus has a high infection and mortality rate. We're seeing bodies dumped outside houses and in the streets. This could get away from us in only a few hours. Hell, it could be too late to stop it already. I can't come in. To have any hope of getting ahead of it, I have to identify the strain. If I don't, we could be looking at a staggering number of dead and a virus that's out of anyone's control."

"A pandemic."

"Yes."

"You're not blowing hot air up my skirt?"

"No, sir."

The following pause was more than a little bit pregnant. "What do you need?"

"Thank you, sir. I want a full Special Forces team, another portable lab, along with a few extras I can have my assistant prepare. I also want a series of supply drops made close to dawn as cover for the team as they come in. We have armed men keeping the people here from coming and going. Sir, there's a deep game going on here."

"Akbar?"

"I don't know. I've seen no sign of him, just well-armed men looking for Americans and me. That bounty is becoming a pain in the ass. Bull did overhear some of the men that held him captive mention a very scary man in charge."

Another pause, then General Stone barked, "Tell your assistant to have whatever gear you need ready in one hour. I'm sending you a dirty dozen along with the hardware."

"Thank you, sir."

"Stay alive, Max."

He knew the general wasn't just referring to himself, but all of the men on the mission, and the woman too.

"I will." He ended the call.

Tom glanced at him. "Get what you wanted?"

"General Stone is no fool."

Tom grunted. "I don't know about that. He sent his daughter out on a mission that had danger written on it with radioactive letters."

"I had no idea you cared so much, Tomahawk."

Both men turned to find Alicia coming out to join them.

"It's a lousy thing for a father to do, put his daughter in danger," Tom told her, censure in every word.

Max winced. Ali was going to go ballistic.

"Fuck you very much," she said to Tom. "No one has to explain jack-shit to you, but since all our asses are on the line, I'll do it just this once. I made the request to be on this team. You know why? Because I'm a woman and women are still not allowed on active duty as Special Forces soldiers. I can beat any man out there. I *train* you sonsofbitches. This is as close as I could get to doing the work I should have been doing years ago."

"He's still your dad."

"Yeah, he is. Where do you think I got my charming personality and winning smile?" She showed off those teeth in the most dangerous smile Max had ever seen.

He cleared his throat and glanced at both soldiers. "Stone, what do you think is really going on here?"

"Colonel," Alicia said lowering her voice, "I think someone went fishing and you...*we* took the bait."

Tom nodded in agreement.

They thought he got suckered?

"I should have let a viral plague just go on its merry way?" he asked them. "Despite calls for help? Despite my team's mission to eradicate these kinds of biological threats before they can become weapons in the hands of ruthless people?"

Alicia lifted her chin. "No, you have a duty to react to shit like this, and you also have a duty to make sure your intel is high quality so you don't lose any men or any of your fancy microscopes."

"Sometimes," Max said, leaning close, "no matter

how much you know or how hard you try, things still go wrong. The job still has to get done."

"Fuck, Dad," Tom said. "You sound like a recruiting ad on TV."

"Did you or did you not volunteer for this mission?" Max asked him.

"Stuck my hand in the air as high as it would go." The soldier grinned. "I guess we're all a bunch of fuckwits."

"Lovely," Max said, punching in the number for Eugene's personal cell phone.

"Sir?" Eugene answered.

"We've run into a few problems. I'm going to need another portable lab, plus a few other things. I have a list."

"Yes, sir." He paused, then said, "Shoot."

"Viral identification packages three, four and six. The hot vaccine package and enough materials for five hundred doses."

"Got it. Anything else?"

"Add some basic medical supplies to the drop General Stone is going to authorize shortly."

"Very good, sir."

"Excellent, thank you, Eugene." Max hung up, then studied the two soldiers scanning the village and surrounding area through their scopes.

"Which of you wants to take the first watch?"

"I will, sir," Tom said.

Alicia slid away from the edge of the roof. "I'll relieve you in three hours."

Max went down the ladder first and was met by Ferhat.

"What is happening?" he asked, his face tight with worry and lack of sleep. "We could hear fighting."

"People tried to leave. Men with guns wouldn't let them. They killed children. Where are your boys?"

"Sleeping."

"We will also, down there," Max said, nodding at the hearth and its hidden stairway. "One of my sons will watch for unfriendly people." He glanced up to indicate Tom on the roof.

The man nodded. "Thank you."

"It is us who thank you."

"Your son protected my sons," the man said. "This makes us more than friends."

Alicia took that moment to slip past them and disappear down the stairs. After a nod to Ferhat, Max followed her.

Bull was already lying along one wall in full gear, his rifle on his chest, asleep.

Ali pulled a drop sheet out of her pack and spread it out on the dirt floor. Max did the same, a couple of feet away from her. She lay on her side, facing Max, a solemn expression on her face.

He wanted to offer her the comfort of his body, hold her, show her she was okay and had done the right thing by killing the man who would have killed a child. "You did good," he whispered. She'd taken lives today, but if she hadn't those two little boys would have died along with her.

Her face softened, and for a moment she looked as emotionally open as she had when they were in bed together. A tear rolled across her face.

He reached out and offered his open palm to her. No censure, no hesitation.

She put her hand in his and he wrapped his fingers around hers, brought her hand to his mouth and kissed it.

She gave him a weak smile and though he knew she wasn't right with it, she was functional.

Mostly.

Max went to sleep with her hand in his.

# SIXTEEN

ALICIA WOKE THANKS to the vibrating alarm on her watch. The room was dark, but her position hadn't changed since she dropped off into sleep.

She and Max were still holding hands.

For a moment she'd been afraid she wouldn't be able to sleep at all. The face of the man she'd killed with her hands was all too clear in her mind, but Max had held out his hand, his expression completely open… and accepting.

She'd placed her hand in his and he'd wrapped his fingers around hers like he planned to never let go.

She'd slept. He'd only said three words, but they'd been the right ones. Her unconscious brain had known how he felt, and that had taken her gut-deep wound and sewn it shut.

That scared her a lot more than anything else.

She was becoming emotionally connected to him. Bonded. If anything happened to him, she'd either lose her shit and go on a rampage, or shut down altogether.

Neither was a good thing.

It was a vulnerability she couldn't afford.

She carefully pulled her hand away from his, then got up and quietly moved up the stairs. The room was dark, silent and empty. The ladder leading to the roof looked like shadowed shelves empty of knowledge. She opened the hatch and slipped out onto the flat surface.

Tom was a dark, unmoving mass.

She crouched next to him. "All quiet?"

"For the past thirty minutes. There has been some sporadic gunfire out past the tents, mostly to the north. A half-dozen times within the village and tents, someone has started wailing, so people are still dying."

"Got any good news?"

"It's not us dying yet."

"Wow, so upbeat I don't know how I will contain my enthusiasm."

Tom's white teeth showed up better in the dark than the rest of his face. "So, you and Max seem cozy."

"I'm his bodyguard. We're supposed to be cozy."

"Right," he said, drawing out the word.

"Listen, asshole," she said. "There're a dozen ways to die on this mission, don't make *me* number thirteen."

"I'm just calling it like I see it, and if I can see it, everyone can."

"What, exactly, can you see?"

"The guy has a near constant hard-on for you."

*The son of a bitch.*

"Why are you watching his crotch? Is there something you want to share?"

"Nope, but you'd better cool it off or it's going to hurt you in a big way."

She couldn't be hearing this one from one of her military brothers, a man she'd trained and chosen for this mission. "What the fuck?"

"Who's it going to damage worse if everyone knows you're knocking boots with the colonel?"

It was a kick to the head. "You know what? Fuck you. Fuck you for thinking either one of us would be thinking about that shit right now. Fuck you for spending too

much of your time and limited brain power looking for
that shit. Fuck you for jerking my chain with that shit."
She was so angry she could have choked him. She settled for squeezing her rifle hard enough to leave finger
impressions. "Now get the fuck out of my face."

He looked at her for a moment and didn't say anything.

She ignored his stupid ass because she'd wasted
enough energy on the moron as it was.

He wiped his face with one hand. "Ah shit, I'm sorry."

"Like I said before," Alicia growled, "fuck off."

"Yeah, I'll do that." He got up and went down the
ladder.

Alicia didn't relax until she heard the hatch close
behind him.

*Asshole*.

She'd thought him a decent guy until now. What the
hell was wrong with him? She and Max hadn't done
anything even remotely improper since they left on this
mission.

*Improper*. Listen to her, going all British.

His little observation had pulled her focus off the
shitty situation they were in. Something none of them
could afford to do.

It took conscious effort to settle in and use her scope
to scan the village, tents and surrounding area. Not a
lot of movement inside the village. There were a few
people moving around in the tents and she could hear
the distant sound of many people coughing. Crying too.

No gunshots from beyond the tents, but it didn't take
long to see people moving around in the distance.

This was a shitty situation. Trapped in a village filled
with sick and dying people, with armed men preventing anyone from leaving.

Fish in a barrel.

Max probably thought he was in exactly the right place to do the most good.

She really had to come up with a superhero name for him.

The hatch behind her opened again and she glanced back to see who it was.

Max. He should still be sleeping.

He crouched down and came over to where she was lying down, keeping watch. "We can't stay here," he said without preamble. "We need to find another place to set up my new lab that's reasonably easy to defend."

"We've got no friends here, but the man whose home we're sitting on."

"So, let's ask him."

"Just remember what happened to the last house we tried to use as a lab and hospital. The people who are trying to pick a fight with us enjoy setting things on fire." She scanned the village through her scope. "And there are a lot more people trying to find a safe place to sleep than there are houses."

"I'll be back." Max scrambled away and she shook her head. The guy had more energy than a damned bunny.

Max was back within a couple of minutes.

"That didn't take long," she said when he joined her at the edge of the roof.

"He says he has the best place to set up a hospital."

"Oh yeah? Where?"

"The village hospital."

She squinted at him. "Are you trying to be funny?"

"No. This village is old. It's been inhabited for hundreds of years. There's a place that they've used as a hospital and a school for most of that time. It's built deep into the rock of the hills and the majority of the rooms haven't been used since the owner of this house was a boy. This place wasn't always a small village. At one time, it was a large town on a major trade route."

"Is anyone using this building now?"

"Nope, there was a cave-in about six months ago. The locals are too afraid of more happening."

"Are they right to be afraid of more?"

"I don't know. What I do know is that our host knows of a way in that goes around the cave-in."

"Fabulous," she muttered. "Sounds like the perfect place to hide out." The militants weren't going to have to shoot them—they were going to die of their own stupidity. And rocks. Lots of heavy rocks.

Max moved away toward the hatch.

"Where are you going?"

"To wake the others. We need to see this place before the rest of our family gets here."

"You go ahead. I'm going to keep watch from here."

"A good idea." Max grinned, then disappeared.

The rest of the village was so quiet, she could hear their host talking to Max inside the house. A couple of young voices threaded through the conversation.

Were they going to take the children with them to check out this place that sounded less than safe?

The roof hatch opened again, but this time it wasn't an adult who came out to lie down next to her. It was Berez.

He stared at her with wide, pale blue eyes.

Or maybe it was her weapon he was staring at.

The door to the house opened and several figures slipped out. Four adults and one child.

She was going to snarl in Max's face when she saw him next. Babysitting duty with a high-powered rifle was never a good thing. She'd already killed one man in front of Berez—he didn't need to see more shit.

She'd probably stunted his growth already.

He inched a little closer, cuddling up to her like a baby chick.

She examined his clothes and realized he must be cold. She opened her poncho and he snuggled right in against her. She was able to partially cover him with her poncho and he sighed, put his head down, then seemed to drop off into sleep.

She stared at the child, uncertainty holding her in stasis. Breathing was difficult, her chest too tight.

He *trusted* her.

She forced her attention back to what she was supposed to be doing, keeping watch on a village balanced on a knife's edge of horror. Fall one way and it would explode into violence. Fall the other and it would succumb to illness.

Movement along the edge of the permanent buildings had her watching that area closely. It wasn't just one or two. There were a lot of people moving around. Coming closer.

A few seconds later, she was able to make out a dozen men walking quietly up the hill, around houses, straight for the house she was on.

She didn't know why she felt certain they were zeroed in on the child's house, but she'd learned a long time ago not to ignore her instincts.

One or three men she might try to shoot. A dozen, nope.

She shook the child awake, then crawled backward, bringing the kid with her. Once they were away from the edge and out of sight—if she couldn't see them, they couldn't see her—she picked the boy up and moved to the back edge of the house.

It backed onto the hill and there were other houses to either side of this one, but they were a few feet lower down the hill.

Which way?

The boy in her arms pointed and wiggled to be put down. She set him carefully on his feet, then put a finger over his mouth. If he wasn't quiet, they were both dead.

He took her hand and pulled her to the very back edge of the house, then pointed down.

A trail.

Narrow, steep and completely unsafe, but a trail.

The boy hopped over the edge and in two seconds was gone from view. She followed and discovered the trick to staying on the trail wasn't just putting your feet in the right places, but your hands too.

The kids around here must be part mountain goat.

Alicia followed him until they were four or five houses away and about one hundred feet from the boy's home. The trail continued on, but they'd be visible to the men approaching, so she gave the boy hand signals to stop and crouch down behind the wall of a house that hid them from view.

She listened hard, but the men didn't speak. Judging by the footsteps, they were almost there.

A door slammed open and gunfire erupted.

Shouting now in Arabic, too many voices to make out individual words, and more gunfire. The voices grew heavy with anger, the weight of them pounding against her ears. The crackle of wood smashing against wood sounded five times too loud. The sounds of bullets never stopped.

Whoever lived in the house she and the child were hiding behind dashed out their front door. More than one person, probably the whole family.

Alicia grabbed the kid, hugged him tight and hurried after the fleeing family.

The boy clung to her, his hands tight on her poncho, front and back, his legs around her waist.

Other people came outside to see what the commotion was about, then ducked back inside.

"Do you know where your father and brother are?" she asked the boy in a whisper.

He nodded and pushed at her to be let down.

She put him on the ground, he took her hand and trotted down the hill.

Alicia kept checking for pursuit, but no one seemed too interested in her and the child. They reached the halfway mark on the hill then the child made a left-hand turn and led her away from the noise and confusion.

They rounded a corner and someone running knocked them down.

Alicia scrambled to her feet, turned to see who they collided with and discovered a man with a rifle. A SCAR rifle. There were only two ways for anyone else to have one of those here.

One, he was a member of the team coming in to help.

Two, he was one of the militants who'd captured Bull and had taken his weapon.

A single look at the man and she knew he hadn't come through door number one. He had none of the lethal grace she was used to seeing in her fellow soldiers. This man didn't know what he was doing.

Still, he knew enough to be dangerous.

He yelled at her and lifted the muzzle of the rifle in her direction.

If he fired, someone else might decide to investigate the noise.

She couldn't let him fire.

Goddamn it, this was going to suck.

Bending over to shield the little boy by turning him away from the man, she pulled a throwing knife out of the sheath inside her right boot and threw it hard.

The man with Bull's weapon dropped in an awkward sprawl.

"Don't look," she told Berez in Arabic as she pulled her knife out of the militant's eye and removed Bull's rifle from around his neck. She wiped the blade on the dead man's coat, put the knife into its sheath, then herded the boy away from the body. "Go, go."

He ran ahead of her and she followed. They were a few houses away when shouts from behind her told her the dead man had been discovered.

Berez led her to what looked like just another house, though this one seemed unused. Broken furniture littered the ground around the front door and windows. He went through the empty maw that should have had a door guarding it and into the dark.

All it would take was one wrong step and that little boy would be injured.

She rushed after him.

The darkness of the interior was nearly complete, but the boy's hand glomped onto hers and he tugged her deeper into the room. She ran into a couple of unidentifiable items before passing through an interior doorway.

Footsteps crunched on the debris-littered floor.

They weren't alone.

# SEVENTEEN

A WARM STIR in the air raised the hairs on the back of her neck. A man stood right behind her. Adrenaline hit her system. She elbowed him in the chest, knocking the wind out of him, and had the heavy breather on the floor a second later, one of her knives at his throat.

"Ali," hissed a male voice from several feet away.

"Max?" Relief released her from the battle high.

"Let him go," he whispered. "That's our host."

The boy's father.

*Oops.*

She released him and backed away. "I'm sorry," she said in Arabic. "I didn't mean to… I'm so sorry."

"You are fierce," Ferhat said, getting to his feet. "Do not apologize for protecting yourself or my son."

She could make out the shapes of Max, the boy and his father now. Somewhere deeper into the structure there was light.

"This way," Max said, pointing in the direction of the light source.

Berez and his father led the way with Max and her bringing up the rear.

"He was going back outside to look for his son," Max said to her quietly. "The kid slipped away when we were leaving their house."

*The little shit.*

"He joined me on the roof, then showed me a rough

trail to take to avoid the militants," she said. "I had to kill another one, though this time I threw a knife."

He glanced at her, but there was no censure in his gaze. "War is a crazy business."

She grunted. "It's a brisk business today."

They walked down a hallway, turned, walked through a room, then down another hallway. The light got steadily brighter until the second hallway was lit up enough to make out the state of disrepair all around them.

There were tables set up in rows, most of them standing, though a few had been knocked over. Along the walls were counters covered in an odd fusion of school and medical bits and pieces. Chalk, syringes, a few books, a broken blood pressure cuff and other odds and ends were scattered around.

Max walked into the next room, the one containing the light source. It was a flashlight that someone had stood on its end with the light hitting the relatively low ceiling.

This room wasn't as messy and dirty as the rest. A long metal table was in the center of the room with a huge spotlight pointed toward it. Tom and Bull were moving what resembled an ancient computer from next to the metal table to the far wall.

"Was this an operating room?" she asked.

"I think so," Max replied. "It's certainly cleaner than all the other rooms. I want to set up my lab in here." He turned to the man who'd sheltered them, risking his life and the lives of his sons. "My friend, do you have family you can stay with? This place may not be the safest if those gunmen find out we're here."

"There is no safe place. My wife is dead. Her parents died last night of the fever. Everyone else is sick. I will find another room where my sons can sleep. We have nowhere else to go."

Damn, now they had civilians to look after.

"Okay." She checked her watch. "Dawn isn't far off. How do you want to do this?"

"Bull and Tom will meet with the Special Forces team, while you set yourself up somewhere high and keep watch. If things go bad, you can provide cover fire to help them get away."

She raised a brow. "What about you?"

"Preparing this room so I can set up my equipment as soon as it gets here." He let out a breath. "I'm going to need samples from the sick."

"I can get those," she suggested. "Being small makes me less threatening to most people."

"Only stupid people," Bull muttered. "Smart people know you're more dangerous than a tiger caught in a burlap sack."

Alicia opened her mouth to verbally smack him, but someone else beat her to it.

"Bull," Max said, "shut your mouth before I put you in the sack with her."

She blinked and Bull started laughing.

Max frowned for a moment, then shook his head. "That's not what I meant."

Bull slid down the wall to sit on his butt, laughing quietly.

She had better luck choking her chuckles back. Bull looked like he couldn't even breathe.

"You're going to give yourself a hernia if you don't stop," Max warned him. "Pull your mind out of the..."

"Sack?" Alicia offered, amused by the entire episode.

"Fine," Max said with a brief glare at her. "Sack. Get yourself up on your feet and get out there to meet with our incoming team."

"Yes, sir," Bull said, still laughing as he and Tom left the room.

After they were gone, she said to Max, "You do realize they're never going to let you forget you said that."

"It won't be the first time I've tried to eat my boots." He shrugged. He attempted to move the large light fixture in the center of the room, but it was bolted to the floor. The metal table was on wheels and was easy enough to put up against a wall.

"How much room do you need?" she asked.

"This is more than enough. I've got plastic sheeting in with the portable lab, so I just have to throw that over the counter and I'll be good to go."

"How long until the team gets dropped?"

Max glanced at his watch. "Soon, about ten minutes. They'll be dropped a couple of miles out to keep from alerting anyone in the village. The supply drops will happen about the same time as the team is ready to enter the village."

"Do I have a few minutes to scout for the best spot to shoot from?"

"Yes, of course." When she didn't move, he asked, "What's wrong?"

"I shouldn't leave you alone. The first rule of bodyguarding is stay with the body."

"Why do I suddenly feel like a walking, talking cadaver?"

His sideways approach to everything never ceased to be a source of amusement for her. "If you are, you look damned good for a dead guy."

He snorted. "Go."

"I think you might have to convince me."

He put down the piece of junk he'd been moving and walked over to her. His hands came out to cup her shoulders and bring her closer to him. "There's a grieving widower and his two small children here. No one else knows where we are. We're as safe as we can be." He ducked down to catch her gaze. "I promise to scream for help if someone happens to come into the building."

"Don't scream. Speaking softly into the radio will work just fine and attract less attention." She looked into his face and found a determination there she hadn't seen before. "If you have to defend yourself or the kids, remember, you're *saving* them, *defending* them. Not attacking someone else."

"I will."

Something about him was different. Harder.

"I'll be back as soon as the new team is here." She left the room and made her way back to the entrance. Once outside she headed for the house one level up and used it to gain access to the roof. The pre-dawn light revealed a dense cluster of brush clinging to the rock face rising above the building.

She wiggled her way inside it and managed to eke out enough room to assume a crouched firing position. The scope showed her a good view of the village as it spread out over the hill and valley to her right.

There were more people out and about, along with militants who seemed to be searching for something or someone. Probably them. Some of the non-militants were performing ordinary tasks—feeding chickens, getting water from the well—others seemed disorientated or lost.

Coughing echoed through the village and down into the tents like the conversation of a room full of people. It came from everywhere and went nowhere.

The distant hum of airplane engines became audible, and got louder and louder by the second. People stopped to look for the source and there it was, a large military aircraft flying low and headed for the valley below the village.

Shouts brought more people out, some in fear, some with hope on their faces.

Alicia looked for the team of Special Forces soldiers that should be approaching the village from the west.

The first crate and parachute came out of the back of the airplane.

Another.

Another.

And another.

Six altogether.

The villagers and refugees poured out into the valley like someone had taken the plug out of a tub. The gunmen trying to keep people inside, the ones who weren't racing toward a crate, were overrun.

Alicia smiled.

Off to the west, a group of men ran at an oblique angle toward the crates, intersected with the edge of the tents, then disappeared into the mob of people.

Seconds later she found them again, moving steadily toward the village proper at a fast walk. They didn't maintain a formation, or specific order, more of a fluid movement of people. Most carried duffel bags, all had backpacks.

No gunmen or militants seemed interested in them—most had hightailed it toward the dropped supplies.

A woman's screams from closer by, inside the village, drew Alicia's attention.

She quickly located the source of the noise and found a couple of armed men wrestling with a woman. They hit her, threw her to the ground. One man fumbled with the front of his pants.

Not on her watch.

She didn't think. She reacted. Found her target, waited for a clear shot and fired.

The man went down. The other man stared at his dead friend for a moment, then ran away.

The woman they had been assaulting scrambled to her feet and disappeared into a nearby house.

The whole thing had taken only a few seconds. A few seconds was all a catastrophe needed. She switched her attention back to the group of men working their way toward the old hospital building.

They were close enough now that she could see the expressions on their faces as they passed dead bodies left outside houses, and a few of the sick who were drawn out of their homes by the supply drop.

The incoming soldiers had all adopted the camouflage Max had insisted on—a scarf tied over the face to obscure the medical mask underneath—but their eyes were visible and reflected horror at what they saw.

It wasn't until they were just twenty feet from the entrance to the old hospital that she noted anyone paying the team any attention. Maybe it was the number of men—fourteen was substantial—or perhaps it was the building they were headed to. Supposedly abandoned. Whatever the reason, two men watched the team from a few houses away. Watched them enter one by one.

The men followed and began yelling at the last couple of team members, one of whom was Tom.

"Don't go in there," one man shouted.

"You strangers must leave," the other said.

Tom turned and shouted back in Arabic, "We're all sick. Do you want us in your homes or here?"

The two men paused, engaged in an intense whispered conversation, then waved at Tom to go inside. They backed away, talking to each other before splitting up and going in different directions.

Great. The whole village was going to know a bunch of sick guys were in the old hospital. A bunch of guys who weren't villagers.

Unfortunately there was nothing she or they could do about it.

Off in the distance, there was the faint sound of gunfire. Rapid, repeating shots. The supplies dropped would have landed that way. The militants and anyone else in the vicinity must be fighting over them.

Had most of the militants gone after the supplies?

She looked over the village and found a knot of women at the well gathering water. Other people seemed to be taking advantage of the lack of armed men to do needed errands, as there were more people out and about than she'd seen since they'd arrived.

A head popped up over the edge of the roof. Tom. He looked around, but couldn't see her, hidden as she was in the brush.

She slid out and he nodded in appreciation of her hiding spot.

"Taking over?" she asked when he got close.

"Yeah, Max wants you inside."

"Got it, thanks. Most of the militants took off after

the bait. The two guys who challenged you split up to spread the word. We're going to have trouble."

"Shit. Well, we'll see how far we can stretch the *I'm sick* card."

"Cough convincingly," she urged as she left.

She was careful to look for any watchers as she got off the roof the same way she got on it, then went inside the building.

Daylight made it easier to see the dilapidated entranceway filled with leaves, dirt and other debris that must have been blown inside during the time it had been uninhabited.

Chairs were collected in an intricate knot of legs in one corner.

Chirping alerted her to a bird's nest clinging to the wall and ceiling in another corner.

Movement deeper inside the building grabbed her focus. A man dressed like she was watched her, his rifle cradled in his arms, ready to fire.

"Stone?" he asked.

"Cold," she said, making light of the name she was often called after a particularly hard training session.

"Colonel wants to see you."

"You are?" All bundled up the way he was, he could have been twenty different men she knew in the Special Forces.

"Frank Jessup."

"Demolitions," she said, his face appearing in her mind's eye.

"Gotta love the boom," he replied as she passed him. "Later."

Alicia walked toward the operating room Max had been trying to clean when she left, and found it full of men, duffel bags of medical and scientific equipment, and weapons. At first she couldn't see Max at all, then he appeared from behind a group of four soldiers who'd found a way to get the big spotlight moved out of the way.

A small hand grabbed the back of her pants and she glanced down to find Berez standing behind her, peeking around her leg to see what was going on.

One of the soldiers saw the kid. "What's he doing here?"

Everyone in the room stopped to look.

# EIGHTEEN

MAX LOOKED UP at team commander Sergeant Greg Nolan's question to see Alicia in the doorway of the room, the smallest boy hiding behind her.

"The child," Max said into the silence, "along with his brother and father, is under our protection."

"For fuck's sake, we don't have time for that," Nolan said, irritation making his tone harsh enough to make the child duck behind Ali a little further.

"No, *I* don't have time for it," Max corrected him. "You, however, have plenty of time to play nice with the locals. Sergeant Stone is going to collect a few samples for me to test while you and your team keep the militants from killing everyone."

Nolan stared at Max, his face immobile for several seconds. "Twelve men aren't enough to keep the peace in a place this size."

"I didn't say you had to pin a sheriff's badge to your chest. The militants are a dangerous and unpredictable threat. They've burnt down one building with a significant amount of my equipment in it and killed a number of people. They seem especially interested in capturing Americans. I'd like to know if they're just fishing or if they've already taken Western aid workers captive with the idea of demanding a ransom."

Max watched Nolan chew on that for a few moments. "Yeah, that we can do. I'll leave a couple of guys here

to keep people out." Nolan glanced at his men. "Hunt
and Jessup can stay. The rest of us will move out. We'll
check in with you in one hour."

"Very good," Max replied. He wasn't sure Nolan
would have heard anything else.

Alicia shuffled out of the way, her young tagalong
still stuck to her legs as the team left.

"Sir," said the one man who'd stayed behind. "I'm
Sergeant Jimmy Hunt, medic."

At least this one wasn't throwing sarcasm into his
face. Yet. He began sorting the duffel bags into a sem-
blance of order. "Well, Sergeant Hunt, care to tell me
why Commander Nolan has his panties in such a twist?"

"It's not you, sir," Hunt explained. "He's pissed off
at the rotten intel we've been getting on this situation.
There weren't supposed to be militants in this place at
all, but there are. And now they seem to be multiplying."

"Given the rapid way people are dying here, that's
saying something," Ali put in.

"The loss of your equipment and the need for a second team makes his neck itchy, sir."

"I knew I was at fault somewhere." Max opened the
first duffel bag and pulled out a roll of heavy duty plastic sheeting and some duct tape. "Here, take this end,"
he ordered Hunt, then rolled the plastic over top of the
long counter that ran the entire length of one wall. Once
the plastic was cut and taped into place, Max went back
to the bag and pulled out a package of nasal swabs.

Alicia came over, with the boy still clinging to her
like Velcro, and took the half-dozen swabs he handed
her.

"Go now," he ordered her. "While people are still

distracted by the supplies. Who knows how difficult it will be to get samples once things start to calm down."

She glanced at Berez.

Max smiled at the child, not much more than three years old, and held out his hands. The boy hesitated only a little before moving into his arms. "Come on," he said to Alicia. "I'll return him to his father."

Max glanced at Hunt. "Do me a favor and cover the other set of counters? I won't be long."

"No problem." Hunt's relieved smile told Max he'd have to make sure the kids and father stayed away from the operating room.

Ali walked out ahead of him and down the hall to the room the boy's father had claimed for them. The father and older brother were sleeping.

Max put the younger boy down and said to him in Arabic, "Time to sleep."

The little one lay down and closed his eyes.

Ali, who'd stayed by the door, led the way out, but Max stopped her before they reached the OR.

"Are you sure you want to do this?"

"No, but I think I'm the best one for the task."

"Okay, I agree, but we both need more sleep. After you take the samples, I want you back here for some rest."

She rolled her eyes. "Max, stop mother-henning me. You don't have the right equipment for it."

He smiled under his mask. "I'll take that under advisement. Carry on."

She saluted smartly and headed out.

In the OR, Hunt had covered the other counter and was going through the bags. He glanced up as Max came in. "This is an impressive setup, Colonel."

"Every man has got to have a hobby." Max began removing items from the duffel bags and placing them on the counters.

Identifying flu viruses was easy up to a point. There were a number of faster detection testing methods available to positively identify influenza. Some of those tests could also differentiate between influenza A, B and C. But determining the specific subtype of influenza—the most common of which were H1N1, H1N2, H3N2—required testing that was neither easy nor cheap. Determining the specific genetic code of a virus to ascertain if it had the potential to become a pandemic threat required a very well-equipped lab.

Max was using one of a handful of analyzers that could accurately determine the specific strain of flu of a sample in very little time.

By the time he had all his equipment unpacked, plugged into the rechargeable batteries and ready to go, Ali was back with the half-dozen samples she'd volunteered to collect.

Her face, what he could see of it, was pale, her eyes almost black.

"What's wrong? You look…" he studied her face "…sick."

"I found a lot of dead people," she said, her voice heavy with sadness and a note of fear. "A lot more of them are sick and soon to be dead."

"How many dead? Sick?"

"I counted fifty dead and twenty or thirty sick, just collecting those samples." She met his gaze. "I stayed close by. I have no idea what's happening on the other side of the village or in the tents." She swallowed hard. "I also found one body in the street, not far from here with a note written on a piece of cloth covering the dead man's face."

A note? Horror took hold of Max's vocal cords. "What did it say?"

"'The wrath of God,' in Arabic."

"It's Akbar," Max managed to say. "It has to be."

"Does that change our plan?"

It was a valid question. "We don't have enough information. He's playing head-games. We should know if there are extremists holding hostages soon from Nolan."

"Don't expect good news, Max." She walked to the wall, leaned her back against it and slid down to sit on the floor. "I'm just going to rest here, if that's okay."

"Ah, yes," Max said sagely. "The first rule of body-guarding is to stay with the body. Of course you can stay."

"Is that the reason you're here, Stone? As the colonel's bodyguard?" Hunt asked.

Ali gave him a sideways glance. "No, I'm after his Italian recipe collection." She frowned. "Why did you think I was here?"

Hunt slid Max a look before answering. "Rumor had it you and the colonel are knocking boots."

"Huh, that must be why Nolan was giving me attitude," Max said.

Ali laughed. It was a tired and sore sound, but it was still a laugh, and Max would take it.

"I'm here because his aim is terrible and he couldn't win a wrestling match with a fly," Ali said, the humor in her voice making her sound almost normal. "Do me a favor and spread that around, okay?" She closed her eyes and appeared to drop off into sleep.

"Was that really the rumor?" Max asked Hunt as he began the first round of testing.

"Yeah, someone saw her coming out of your room one night."

Sometimes the best way to combat an insidious rumor was with the truth. "She did."

"Sir?" Hunt asked.

"She snuck in to demonstrate how easy it was for an enemy to lie in wait. Scared a couple of years off my life and smacked me down hard. It nearly made me ask for someone else, but…" Max shrugged. Was misdirection a lie? "She's the best."

"She is. She's one of us."

The simple statement confirmed Max's theory about where Nolan's sarcasm had come from. Out of some misguided attempt to protect her or show solidarity with her.

"I've worked with several other Special Forces soldiers and I respect your training and your trainers. I need her and I need you and your team. I can't do this—" Max waved his hand at all the lab equipment "—without your help."

Hunt nodded as his expression shifted, became resolute and determined. "How bad do you think this outbreak is going to get?"

Max didn't respond right away. The question only sounded simple, but it wasn't. Viruses weren't known for following rules or staying between the lines. "Any answer I give you would be sophistry, because I just don't know, but…"

Hunt proved he was a smart communicator by staying quiet and letting Max pick his way through what he wanted to say and what needed to be said.

"…I'm afraid the death toll is going to be very high, and we'll be lucky to keep it confined to this village."

"Lucky to keep it confined?"

"If this virus spreads and its infection and mortality rate stays as high as it is now, we could be looking at the next great plague."

"Like the swine flu epidemic in 2009?"

"Oh no," Max told him. "Nothing like that."

Hunt appeared to relax.

"Much, much worse," Max finished.

Hunt's eyes widened. "Shit."

Max fell silent as he finished setting up the first test.

Hunt alternated between watching him and keeping an eye on the interior of the building.

Alicia seemed to be deep into sleep. A good thing. She'd been on alert for a long time, over twenty-four hours, with very little rest. Despite how tough she was, he worried that she was pushing too hard.

She wouldn't like it if she knew what he was thinking, letting her sleep longer than she probably wanted.

As he started the test, he realized the chatter over the Special Forces radio had fallen to near silence.

He walked over to Hunt. "Should I be worried about the lack of conversation over the radio?"

"Sir, Nolan used the code word for *our communications are being monitored*. Someone out there is listening in."

Max's jaw dropped. "How is that possible?"

"Someone probably got a hold of at least one of our radios."

"Theft? From where?"

"Things have been going missing," Hunt said, his

voice low and unhappy. "From a number of places on the base, some ours, some locally run."

"That fits Akbar's SOP. He likes to work havoc from the inside, and has been behind at least two of the most recent attacks in this part of the world. He's ruthless and completely without conscience. He doesn't even care if he kills himself."

Max kicked himself for the umpteenth time. If he'd figured this out just a few hours sooner, a lot of deaths could have been prevented.

"We were all briefed on him. Scary bastard." Hunt went back to watching the door. "Here comes Nolan." He disappeared out the door.

Max glanced at Alicia. Still asleep. She'd earned it.

He left the room and met Nolan along with a half-dozen of his team in the hallway outside the operating room. Hunt was speaking in a low tone to him and Nolan's gaze met Max's for a brief, intense moment.

Was his love life or Ali's that fucking important?

"Someone's listening in?" Max asked the team leader.

"Yeah." Nolan shook his head. "We've got a hell of a clusterfuck brewing here, Colonel. We counted at least thirty armed men and more were coming in. The supply drop was a good idea. From what we could see, these people have been isolated for long enough that they were running out of food and basic supplies."

"Did the militants get it all?"

"No, sir. They got a lot of it, but the locals got to a couple of crates before anyone else could come in and chase them off." Nolan stopped to take a breath. "Sir, I estimate that a third of the population is dead." The last word almost seemed to echo. "Another third are sick."

"What about aid groups? Did you find any that are operating?"

"Not really. Pretty much all of them are dead already, although I did find a couple people from the Red Cross, but they're both sick and refused to let us get close enough to them to ascertain how sick they are."

"Damn it."

"The militants are going to be a problem very soon. You're right about them looking for Americans. They're searching tent to tent and house to house, but they are avoiding places with sick and dead."

"Are they aware of you?"

"That's how we found out they're tuned in to our station. One of my guys found a bunch listening in. Now, we told everyone we came into contact with that we were sick and got chased out of a lot of places, tents and houses. That might buy us some time, but we're going to need a shoot-and-run plan or three ready for when they do finally come after us."

"I'll leave that up to you and your team," Max told him. "You're the experts." He was about to turn back to his makeshift lab, but stopped to share the piece of information Nolan needed to know at the moment. "The only person you have to impress is Sergeant Stone. She gets final say on any plans that involve me running, shooting or fighting in any way."

Nolan frowned. "That's not how we usually do things—"

"I don't give a shit." He didn't. "Her mission is to keep me safe, so it's her ass that's on the line if something goes wrong on your shoot-and-run plan." Max pointed his index finger at Nolan to punctuate his next

words. "You clear it with her or it doesn't happen, do
you understand, Sergeant Nolan?"

Except for a slight raise in his eyebrows, Nolan managed to keep his face neutral.

Max wasn't sure if it was because the other man
was surprised, impressed or disgusted by Max's words,
and he didn't care. All Nolan had to do was follow his
own orders.

"Yes, sir," Nolan said with a salute. "I've got a few
men in watch positions around the neighboring buildings, so we should have some warning if things are
about to get FUBAR."

"Good." Max turned around and took a step toward
his lab.

Alicia was standing in the doorway with her arms
crossed over her chest and a scowl on her face.

# NINETEEN

ALICIA LET HER gaze rest on Max for another second before she glanced at Nolan and nodded. The soldier nodded in return and headed out, leaving behind Jessup and Hunt again.

"I apologize, Sergeant," Max said formally.

Even as tired as she was, she couldn't keep one eyebrow from climbing her forehead. "For?"

"Disturbing your rest."

*Disturbing my...* For Christ's sake, he sounded like a bloody Brit. She was going to have to haul him off to some dark corner and have her way with him. Again.

He didn't seem aware of her reaction, continuing with, "Sergeant Nolan didn't bring any good news."

"Nolan doesn't like good news," she said, restraining herself from rolling her eyes. "He says it's boring."

"I think the situation is plenty exciting enough even for him," Max said with a double handful of sarcasm. "How much did you overhear?"

"The part where he has to impress me with his shoot-and-run plans."

"Then you missed the really depressing news about a third of the people here being dead and another third sick. And we're surrounded by double our force and the only thing keeping them away is the *I'm sick* lie."

"See, this is what Nolan means. This is not boring."

He stared at her like she had gone nuts. "You really need to get a few more hours of sleep."

She knew herself, knew her capabilities. "I'm good for a few hours now."

His expression flattened out. "I might need you in a few hours. Right now I *don't*."

*He did not just say that.*

*He did not just question my judgment.*

*In front of an audience.*

She stared at him as the cold truth spread icy fingers through her chest. If he could decide to ignore her decisions now, when else would he ignore them?

She waited. Waited for him to realize what he'd said and how he'd said it. Bald. Cold. An order and nothing else.

Someone whistled, and out of the corner of her eye she saw Jessup take a step back.

Max glanced at Jessup and Hunt, both of whom were frowning at him, then back at her. She saw the moment he comprehended what he'd said bloom on his face. His eyes widened and he sucked in a breath.

*Too late.*

She saluted. "Sir," she said, her voice as cold as his had been. Then she turned on her heel and returned to her patch of wall where she'd been napping earlier.

"How badly did I just screw up?" Max's voice was clearly audible out in the hallway. Was this his way of sucking up?

"Sir," Jessup replied. "We all complain about how hard she puts us down during training. How she pushes and pushes us to put the extra effort in, because that little extra bit might be the difference between living and dying. She does that because she gives a shit. You just told her you don't."

"That wasn't my intention. I was worried about her not having enough sleep when the fighting starts."

"If you think she hadn't already thought of that, you're the one who needs more sleep. With your permission, sir, I'm going to relieve Tom at the watch so he can sack out."

"Sir," Hunt said. "Do you need me here, or can I set up a watch near the front entrance?"

"That's fine."

Footsteps moved away.

Max came into the lab only after one of his machines beeped.

Alicia cracked open her eyes and watched him tear off a piece of paper the machine had spit out.

When he didn't move, didn't speak, just stared at the paper, she knew the result was not a good one.

"How bad is it?" she asked.

"It's the bird flu, Influenza A H5N1."

"What does that mean?"

"It's highly contagious among birds, domestic and wild. It's everywhere. In humans it has a high mortality rate. It *was* relatively hard for humans to catch the virus. The usual victims are people who working closely with chickens, but…" His voice trailed off for a moment before he finished speaking. "The medical community around the world has been watching this virus closely. It's predicted to be the most likely cause of the next big pandemic, if it mutated to a strain that prefers the tissues of the upper respiratory tract of humans, rather than birds."

"What do you mean by pandemic? Like the Ebola thing that keeps popping up in Africa and Asia?"

"No," he said with a sad chuckle. "Ebola is nothing compared to what this virus could do. Some estimates say five million dead, others fifty million dead. I tend to be on the alarmist side myself. I think it could be far worse."

"Worse than fifty million people dead?" She couldn't imagine that many people gone all over the world.

"Fifty million dead and another thirty-five million infected. That means eighty-five million people will be out of commission, a lot of them medical personnel. Guess what happens to a society when that many people are unable to do their jobs?"

"Anarchy," she whispered, horror strangling her voice.

"Yes."

"How…" She had to swallow to wet a suddenly dry throat. "How can anyone calculate accurate infection and mortality rates that high? Isn't all this just academic?"

"The Spanish flu at the end of the First World War killed at least that many people. Some say as many as one hundred and fifty million people died. There aren't any hard numbers because people were dying so fast, and in some places entire villages of people simply ceased to exist. Not enough records were kept."

"Oh."

"What makes things different today is how mobile the world population is. It's almost a given that any quarantine that's put in place will be too little too late."

"So, we start right now," she said, getting to her feet.

"We get out of here with the samples and get the pharmaceutical companies to produce a vaccine."

"Normal vaccine production takes three months."

*"Three months?"*

"Even if a vaccine could be produced faster, no one is going to rescue us, Ali. We could be infected."

"We have to do something," she whispered. "Anything."

"We can get the information out to our command and make sure samples are picked up so the process of creating a vaccine can begin, but again, that won't help us or any of the people in this village."

"What would help these people…us?"

"Passive antibodies, maybe, from someone who's had the flu, survived and is now healthy." He glanced at his equipment. "I've got everything I need here to isolate the antibodies…" His voice trailed off as he stared. "I'd need more than one survivor to get enough of them."

"I met survivors when I collected those samples," she told him, hope speeding up her heart rate. "How much blood would you need from each person?"

"A unit, like when you donate blood."

"Could I offer food or medical supplies in exchange?"

"Yes." He stared at her like he was afraid to hope. Afraid to imagine an end to this nightmare that didn't result in all their deaths. "Yes, you could. I'd need…" His gaze became unfocused. "At least seven or eight donors to start."

Having a plan relaxed muscles in her face she hadn't known were clenched tight. "Do I have your permission to start rounding up volunteers and sleep later?"

He walked up to her until he was only inches away. "I'm sorry. I was an idiot and I won't do it again."

He wasn't getting off the hook that easily. "Do what again?"

"Disrespect you, in front of other people or in private."

Despite wanting to move closer to him, she took a step back. "As much as I would like to insist on your groveling, we don't have time. What goodies can I give away? Where do you want me to bring the donors?"

"One of the rooms closer to the front of the building. I'll have to see if Hunt and Tom can assist with drawing the blood."

He looked around then grabbed a couple of bags of face masks, some simple pain and fever medication, and a couple dozen packets of electrolyte powder to add to water.

She shook a packet. "What's this?"

"For anyone who's been sweating or vomiting it's one of the best medicines there are." He watched her put it all into her backpack. "Will it be enough?"

"Yeah, I think so. Some rice or flour would be good too, but I don't know if we have any we can give away." She glanced at him and he nodded.

"Okay. Don't take any unnecessary risks. If you see trouble coming, get out of the way."

Her backpack hardly weighed a thing. "Are you saying I'm reckless?"

"No. You have a protective streak a mile wide and when you see someone in trouble, especially a woman or a child, you automatically try to help." He walked right up to her and said quietly, "You can kick my ass and anyone else's ass in a fair fight. These guys don't fight fair, so be careful."

She came to attention and saluted him. "I will, sir. A lot of lives are depending on me."

"Yes," he said, his eyes full of emotion she wasn't sure she wanted to explore too closely. "They are." He saluted her, and she left.

Hunt had picked out a great perch from which to watch the front door and windows. It was a waist-high counter that probably served as the hospital's reception desk. He was lying on it in a prone shooting position watching for anyone approaching from the street.

"I'm going blood-donor shopping," she told him. "Max needs blood from people who've had the flu and gotten better. So I'll be back and forth. He's also going to ask you to help bleed the donors, so let Jessup know you'll be busy soon."

"Shit, that kind of foot traffic is going to bring attention to us."

She shrugged. "Can't be helped."

Hunt sighed, but didn't otherwise comment.

Alicia went to the door, waited to see if anyone was in the area, then slipped out the door and into the gray day. It wasn't raining, but it looked like it could start anytime.

She went house to house asking for anyone who'd survived the sickness. In the first two houses, all she found was dead people. Not a promising start.

She hit pay dirt in the third house. A teenage boy answered her knock and said that his parents were both dead, but he and his baby sister had both gotten better after being sick. Max probably wouldn't take blood from a two-year-old, but the young man looked old enough.

She brought them both back to the hospital, then

went and got Ferhat. He took the teen and his sister in and got them settled in the room with him and his sons.

"I can't leave the tests right now," Max told her. "Can you track down Nolan and ask if his other medic can give me a hand?"

"Sure." She looked at the tired kids and the even more tired father. "Watch your back. Never forget, we're in a foreign country."

She left and after ten minutes of careful searching, found Nolan and a couple of his guys talking with an older man in one of the tents.

Nolan saw her, excused himself and walked with her a few feet away. "Problems?"

"Max needs your other medic to help collect blood donations. He has an idea. Wants to try creating a treatment from the blood of people who've survived the flu."

Nolan grunted. "That is an idea. I'll send him as soon as I'm finished talking with the elder."

"Thanks."

"The militants have been conspicuously out of sight for the past thirty minutes. I don't like it. Don't relax your vigilance, not even for a second."

"I won't. Do you need anything? Any news for Max?"

"There were a few Western aid workers still trying to help these people, but militants went through the tents like locusts and took them all. No one knows where they were taken, or at least no one is willing to admit they know where."

"It's like they're one step ahead of us all the time."

"That is what has me worried. We could be caught in a very large, lethal trap." Nolan nodded at her and went back into the tent.

She continued her search for flu survivors and found three more, all in the same family, who were happy to get out of their tent and into a solid structure even if it was messy. All five of them went together, the other two sick but of the opinion that the best place to go was the abandoned hospital.

The next two tents she went into, everyone was dead. In the second tent, their fire was warm and still smoking, so someone had been alive until not too long ago.

The speed at which people were dying was…scary fast.

She put it out of her head and continued looking for more survivors. It took her twenty minutes to find another survivor, this time an old woman who was weeping over the bodies of her children and grandchildren.

Alicia asked if she'd help to save the lives of other children, other grandchildren, but she pushed Alicia away and continued to wail.

Ali left her to her grief.

She found a young mother who was staring down at the dead faces of her husband and son.

"Why?" she asked Alicia. "Why did I survive when they did not? I would have rather died with them."

"Perhaps so you can help other people."

"I cannot even help myself," the woman whispered.

"You can. You did survive and the secret to helping others is in your blood."

The woman looked at Ali for the first time. "My blood?"

"Would you give a little of your blood to help?"

The woman didn't respond for a long time, stood and stared at the bodies she'd wrapped in blankets. Finally she said, "I will help."

Alicia led her toward the old hospital. The tents and village felt even quieter than before. There were very few voices talking. Coughing was almost the only noise she could hear.

They left the last of the tents behind and passed the first house. It boasted a tall back wall of stone, with no windows until twelve feet up.

As she and the woman passed the wall, men with covered faces rushed them.

# TWENTY

A MAN GRABBED Ali from behind, wrapping his arms around her, trapping her arms against her body. Another man was reaching for her legs when she bent over, forcing some space between her and the man behind. Then she elbowed him hard in the kidney at the same time as she stomped on the top of his foot.

His hold faltered as the second man grabbed her legs. Her arms were free now and she punched him in the throat. When the man who'd grabbed her from behind tried to catch her again she turned, kneed him in the balls, then punched him in the throat too.

The other woman screamed as two men tried to carry her away, kicking and punching for all she was worth.

*You go, girl.*

Distant shouts in Arabic told Ali she didn't have much time before the four kidnappers were going to have help. And while she'd love the chance to beat the shit out of every single man who arrived thinking he could cart a woman off, she wasn't alone.

She pulled out two knives hidden inside her sleeves in arm sheaths, one for each hand, and launched herself at the two men carrying the woman off. She flowed toward them like she was riding a wave, stabbed the one who had the woman's feet in the neck. He went down and Ali avoided his flailing legs as she moved without pause after the other one.

He tried to block her by yanking the woman around, using her as a shield.

Ali went one way then dove the other, ducking low and coming up to puncture his femoral artery.

He fell and dropped the woman at the same time.

She didn't stop screaming, but she did scramble to her feet and kick the man frantically trying to stem the flow of blood from his leg a few times.

Another man, this one armed with a gun, came around the wall and Ali threw one of her knives at him. It took him in the throat and he flopped onto the ground like a dead fish on ice.

Alicia tugged at the woman's arm and managed to get her moving back into the tents before more men arrived.

The other woman clutched at Ali, thanking her repeatedly. Ali found herself in the awkward position of having to shush her so as to not attract more attention from the wrong people.

Speaking of which, the five or six people she'd found better be enough, because it was obvious the militants were going to be looking for her.

They took the long way around to the abandoned hospital, adding a solid fifteen minutes to the time it should have taken to reach it. Time well spent if it saved them from being attacked.

Jessup was off the roof and watching the entrance in Hunt's place.

He nodded at her, but didn't otherwise move.

Hunt was back in the room Ferhat had taken over. Now it housed all the others she'd either delivered or sent for blood donation. Hunt had two people lying down with blood slowly flowing into donation bags from tubing attached to a needle in their arms and was inserting a needle into a third person's arm.

Alicia turned to the woman. "This man is going to take some blood from you. There is a doctor with me who is going to use your blood to hopefully create a medicine."

The woman looked at Hunt dubiously, but before she could speak, Max walked into the room.

His gaze found Ali's first, and though he wore his medical mask openly, she had no trouble seeing the relief in his eyes. He approached her, stopping a socially acceptable three feet away. "Are you all right?" There was nothing socially acceptable about how intense his stare was. It was as if he touched her with his gaze and she found herself growing hot and damp in uncomfortable places.

"Yes. I had a bit of trouble with a group of thugs who thought they were going to carry my friend and me off, but it wasn't anything I couldn't handle." Alicia nodded at the woman and continued in Arabic, "She has come to donate her blood."

"To make a medicine," the woman said firmly.

Max looked at the woman. "Thank you. Your generosity will save lives." He included Ali in his glance. "I must get back to the lab. Please excuse me." He left as precipitously as he'd arrived.

"Your husband is a learned man," the woman said to Ali.

Alicia managed to contain her start of surprise, but Hunt didn't bother camouflaging his bark of laughter. So much for pretending to be a young man.

No point in pretending she was something she wasn't. The female part, not the *wife*. "When it comes to caring for others, he is, indeed, intelligent and thoughtful. His own care…" She shook her head. "I must constantly remind him to look after himself too."

The woman nodded sharply. "That is always the way between husbands and wives. My name is Fatima."

Wait, she and Max acted married?

"I am Alicia, but please call me Ali."

Fatima was looking at the children, the teen and his little sister. "Where are their parents?"

"Dead of the illness."

For a moment Fatima's face reflected intense grief, then she smoothed it over. "May I care for them?"

"I think," Ali said slowly, "that would be good."

"Is there food?"

"Yes, here." Ali showed her a collection of Meals Ready to Eat, as well as bottles of water. Ali demonstrated how to use the heat packs on the MREs and Fatima seemed impressed with the crappy food.

She went to the children and asked if they'd had anything to eat.

Hunt continued monitoring the blood donations and when she caught his eye, he shooed her away.

She walked the short distance toward the lab and found Max writing in his journal. He didn't look happy.

"Got any answers?" she asked quietly.

"Yes, unfortunately." He sighed. "None of them good." He looked at her and his laugh held a razor-sharp tone of irony. She was surprised it hadn't cut anything off her.

"Tell me, Max."

He blew out a breath. "This H5N1 flu is different from the one we've seen so much of in the past few years. This one has a preference for human lung tissue, not avian, or we'd be seeing dead chickens everywhere and we're not."

"That sounds deadly."

"Lethal. On a large scale."

*Large scale?* He was talking about that worldwide pandemic again, but it had to start somewhere.

"Where did it come from? I mean…did people catch it from the local chickens first and it changed? Or did it come from somewhere else?"

"Chickens?" Max said, staring off into space. He glanced at his journal and flipped through several pages. "Death occurs within twenty-four to forty-eight hours after symptoms begin to take their toll."

He paced the length of the room and back again. He looked at his own latest entry. "This is very close to the Indonesian strain, but not quite." He shook his book at the air. "Not quite."

"Max?" she asked carefully. "You're not going all mad scientist on me, are you?"

He muttered to himself for another minute, then seemed to find something significant in his journal. He stared at the page, then closed the book with a snap. "We have to prevent people from getting sick. We need to create a vaccine."

"You said a vaccine would take a few months, so that's out."

"Maybe not. I said the drug companies would take three months to create large-scale doses of a vaccine. If I do it the old-fashioned way, I could cook up a vaccine here, but we'd have no way to test it to find out if it actually works."

"Well, get started already."

"It could just give us the disease."

Fuck, he wasn't giving her too many options that had a reasonable chance at success. "Can we call in an extraction?"

"If we leave we condemn most of the people here to death, and so far, we have a disproportionate number of previously healthy adults dying. That would leave a lot of children to fend for themselves with only the very elderly to care for them."

"What about all the millions in the rest of the world?"

"I can't risk exposing the extraction team to the virus. We could all be infected. I could request more supplies, but the militants might get it, and those supplies in their hands would not be good." He paced the room again, rubbing his eyes with one hand. "Things are too volatile. We've got an unknown number of militant extremists in the area, missing aid workers and a deadly outbreak in progress."

"Maybe there's no perfect answer. Maybe we need to decide on the one that has the best chance of succeeding?"

"I wish I knew which one that was."

"It's been a while since you got some sleep," she said, taking a closer look at his eyes. *Yup. Bloodshot.* "You'll think better if you sack out for a little while."

"A nap," he said pointing an index finger at her. "I can't afford to lose too much time."

"Thirty minutes?" she offered.

"Yes, okay." He nodded. "I need a clear head for this." He headed toward her patch of wall where she'd zonked out for a little while. "Have Hunt collect a unit of blood from everyone who's had the flu and survived."

"He's working on it."

"Good, good." Max sat down then lay down on his side, his head on his backpack. "I'd like a few more donors."

"I'll see what I can do after you wake up." She walked to the doorway. "Sleep."

He closed his eyes and appeared to drop off immediately.

The man was going to work himself to death. When this was all over, she was going to have to insist on a few changes in the way he did things. Take care of himself better. Ali shook her head, then went to check on Hunt and the donors.

Fatima was donating blood now, along with the teenager she'd decided to take under her wing. His baby sister slept between them.

Ali grabbed a bottle of water and a couple of granola bars and put them where Fatima could reach them.

The woman didn't smile, but she nodded.

Hunt looked up when she came in and gestured with his chin at the door. He followed her out.

"Sorry, didn't want to wake up the ones who are sleeping. They're all worn out."

"Max is sleeping too." She glanced into the room. "How many donations?"

"Six."

"Max wants a couple more for sure," she told Hunt. "He's figured out which flu virus it is and he's pretty scared. He wants to try to create a vaccine."

"Here?" Hunt's skepticism wasn't a surprise. "Now?"

She shrugged. "He said something about doing it the old-fashioned way."

Hunt glanced into the room and Ali followed his gaze. Berez was coughing, a wet, rattling sound that had her gut tight with worry.

"He started coughing after we got here, and it's only

gotten worse since. He's got a fever too. Max gave him some acetaminophen and a decongestant while you were outside, but it hasn't made much of a difference."

"Did Max take samples from him?"

"Yeah, a couple."

Then there was nothing she could do but watch over him and his family, and wait.

She looked at Hunt and noted darkened eyes. "How are you feeling? Any symptoms?"

"I have a headache, which is unusual for me. Max took a nasal sample from me too. You?"

"I'm tired and sore, but that's to be expected after a couple of bouts of close-quarters combat."

"How many times have you gotten in a fight this trip?"

"Twice. A bunch tried to carry Fatima and me off."

"Did they appear well trained?"

She thought about it. "They seemed to know one end of a rifle from another, but were ineffectual against me and my knives."

"Their lack of training is an advantage for us."

"That and the fact that they don't expect someone my size to know how to fight back."

"When was the last time you heard from Nolan?" Hunt asked.

"About forty-five minutes ago. He was in the tents, I think, negotiating with some elders. He was supposed to send the other team medic."

"No one has shown up." Hunt frowned. "He's fifteen minutes overdue for a check-in."

"You want me to track him down?"

"No, not yet. If things have gone bad, we're going to need your weapon and your aim."

Footsteps approached from the direction of the entrance of the building. A moment later, one of Nolan's team appeared in the gloom.

Mike Holland was the team's other medic and looked like an extra out of one of those Viking shows. His hair was regulation, but his blond beard and mustache were a little overgrown.

"Hey," he said to her and Hunt. "Sorry I'm late, I had a tail I had to get rid of."

"You were followed?"

"Not very well. It didn't take me two minutes to figure out the two fellows behind me were out for more than a casual stroll."

"What's going on?" Hunt asked.

"A whole lot of dying," Holland said, pulling a granola bar out of a pants pocket, ripping it open and eating it. "It's more than moderately horrible."

"What about militants?"

"Oh they've been busy, mostly questioning and killing people. Between them and the virus, there isn't going to be anybody left alive in this place."

"What are they questioning people about?"

"They keep asking about Americans and other strangers in the village. They've grabbed people from homes and tents alike and taken them somewhere. We don't know where, though we're searching for the place. Nolan has talked with a fair number of the surviving village elders and found out that this sickness just appeared a week ago, like someone dropped a bomb on the place. The refugees had arrived two weeks prior."

"That doesn't sound good," Ali said.

Hunt grunted. "That sounds like a weapon."

## TWENTY-ONE

MAX WOKE TO the sound of his name. He forced his eye-lids open, though they seemed to weigh far more than gravity could explain.

Alicia knelt next to him, a small smile curving up one corner of her lips. "Hi, sleepy head."

Relief surged through him. She was here. She was *safe*. "How long did I sleep?"

"Thirty minutes, as ordered."

He pushed himself into a sitting position then took in a couple of deep breaths. Alicia was only a couple feet away. Behind her sat a line of laboratory equipment and the sight brought the situation into clarity.

He refocused on her face and realized there was one other thing he could do to help the people who lived here.

"Do you have the flu?" he asked her.

"I feel fine, normal, so I don't think so."

"What about Tom and Bull, do either of them have it?"

"Tom thinks he might be coming down with it. I don't know about Bull."

Max pushed to his feet. "Let's ask them."

"You thought of something?"

"Yes," Max said, walking out of the room and into the one where Hunt and Holland were collecting blood from the last person. Tom was there too, helping out.

Max walked up to Tom and put a hand on the other man's forehead. "You're a little warm. Are you coughing? Any trouble breathing?"

"The cough only gets bad when I lie down. No trouble breathing."

Max put his stethoscope in his ears and got the other end past several layers of clothing so he could listen to Tom's lungs and heart. "Chest is clear." He removed the stethoscope and wrapped it loosely around his neck.

"Here's the big question. Have you had a flu vaccination in the past six months?"

Tom's confused face cleared. "Yes, sir."

"Does that mean…" Ali began.

Max was quick to cut off that thought. "I don't know. The vaccine you got was for a different strain. It was close, but not quite the same. Still, it might provide some protection." He looked at her, Tom and Hunt and held their gazes so they paid attention. "One case doesn't mean we're in the clear."

"But, there's hope?" Tom asked.

"There's hope," Max assured him. "I need you to keep a detailed journal of how you feel. If it gets worse, I need to know how it gets worse. Okay?"

"Yes, sir."

Max looked around, but Bull wasn't in the room. "Where did Bull go?"

"Next room over," Tom said. "He complained that it was too crowded in here."

Max got up and went to the next room. Bull was a dark, quiet figure on the floor.

"I'm sorry to wake you," Max said as he crouched next to the big soldier.

No response.

Max shook the other man.

He felt cold, his muscles too lax.

The stethoscope told him what he already feared. He looked over Bull's body to see if there were any physical indicators of what killed him, and discovered a trail of blood from his ear. When he turned him over, blood had leaked out of his other ear as well.

Max got to his feet and walked back into the other room. Everyone's energy levels seemed a bit higher.

This was going to suck.

"Bull is dead."

Every American turned to stare at him. No one moved for two seconds, then Tom exploded to his feet and was out the door and in the next room before Max could take another breath.

Max followed, but didn't approach. Most soldiers needed space at a time like this.

"Was it the flu?" Tom asked.

"I don't know. I'll have to do an autopsy to determine the cause of death, but I don't remember hearing him cough a lot."

"He did have one, but it wasn't bad." Tom shook his head. "He said he felt really tired and had a bad headache. That was a couple of hours ago." He turned to stare at Max, a resigned expression on his face. "He had his flu shot."

"It might not protect everyone. I won't know more until an autopsy is done. It's too early to speculate."

"How could he die in just two hours?"

"During the Spanish flu pandemic at the end of the First World War, millions of people died. Some of them died within hours."

"Why is there blood coming out of his ears?"

"The virus must cause damage to the mucous membranes, leading to hemorrhages. I'm very sorry."

"Not your fault, Colonel. He knew the risks just like the rest of us. But if you find out this bug was manmade, I want a crack at the fucker who cooked it up."

"There's a lineup for that, but I think I could squeeze you in." Max took a good look at Tom's face and saw anger and grief, but what one would expect. "I have to call the base. Can I leave you in charge of the body?"

"Yes, sir."

"Very good."

When Max turned to leave, he found Ali in the doorway. She looked sad and angry, but the expression she gave him was supportive.

"Reporting this to the general?"

He nodded and went around her to go to his lab. "I'm going to ask for another supply drop. A small one this time."

She followed. "How small?"

"I'm thinking it could be dropped by a drone on a specific target." He began to clear a space to set up the equipment he was going to need to separate out and harvest the antibodies in the donated blood.

"That would be better than the stampede we had for the last one." Her voice was dry.

"Yes and no. The distraction was valuable." He glanced at her and she seemed awake and very able to do anything needed. "There's one thing I'm going to need if I'm going to try to create a vaccine from this specific virus. Something that would not likely survive a supply drop."

"What's that?"

"A dozen or more eggs."

"Eggs? Like chicken eggs?"

"Yes, fertilized."

"I'd be happy to go shopping for you, Colonel, but how can you tell a fertilized egg from an unfertilized one?"

"It's called candling. You literally shine a light behind the egg and look for shadows that aren't just a yolk and egg whites. With so many people dead, I think we should be able to find enough eggs from chickens with no current owners."

"Yeah, probably." She sighed. "I suppose you want these eggs sooner rather than later."

He smiled. "You read my mind."

She sighed and sang, "Hi ho, hi ho, it's off to grab eggs I go."

She was almost out the door when he called out to her. "Ali?"

She looked over her shoulder at him. "Yeah?"

"Be careful." He couldn't show her how worried he was, couldn't tell her that if she didn't take care of herself he'd be very, very angry. All he could do was ask.

She paused, then walked back toward him.

And kept coming until she stretched up on her toes and kissed him square on the mouth. "I," she whispered against his lips, "will be very careful if you promise to do the same."

"Deal," he breathed, then cupped her head and ducked down for another kiss. He could nibble on her soft, full lips all day.

And then she was gone.

Max stared after her for a moment, then moved to a part of the building away from the rock face where he could get a signal and pulled out his satellite phone.

"Stone." The general's voice was as professional as always, but there was a note of worry or perhaps impatience in it.

"Sir," Max replied. "I'm requesting a quarantine of this area. I've identified the virus and if it gets out the death toll could be catastrophic."

"Define catastrophic."

"Millions, sir. Hundreds of millions dead. Everywhere."

"Is it Akbar?"

"My gut and the message Ali found on that body earlier are telling me it's him."

For a moment Stone didn't say anything, then his voice came back over the connection. "What do you need?"

"I need vaccination supplies and enough doses of the latest Influenza A H5N1 vaccine for three hundred people."

"Will that vaccine help?"

"It's a long shot, but it's better than doing nothing at all. None of the locals here have been vaccinated and the mortality rate is around thirty-five percent."

"Is it contagious?"

"Extremely. One of our own appears to have died of it about hour or two ago. He'd reported a slight cough, went to grab a few hours of sleep and died. Another of the men is reporting flu-like symptoms, but his illness isn't progressing. His appears to be like any other flu in a healthy adult. Irritating, but not lethal."

Max took a deep breath and continued. "But two cases don't tell me much. That's why I want to attempt to vaccinate the remaining population here. If it helps hundreds of people, then I'll have hope that the vaccine is helpful."

"What's your plan B?"

"That is plan B. Plan A is two-fold. We've collected blood from survivors so I can harvest antibodies to the virus, to use as a treatment for those who are gravely sick. I'm also going to try to culture a vaccine here from the full virus. In case plan B doesn't work. That's forty-eight hours away, though."

"Which soldier died?"

"Bull. I mean, Sergeant Bullard."

"Good man."

"Yes, sir."

"I'm going to give the phone to your assistant he can get your stuff. We'll have to coordinate a covert drop for this one."

"My thought as well, sir."

"Don't risk yourself or any of our soldiers if you don't have to."

He didn't say "take care of my daughter," probably because that sentiment would earn him a nasty reaction from said daughter, but Max didn't have difficulty in inferring the meaning.

"No, sir, I won't. I need every one of them able to perform at their current impressive level."

"Good."

There was a bit of static, then Eugene greeted him and Max began to list off the supplies he'd need.

"Have you heard anything on Akbar's movements?" Max asked when he'd finished.

"No, sir. It's been quiet. No suspicious letters or packages." He paused. "Do you think he's in Northern Iraq?"

"I really hope not, but I think I'm going to be disappointed."

"You need biohazard suits if you're dealing with him."

"That would be like closing the barn door after the horses have gotten out. Too little too late."

"Sir, do you need assistance?"

"No, Eugene, I've got three Special Forces medics assisting and Sergeant Stone is off right now gathering eggs for me. I'm good."

"Eggs?"

He sounded flabbergasted.

"It's a little old school, but I want to try to culture a live but weakened version of the virus. The deadly version isn't safe to work with."

"Very good, sir. Anything else?"

"Not now. Thank you, Eugene, and carry on."

"Yes, sir." There was a pause, voices in the background. "Sir, I have the information on your covert drop."

"Excellent." Max took down the coordinates and time—just after sunset—then he ended the call.

He went out to Jessup, who was guarding the front door. "Can you get Nolan to come in? I've requested a covert drop and we need to send a team to intercept it."

"He's got eyes on the front door of the building, so that's no problem." Jessup went to one of the windows next to the door and moved the old, ratty curtain so it covered about a third of the window.

"That's it?"

"Simple is always better. Of course the next signal isn't the same."

"Huh, you have a whole list?"

"Yeah, six or so."

Movement outside caught both their attention, but it was Alicia returning. She didn't arrive via the shortest or most direct way. She zigzagged all over the place.

After a few minutes she walked slowly up to the entrance and eased her way inside carrying a sack filled with lumpy egg shapes.

"How many did you get?" Max asked, pleased to see so many eggs in the bag.

"A couple dozen," she replied.

Max nodded at Jessup and led the way to the lab.

"You were right," she added. "There were a lot of chickens whose eggs haven't been collected in a few days. A lot of people are dead. If the sun ever comes out, it's going to stink worse than a funky Cadillac for miles."

"Did you see any militants?"

"Not close up. They seemed to be moving out into the tents. I hope Nolan isn't in their sights."

"No, I had Jessup give the secret handshake to call him in."

Ali began pulling eggs out of the sack and placing them carefully on the plastic-covered counter. A few of them had cracked, but most, twenty-three, were intact and appeared to be fertilized.

Max smiled and turned to thank her for a job well done, when a deep-throated explosion rolled through the air and shook the building.

# TWENTY-TWO

ALI RAN.

The explosion hadn't sounded like it impacted the old hospital itself, though dust continued to rain down from the cracked ceiling as the seconds passed. Behind her, their booted feet pounding like bullets on the fly, ran Max, Hunt, Tom and Holland.

As they approached the entrance, gunfire became audible. A lot of gunfire.

Jessup was crouched a couple of feet behind one of the big glassless windows, his weapon braced on a chair, but he wasn't firing.

"What the fuck?" hollered Max.

"We're not under attack," Jessup said. "Not yet anyway. The explosion detonated farther out in the tents."

Hunt, Tom and Holland took up positions in the other windows.

"Is Nolan or any of our team back?" Max asked Jessup.

"No, sir."

"Fan-fucking-tastic."

"Kid at three o'clock," Hunt called out.

"Looks like a couple more behind him," Jessup said.

"We're not a fucking daycare," Tom snarled. "We've got too many civilians in here as it is."

Ali was about to tell him to shut up when the air rattled with the sound of multiple bullets. But it was too far away for it to be a rifle.

"That was no rocket-propelled grenade," Jessup said. "What the hell are they firing, a Howitzer?"

"Whatever it is," Max replied, "I hope to hell they don't point it in our direction."

"Where did those kids go?" Hunt asked.

Ali glanced in the direction that they were coming from, but saw no one. "Maybe the noise made them duck into a house."

Small arms gunfire popped faster than Fourth of July fireworks somewhere outside their field of vision.

"Someone is getting their asses handed to them," she said under her breath.

Max must have heard her because he said, "If Nolan or someone from his team isn't back within five minutes, I'm going to need a volunteer to find out what the hell is keeping him."

"I'll go," she heard herself say.

Max didn't respond right away. A few seconds passed. A few seconds that lit an angry fire in her gut. If he was hesitating because she was a woman, she was going to kick his ass.

"I'm concerned that you've been seen a lot in the village. People might have a pretty good idea of who you are and who you're with."

"Who I am?" He didn't want to assign her this task because she was a certain general's daughter?

"An American soldier."

Okay, that distinction was one she could accept, but he was forgetting other things. "You need the medics to help you with the people who are already here and any wounded who may arrive. I'm the one soldier you've got who can leave without leaving you shorthanded."

He glanced at her, his face grim. "You've convinced

me, Sergeant Stone. Use extreme caution while searching. Do not risk yourself any more than you have to."

Ooh, he sounded pissed. "Yes, sir."

Ali slipped out the doorway and was across the empty space between the front façade of the building and the nearest house in the time it took to breathe twice.

She needed to see what was going on before running headlong into a firefight that might not have anything to do with Nolan's absence. She chose to go up the hill, looking for a spot that would give her a view of the valley.

She climbed the hill the way the Berez had shown her and found a good spot within a couple of minutes.

She crouched behind a tree and used her scope to find the source of all the fighting.

There were a couple of craters in the ground in the tented area, smoke from several fires that were blazing without hindrance among the tents. A number of men with small arms shooting at each other, engaging in small skirmishes and running for cover.

Nolan and his men were conspicuously absent.

One of the groups of men fighting rolled something ungainly across the uneven ground, then they hauled ass in several directions.

Holy fuck it *was* a Howitzer. Where the hell had they gotten that?

Only two men stayed with the piece of artillery. She watched them fire it a fraction of a second before the shells hit and the sound of it rattled the teeth in her head.

She watched them load fresh ammunition and prepare to fire it again.

She braced herself for it, but it didn't happen the same way. This time, the Howitzer disintegrated with an explosion that screamed of torn metal and old age.

The men on the side of the artillery gun looked at the crater where the piece of hardware, and its operators, had been with a deep shock she could see through her scope. They staggered like drunkards or extras from a cheap zombie movie.

Was this good news or bad news?

She had no idea if either of the two groups shooting at each other was sympathetic to the civilians that lived here or the Americans in their midst.

There was still no sign of Nolan or his team.

Where the fuck had they gone? Or were they all dead already?

The group that had been under attack by the Howitzer charged toward their enemy with a roar she could hear. The other side broke and ran. Those who could run anyway. The rest were overtaken and beaten or shot. It didn't look like the attackers had any interest in leaving anyone alive.

That was not good.

Even worse, she didn't know who any of these people were. They could be offshoots from militant groups from anywhere, or they could be family members of the people who lived here.

Not that there were many of them left. The flu had killed more than half the people in the village and the tents. This fighting was only going to result in more deaths.

By the time they were done, this place was going to be populated by ghosts and those it would have been kinder to kill outright.

She shook herself. Defeatist, that's what that was and she didn't have time for it. She had some soldiers to find.

*Okay, if I were Nolan, where would I go to ground?*

The tent-town was three-quarters destroyed, either from artillery blasts, fire or people tearing it down. Not a good hiding place.

The village, with its stone-walled houses—now that was a better bet. Where did it look the quietest?

No one was out and about. She'd have to start someplace logical and work her way through the buildings until she found them.

Ali abandoned her perch and went to the closest home. After a knock she went inside. She found nothing in the first room, a kitchen and main living area combo, but she could smell something rotting.

The whole family lay dead in a bedroom. She couldn't see any obvious injuries, so it must have been the flu.

The next home was the same.

The third home had only two survivors in it, both of them very elderly women.

"What do you want?" one of the women asked.

"I'm looking for strange men with expensive guns."

They shook their heads. "No, we haven't seen anyone like that. Have you been in other houses?"

"Yes."

"Is anyone alive?"

"No," Ali managed to get out. "You are the first living people I've found so far."

"Kill us," one of the women said.

"What?"

"We have nothing. No children or grandchildren. No husbands. Kill us."

Ali stared at them, horror filling her throat until she was choking on it. She couldn't speak. She shook her head and backed out of the house, rushing to the next one and just standing outside the door trying to get air into her lungs again.

Jesus Christ, how bad would the situation have to be before she begged to die?

A few seconds later, she pushed herself to move and went into the house. This home was empty of people, living or dead.

She moved on.

The fighting in the tent area sounded less furious. The Howitzer blowing up must have demoralized the group that had been using it.

She checked another three homes, finding only the dead, before screaming and single gunshots outside caught her attention. Instead of going outside to investigate, she stayed in the home she was in and peeked out a window pointed in the correct direction.

A group of armed men had rounded up some women, children and elderly people. The men and boys were separated from the group and were made to kneel on the stone street. One of the gunmen shot an old man at the end of the row of people.

All of the women began to scream, punch and kick at their captors.

A silent snarl curled her lip and she had to make herself stay where she was and think through the desire to run out there and kill every man with a gun.

There were twenty or more armed men. Could she do *anything* that would help the situation without making her own worse? She had a duty to protect herself and her men, to protect those civilians she'd already accepted responsibility for.

The front door of the house she was in slammed open.

The choice to fight these disgusting creeps might be

taken from her. She was out of the direct line of sight from the door, but once the person who kicked the door in moved four or five feet farther in, they'd see her across the room near the window.

Her position wasn't all that good, so she turned to face the incomer and crouched with her rifle butt settled in the cradle of her shoulder, ready to fire.

Someone took a step, two, three—on the fourth one, the gunman came into view, but he didn't seem to see her for the first couple of seconds.

He was looking at head height and wasn't expecting a small person to be crouched on the floor, she supposed.

She saw the moment he noticed her. His eyes widened and he sucked in a breath, but before he could yell a hand slapped over his mouth from behind as a knife cut his throat.

The gunman sagged and the assassin behind him caught his body before it could make much noise.

Ali stared the knife-wielding shadow, who lifted one hand to make a shushing gesture over his lips.

Nolan.

She looked beyond Nolan and noted several other Special Forces soldiers slipping into the house and closing the door.

She stood and walked over to him. "Where the hell have you been?" she whispered.

"Someone brought artillery to a gunfight," Nolan said. "I lost four men in the cross fire."

"What?" She glanced at the other soldiers and realized he was short four of them. She also realized that some of them had injuries. "Holy fuck."

"We saw you duck in here, then some of those bastards started searching house to house."

"So, we can expect more of them to come through the door? Great." She looked him and the rest of the men over quickly. There was blood on all of them, but it was impossible to tell if it was theirs or not. "Injuries?"

"Some. Nothing that will slow us down right away."

Outside there were more gunshots. Three in a steady three-second pattern. "The fuckers are shooting all the men." Her whisper ended on a growl.

"There are women and children out there," Nolan whispered back. "A direct assault will result in too many innocent deaths."

But she could see he was thinking hard.

"We split into two teams," he ordered. "Half of us lead the civilians away from this area. The other half overwhelms whoever is left." There was no question in his voice, but he looked at her as he finished speaking, in a way that begged her to agree.

Not a hard decision.

She nodded once. "Go."

Nolan turned and within a couple of seconds the soldiers had themselves organized. He went out the door with his weapon raised, one man with him.

Had there really been only four of them? They'd seemed like an army. Then again, they were Special Forces. The Snake Eaters, as some called them, were worth three of any other man when it came to warfare.

The rapid, repeat bark of a rifle told her Nolan and his wingman had engaged the enemy.

Shouts in Arabic told her they'd been spotted, and someone called for more men to chase down and kill the Americans.

It sounded like a crowd of men ran past, none of them quietly. It took a minute for the uproar to pass, then another gunshot went off followed by the wailing of women.

Time to put a stop to that shit.

"I'll go in down the middle," she said to the two Berets. "You two come in from the flanks. How many seconds do you need to get into position?"

"Five," one of them said.

The other nodded.

"Go."

Both went out the door in opposite directions.

She waited, counting slowly in her head. At five, she walked out the door and calmly strode toward the crying, screaming mass of women and girls. In front of them by about ten feet was the kneeling line of men and boys. About half were lying facedown, blood splattered all over them and the people next to them.

A gunman was poised to shoot the next male in the head, who was no more than a teenager.

She shot the gunman first.

For a moment the remaining gunmen didn't realize their man was dead and not the teen.

The boy winced as if he expected to feel pain, then raised his head and looked right at her.

Undiluted fear radiated from his wide eyes and tense mouth.

She did the only thing she could do to tell him the situation had changed.

She winked.

Behind him, the gunman crumpled. His weapon bounced across the stone street, then all hell broke loose.

# TWENTY-THREE

THE TWO SOLDIERS working with her charged toward the gunmen from either side, while she picked off the ones in the middle with careful single shots. This was not a good time to go semi-automatic. Too many civilians in the way.

She picked off two before anyone started returning fire. A couple of gunmen grabbed women and used them as shields, but they underestimated the shooting accuracy of the soldiers they faced. They died with bullet holes in their foreheads.

Something punched her diaphragm, hard enough to knock her back and force all of the air out of her chest. She had to work to stay on her feet and catch her breath, but managed both within a few seconds.

She regained her equilibrium and got her rifle into position just in time to shoot some asshole who'd grabbed the teen she'd saved. He was either going to shoot the boy or try to use him as a shield.

*Coward.*

Ali shot him in the throat.

Another gunman went down a few feet away and she looked for another target, but couldn't find one.

Had they killed all the bad guys?

Ali moved in to search the bodies on the ground and the remaining civilians. Her two soldiers did the same.

When she reached the teen she put her hand out and said, "Are you hurt?"

He shook his head then grabbed her hand and allowed her to help him to his feet. It made her sore chest ache. "Is your home close by?"

He nodded, then said, "Everyone is dead." He glanced at one of the bodies that had been shot in the back of the head. "That is my father."

"Shit," she muttered.

One of the crying women came over to him. "Nephew, come with me. Your cousins are dead, but we have each other."

Relief eased the tension on his face so that he looked his age again and not like an old, old man who's seen too much. He went to his aunt and hugged her, but after they'd taken a few steps away, he turned around and ran back to hug Alicia too.

"Thank you. You saved me."

"Be safe," she whispered back to him.

This time when he walked away with his aunt, he didn't turn around.

Some of the women were trying to carry their dead away while others just wept over a body.

"You need to go back to your homes and stay out of sight," Ali told them.

"Our homes aren't safe," one woman shouted at her. "These animals broke in and forced us to come here. Forced us to watch as they murdered our husbands and sons. They would have forced us and our daughters into marriage."

"I will show you how to shoot their guns," one of the surviving local men said.

"Good," Ali said to him. To them all she ordered, "Go now, before any of them come back."

That got everyone moving.

Her two guys joined her in watching for the return of any of the bad guys who chased after Nolan and his buddy while the women, children and remaining men gathered up the weapons and dispersed.

"Hey, Stone," one of her men asked. "Are you okay?"

"Well, other than tired, yeah, why?"

"'Cause you have a bullet hole in your clothes right over your heart."

She glanced down in surprise and discovered that she did, indeed, have a hole through every layer of clothing she wore right down to the body armor. The slug was buried in it. "What the fuck?"

"Did it penetrate?"

She touched the area around the bullet, probing for pain. "I don't think so. It hurts, but not enough."

"Living up to your name again?" the other soldier asked rhetorically. "The colonel is going to have a few words to say about that."

"Shit, do we have to tell him? He'll have kittens."

Both soldiers grinned and tried not to laugh.

"Come on, assholes," she said rolling her eyes. "The civilians are gone. Let's find Nolan."

They headed off in the direction Nolan and his wing-man had run in. It wasn't a hard trail to follow. There were bodies of bad guys every so often.

Then they found the body of Nolan's wingman, and all the energy she had seemed to flow right out of her.

"Fuck, it's Parker," one of her men said.

"We can't leave him here," Ali said. "Could one of you take him to the old hospital?"

"Yeah," said the guy who identified him. "I'll do it."

He picked up his buddy in a fireman carry and strode off.

Ali looked at her remaining man. "I'm sorry. You're Thompson, right?"

He nodded. "Not your fault. We're dealing with some dangerous men. They don't care who they kill as long as their leader is happy."

She started walking again, looking for another crumb on the trail and found another bad guy's body this time. "How do you know that?"

"Before the Howitzer got rolled out, we talked to a bunch of village elders. They had heard enough to know that this whole clusterfuck is a trap."

"A trap for who?"

"Us. You. The colonel."

"Well, that's shitty."

Ali and Thompson kept going in the same direction as the trail seemed to be taking them. Another body, this time a bad guy. Gunfire from up ahead told her that they were on the right track.

As they neared the fighting, they slowed down and approached the area, near the outskirts of the village, very cautiously.

Rounding the corner of a house, Ali saw a group of gunmen firing at one house in particular. Whoever they were shooting at was inside and firing through a window. Two gunmen slipped away from the main group and came toward Ali and Thompson. They both ducked back before they were seen.

The gunmen came around the corner and face to face with Ali and Thompson. Both men opened their mouths to yell at the same time as raising their weapons, but the two Americans were prepared for them and didn't hesitate.

Ali knifed one man in the neck, while Thompson did the same to the other one. Both went down fast and quiet.

With hand signals, Ali and Thompson discussed a couple of options for an attack and decided on flanking positions. Thompson went around to the far side of the militants' positions while Ali counted to thirty slowly.

At thirty, she inched along the stone wall of the house until she could just see around it. She picked out the man she thought was the leader, and shot him. She methodically shot the next man closest to him, and the next man.

Men started to go down on the other side, which meant Thompson was in position and was doing his fair share of damage.

Whoever was inside the house made good use of the confusion and took out a few bad guys, as well. Until there were none left.

"Nolan?" Ali called out.

She was about to call his name again when he responded, "Yeah, I'm in here."

She crossed the street without relaxing her vigilance in case they missed a bad guy, and cautiously entered the house. "Where are you?"

"Back here."

Ali found him slumped below a window, blood smeared across his chest and the wall. She rushed to him and he gave her a watery smile.

"Did you kill those fuckers?" he asked, breathing harder than he should have been.

"Every last one." She examined him, searching for the wound that resulted in all the blood.

"Excellent."

Thompson ghosted into the house and crouched next to her. "Hey, boss. You sleeping on the job?"

"You gonna report me?" Nolan asked, gasping for breath before and after the words.

"No time to sleep, boss," Thompson told him. "We're stuck in the middle of an asshole convention."

"I'm going to need some help. The son of a bitch who shot me did too good of a job. I'm not going to get anywhere under my own steam."

"No worries, boss," Thompson said. "I'll run you home."

"Where are you hit?"

"Left side. I think it was a ricochet 'cause it looks like it came up and under my armor."

Ali and Thompson laid him out flat on the floor and she lifted his clothing to get a look at the wound. It was just inside his body armor and was bleeding sluggishly, but steadily. "You need a pressure bandage or you're going to bleed out."

"I think I'm more than halfway there," Nolan said, his voice fuzzy and slurred.

Ali got her pack off and pulled out her first aid kit. She grabbed a pressure bandage and a large wound bandage and proceeded to wrap his lower abdomen as tight as she dared.

He passed out just as she finished.

Fuck, they had to get him to Max yesterday if he was going to survive.

"If we get him over your shoulder without making the bleeding worse, can you carry him all the way to the hospital?"

"I could carry him all the way home," Thompson said with a feral grin. "With you guarding our backs, it'll be a cake walk."

"Let's do it."

She helped Thompson get Nolan into a fireman's carry that wouldn't dislodge the bandage, then hoisted her pack back on, added Nolan's weapon, and got her own weapon ready in case they met any unfriendlies on their way back to the old hospital.

They didn't see many people out and about as they hurried on careful feet through the village. There was still the odd gunshot ringing out from farther away, but not the sustained number that indicated active fighting between two large groups.

A few of the locals, ones that weren't too sick, were out getting water or other supplies. She saw one kid of about ten with a dead rabbit in his hands.

She nodded at him. "Good job."

When they got to the hospital, Jessup ran out to meet them.

"Tell Max that Nolan's lost a lot of blood."

Jessup ran ahead.

Max met them outside the OR. "Bring him in here."

Max had taken the operating table and moved it away from the wall. It wasn't in the middle of the room, but he could walk all around it.

Ali and Thompson got Nolan on the table then helped Max get the clothes off Nolan's upper body without cutting them to shreds.

"He lost a lot of blood," Ali said. "Most of the rest of the team is dead. Only Thompson here and the soldier who brought the other soldier's body here survived."

ALI SOUNDED MORE tired than Max had ever heard a conscious human being sound. It made him want to pack her in cotton and keep her away from any and all danger.

He snorted to himself. Right, like she'd go along with that. No, she'd probably put him on the floor again and step on him for good measure.

"Do you know what happened?" he asked her.

"Nolan said he lost four in those big explosions we heard. He'd negotiated with the village elders for co-operation, then another group came in and blew it all to shit."

Max managed to get Nolan's body armor off his torso without cutting any of the straps holding it in place, then took a cautious look at the wound. As soon as he peeked under the pressure bandage, blood welled up and out.

He put the bandage back, then palpated his abdomen. It was tight and he didn't like what he was feeling around Nolan's kidney.

"I think the bullet or shrapnel nicked his kidney. He's bleeding internally."

"He bled a lot before we got him back here, Colonel," Thompson said.

Max took a blood pressure reading and it was so low he didn't know how the soldier was still alive. "Eighty over fifty. Get Hunt in here," he ordered. Then he pulled out his trauma first aid kit. Goddamn it, he didn't have the tools, drugs or support to do surgery, let alone a repair on a lacerated kidney.

It was either that or Nolan was going to bleed to death.

*Fuck.*

Hunt came in, but when he saw Nolan he stopped dead. "Jesus."

"How many units of blood have you got?" Max

asked, pulling every piece of gauze and bandage, no matter how small, and arranging them on the counter near him.

"Six." He stared at Max running around like a madman then looked at Nolan. "Sir, you can't perform surgery here."

"If I don't, he'll die."

"Doing it without drugs will probably kill him anyway." Hunt's voice broke at the end.

Max stopped moving to pin the medic in place with a look. "Which would you want? Let you die or try to save you?"

Hunt's face was agonized.

"Nolan has a wife and two kids," Ali said, her voice as hard as her name. "We're doing this. Either you're helping or you're out."

"I'm in."

"I need all six units."

"Yes, sir." Hunt dashed out of the room and came back a couple minutes later with all six.

Max had used the time to set up an IV in Nolan's left hand. As soon as Hunt handed him a unit, he connected it to the IV line and began the drip.

"Don't you have to test his blood to those units?" Ali asked.

"Yes, but I don't have time and Nolan's blood group is A positive which means he can accept blood from approximately ninety percent of the population." Max moved around the table and managed to get another IV line into Nolan's right hand. He hung another unit of blood and started the drip.

He looked over his available supplies. He had the basics and that was about it. Scalpel, scissors, a couple of small retractors that were normally used for small wound repair, a suture needle and suture thread.

He took another blood pressure reading. Eighty-two over fifty-five. He looked at Ali and Hunt. "I'm going to need both of you to help me."

"Yes, sir," they said in unison.

"Good. Ali, I want you to hand me instruments and bandages. Hunt, I want you to monitor Nolan's vitals and continue to hang blood. The rest of you..." He looked at Thompson and the other soldier from Nolan's team who were still in the room. Damn it, he couldn't remember the man's name. "Hold down the fort."

Everyone nodded.

Max let out a breath. "Then let's get to it."

# TWENTY-FOUR

MAX KEPT NOLAN covered above and below the wound, then cut the bandage off and revealed the damage. He used the only anesthetic he had—a local—injecting it around the wound. Blood welled up, but he ignored it. He made a careful incision and retracted the skin so he could see what was happening inside.

Too much blood. Far too much.

"Ali, I need a bunch of gauze pads."

She handed him a pile and he used them to soak up the extra blood. He had to really look but finally found where the piece of shrapnel nicked the top of his left kidney. Blood was pouring out of the small wound at a frightening rate. If he didn't close it soon, Nolan wasn't going to make it.

He grabbed the suture needle he'd prepared and began closing the tear. "Ali, can you use the gauze pads to get some of this blood out of the way?"

"Okay," she said, moving closer with a handful. "Squawk if I do it wrong."

He tied off the first stitch and waited while she cleared the area of blood. "Perfect."

He stitched quickly, despite Hunt having to hang two more bags of blood before he finished. The tear was closed properly, but that was the only good news.

Nolan's lips and fingertips were blue and all his visible skin was pale with a bluish tint to it, indicating an extensive lack of circulation.

He'd never seen a man with this kind of blood loss recover. With a lack of available units of blood, or circulation expanders like albumin, any recovery at all was highly unlikely.

As he stitched the incision in Nolan's abdomen, Nolan began to shift restlessly and moan.

Special Forces soldiers sometimes claimed to be supermen. Maybe this time, this one was.

"He's waking up," Max warned. "Talk to him, Hunt. Hearing is the first sense to come back. Make sure he knows he's safe or he could damage himself or us as he comes around."

"Nolan, boss, it's Hunt. Are you with me?"

"Be ready to help hold Nolan down," Max said in an undertone to Ali. "Most people don't react well to surgery without anesthetic."

"Can we strap him down?"

"That might make things worse."

Nolan continued to moan and Max worked faster, placing a non-stick abdominal pad over the incision and holding it in place with a pressure bandage he wrapped around Nolan's waist.

"Sergeant Nolan," Hunt said loudly into the soldier's ear. "Give me a clue, man, are you back?"

Nolan's eyelids fluttered then rose and he blinked at Hunt, who put himself directly in Nolan's line of sight. "Hunt?"

"Yes," Hunt said with a relieved smile. "You made it, you crazy son of a bitch."

"Made it?" Nolan frowned. "What happened?"

"You took one in the kidney, but Max just sewed you back together."

"Oh?" He continued to blink, confusion all too evident on his face. He looked around, watched Max as he got everything out of the way and Stone covered him with his own clothing. "Stone? What happened?"

"You played Pied Piper with way too many bad guys," she answered drily.

"Oh." He relaxed, seeming to be satisfied with that explanation.

Hunt's expression went from surprised to worried. He opened his mouth, but Max spoke first.

"Where are you, Sergeant Nolan?"

"Fort Bragg?"

"How do you feel?" Max asked, looking at Hunt and pointing at the blood pressure cuff.

Hunt took the hint without further prompting.

"A little fuzzy." His eyes sagged shut, then they popped open again. "Where are we?"

"Seventy-five over forty-nine. Heart rate elevated." Hunt had no need to say anything else. The numbers alone were bad enough.

Max took his penlight and shone it in Nolan's eyes. They both reacted normally but there was a clamminess to Nolan's skin that triggered an alarm deep in Max's head. "Open your mouth, please, and say ah."

The routine question received immediate compliance.

Nolan's tongue looked like a squeezed lemon.

Dehydration. The man might be conscious right now, but he wouldn't stay that way without more fluids.

He might not even stay alive.

Nolan's eyes closed again and his body relaxed.

"Sergeant Nolan?" Max said.

No response.

"Nolan," Hunt said a little louder. He gave Nolan's shoulder a shake.

No response.

"Can we give him another unit?"

"We used them all," Hunt reported.

"Get a bag of saline," Max ordered. "He's on the verge of dying of hypovolemic shock."

Ali ran over to the medical supplies and grabbed a bag of the fluid.

Max hung it and got it dripping into Nolan. Dripping wasn't going to do it. He opened the valve on the tubing all the way and squeezed the bag to send a gush of saline into the man's veins.

"Heart rate?" Max asked.

Hunt put his fingers on Nolan's carotid artery. "Still fast." He began taking a blood pressure reading without being asked. He let the air out of the cuff slowly, frowned and inflated it a second time. "I can't get a reading."

"Shit," Ali said, her voice subdued. One glance told Max she wasn't surprised, but she was very, very sad.

Hunt read her expression too. "We're not going to lose him," he growled.

Yes, they were, but not everyone had to watch. Max squeezed the bag of saline. "Hunt, get me an update on our situation."

"What?"

Max thrust his chin in the direction of the doorway. "Check in with Jessup and our guests."

Hunt's face hardened and he tried to take another

blood pressure reading. "I don't need to go anywhere to know our situation fucking sucks."

"It wasn't a request," Max told him. He'd give the soldier some slack, but only so much.

"Seventy-six over fifty-two."

Max squeezed the last of the saline into Nolan, then checked the man's carotid pulse.

He couldn't find it.

He leaned down, pushed away the clothing covering the injured man and put his ear over Nolan's heart.

Nothing.

"Cardiac arrest," Max said. "Ali, bring the defibrillator."

She rushed to get it while he began chest compressions.

As soon as she returned, Max started charging the machine and got the pads in place. "Clear."

Hunt and Ali stood back and Max hit the shock button.

Nothing.

He charged the machine again. It took eight long seconds, while Hunt did chest compressions and Ali breathed for the injured man, for it to be ready. "Clear."

Again everyone stepped back.

No response.

Hunt resumed chest compressions. Max hit Charge again and checked Nolan's eyes while waiting the eight seconds. No reaction from his pupils.

"Clear," Max said when the machine was ready. He shocked Nolan again.

Still no response.

Max glanced at Ali, who shook her head.

Max had to agree. Nolan was gone.

"What the fuck are you waiting for?" Hunt said as he did chest compressions. "Charge that thing."

"He's gone, Sergeant."

"He's not gone," Hunt snarled. "Do your fucking job."

"Max is right," Ali said to Hunt. "Nolan lost too much blood. It was a miracle he woke up at all. It's time to let him go."

Hunt ignored her, kept pumping Nolan's chest, but after another minute, he finally stopped. He sneered at Ali. "You're just as warm as your name. Do you give a shit about anything?" He walked away before she could respond.

She stood in place, ramrod straight.

"He's wrong, Ali. You're a strong woman, but never cold, never inflexible."

She sighed and turned to look at Nolan's body. "Sometimes I wonder if guys like him are right."

"Don't," Max ordered. "Don't wonder, because there's one thing he doesn't understand right now. Maybe later he will, but at this moment, he can't understand. He's emotionally invested in saving Nolan. We all were to a degree, but no doctor or nurse could ever do their job effectively if they can't set aside their emotions while they're working. If we don't we die a little with every patient. We suffer their wounds, their trauma. It wouldn't take very long for one of two things to happen."

He held up one finger. "Depression and suicide. Or two—" he held up a second finger "—we literally go crazy. You know how to create that emotional buffer, but Hunt has failed to cope. He's going to need help when we get back to the world."

"He'll probably fight it."

"He can fight it all he wants. I *will* ensure he gets the counseling he needs."

Her shoulders were still hunched, making her look defeated. "And we just used up the blood you needed to make your treatment."

"It was a long shot anyway. I've already started culturing the virus in the eggs you brought me. Hopefully in twenty-four hours, I'll have enough to test a vaccine."

"I thought you said forty-eight hours?"

"I did, but I don't know how long I've got, so I'm going to accelerate things as much as I can." He gave her a small, quick smile. "If you find more eggs, I can start a second batch."

"What about the supply drop you ordered? Isn't that due soon?"

"Shit, yes it is."

"I have an idea," she said.

He smiled. "Give it to me."

"Ask Ferhat if we can send out the kids to collect eggs. No one is going to think twice about seeing them doing that."

Max considered and quickly decided she was right. "Okay, you meet the drop. I'll talk to Ferhat about getting the eggs."

Things were moving fast now and Nolan was dead.

"Can you keep watch while I brief Tom, Jessup, Thompson, Holland and the other new guy?"

"Warren. Yes, sir." She glanced at Nolan. "What about the body?"

"We've got a few to collect, damn it." There was a lot that needed to be done, with no time right now to do it. "I'll wrap Nolan and put him next to Bull."

"Yes, sir." She moved to the door. "Are you…okay?"

He quirked up one side of his mouth. "Never surrender, never give up."

She didn't smile in return, but the concerned frown lightened and she left.

He found an old blanket and wrapped Nolan's body in it. Just as he finished, Jessup and Thompson came in. They picked up Nolan's body without saying a word and took it out of Max's lab. When they came back a minute later, Tom, Hunt, Holland and Warren came with them. Aside from Ali, every American soldier he had left alive was present.

"Our situation has changed. We're down too many people to attempt any other military intervention outside this building. We have a few civilians we can shelter, but I won't authorize any other forays outside unless it's to obtain supplies."

"What about your vaccine?"

"It's cooking now. It needs twenty-four hours minimum. Forty-eight would be better."

"What about Stone?" Jessup asked. "She said she's going out to meet the drop."

"Yes, she is."

"Sir, I volunteer to go with her." Jessup shifted his weight slightly.

Max raised a brow at him.

He nodded. "The buddy system."

"Ah, then yes. Go with Stone." He released a breath. "I think we've entered a deep game."

"It's Akbar, isn't it?" Hunt said, his voice rough.

"I think so." Max smiled now, but he knew it wasn't a happy one. He was showing teeth. "There's one thing that Akbar seems to have forgotten."

"What's that?" Thompson asked.

"He's attempting to control the uncontrollable. Most bacteria we come in contact with are harmless, some are even helpful, and only a few are dangerous. Viruses are not bacteria. Most cause disease or have the potential to cause disease. They are quick to adapt and change. Much quicker than bacteria. Much, much quicker than us."

"He's playing with fire," Hunt said.

"Yes, and unfortunately, we might all get burned."

"He's crazy," Thompson said.

"Certifiable, but he's also smart and he has no fear for his own life at all. He's almost as dangerous as the virus that's killing the people in this village."

Thompson snorted. "Then I hope the damned virus wipes his ass off the planet."

"That would be justice in action, wouldn't it?" Max asked rhetorically. "So, now you know. We're facing a madman with a weapon that could wipe out millions of people if it gets out of this place."

Hunt's laugh was cold. "Now give us the bad news."

"Thirty-five percent is a conservative estimate."

"Dude," Hunt said. "Are you always so wicked literal?"

"Ask my ex-wife. She claims I have no sense of humor at all."

The men all relaxed.

"Say no more, man," Hunt said. "Every ex-wife says that."

Ali would be proud of him, bonding with the men under his command. She'd probably find it hilarious.

"I'm sending the two boys out to collect more eggs.

I want to start a second culture of the virus so if the first works, there will be more ready a day or so later."

A couple of the men winced, but no one voiced any concerns.

Coban came running into the room, yelling, "A plane crashed outside the village!"

# TWENTY-FIVE

ALICIA'S STOMACH CHURNED as she ran for the entrance of the building and its wide windows, Max a few steps in front of her. The rest of the team, what there was left of it, crowded around the windows when they reached the trashed reception area.

The smoke from the crash was easily visible down the valley, but that was all they could see.

"We need to get higher," she said to Max.

"Take Jessup with you," he said, pinning her in place with a gaze that was one part horror, one part fear and all the way angry. "I want a report in ten minutes."

"Yes, sir." She glanced at Jessup, who nodded at her.

"You know a good spot?"

"Yeah."

"Lead the way, Kemosabe."

"Call me that again and I will kick your ass," she said in a mild tone most women would use to chastise a four-year-old.

His lips twitched, but he managed not to smile. Good for him. She was in the mood to kick some more ass. She looked at Max again and had to force herself not to react to the change in his face.

Before, he'd been all military, concerned for the team and for the situation. Now, there was a heat in his gaze that made her want to crawl all over him. If there'd been any chance to do it without an audience, she'd have done it.

Instead, she had to stuff her need to reassure him, that she could do this—was in fact, the best soldier to do this—and hope he read between the lines.

"Ten minutes," she said, her voice huskier than was professional. "I promise."

His nostrils flared and she knew he wanted to say something, but he looked so damned combustible she was afraid anything he said would blow up the fiction that they weren't involved to smithereens.

So, she left before he could comment. Left with Jessup on her heels and a single-minded focus of getting the intel they needed and back again as fast as possible.

Despite the speed of her departure, she hadn't sacrificed stealth, making sure no one was following them as they worked their way up the mountain. It took only four minutes to reach the spot she'd used before for reconnaissance. Only a few seconds to determine that the news was all bad.

"Does that look like a drone aircraft?" she asked Jessup as she sighted down the scope on her weapon.

He was doing the same. "Yep, one of ours." He paused for a moment, then asked, "When is that drop supposed to happen?"

"About thirty minutes."

"This couldn't be that plane, could it?"

"Maybe this one was taking pictures for the desk pilots at the base."

"Fuck, I hope so."

They both watched armed men swarm the smoking wreckage, then walk away with pieces of the machine.

"Fuck, that's not good," Jessup whispered. "There's a lot of technology on those birds."

"Hopefully nothing they can use right away."

"Seen enough?"

"Yeah." She broke cover and they made their way back to the battered-looking building they'd taken over.

Jessup was silent for most of the way, but about a minute out he asked, "Do you think Max can cook up a vaccine that will work?"

She glanced at him, but he was watching their perimeter. "If anyone can, it'll be Max. Or are you really asking if any of us are going to survive this killer flu?"

"That too, I guess."

"I don't know." She continued to watch her own perimeter while taking quick glances at Jessup. How worried was he? "I do know that Max hasn't given up and neither have I."

"Don't get your thong in a bunch, Stone, I've just never seen a bug kill this many people so fast. There can't be much doubt that it's a weapon."

She was going to ignore the thong comment. "Was the Black Death a weapon? Was the Spanish flu? Both of them killed large portions of the population, and both were naturally occurring pandemics. Until we know for sure, we can't assume anything."

"Well, aren't you the voice of reason."

"What the fuck is with the sarcasm?" she asked, out of patience for male bullshit.

"I thought since you're banging the colonel you'd have some intel the rest of us don't." It was said in a casual tone, the kind a guy used to talk about the weather. That just made it a bigger insult.

*Hmm, punch him, shoot him...punch him, shoot him?*

"You are, without a doubt, a moron," she told him.

Jessup shrugged. "Just calling it like I see it."

"Go fuck yourself. I don't assume you're fucking the man in front of you when you're nut-to-butt in the dirt, do I?"

"Yeah, but—"

She cut him off with a sharp gesture. "Here's a newsflash, I don't work with morons."

He frowned. "What's that supposed to mean?"

She didn't bother answering. They reached the hospital and went inside. Max and the rest of the team were waiting for them.

"It looks like a drone." She kept her tone tightly professional. "It's too early for it to be the drop aircraft. This one might have been scouting. The machine is already being picked over by scavengers."

"Not good news, but not really bad news," Max said. "For the moment, anyway. How many men did you see picking through the debris?"

"About a dozen, which isn't very many." She thought about that for a moment. "Either we've put a serious dent in the bad guys, or a lot of them are sick."

"Or dead." Max glanced at his watch, then nodded at her. "You'd better get to the drop site."

"I'll leave now, but I'm not taking this moron with me." She angled a thumb over her shoulder at Jessup.

"Moron?" Max asked, his voice hard. "How big a moron?"

She glanced at Jessup now and from his frown, he still had no idea what that meant.

"What did you do, man?" Hunt demanded.

Jessup's surprised face told her he hadn't expected anyone else to care. "I didn't do anything."

His defensive tone said it all.

"All I did was ask a question."

Max stared at him, all trace of understanding mentor gone. "What question?"

"I asked her if this flu was a man-made weapon."

"How would she know the answer to that question?" Max's voice was silky smooth. Bad things happened when he sounded like that.

"Well, she's, uh, sleeping with…you, so I figured you might have told her a few things you hadn't told us."

No one said anything for about three seconds.

"You're right," Hunt said to Ali. "He is a moron." He glanced at Max. "I'll back her up, if that's all right with you, Colonel."

Max looked at her, and she nodded.

"Yes. Go."

Ali and Hunt headed out.

"Stupid fuck," Hunt muttered.

"Sometimes I wonder if I'm the moron," Ali said conversationally. "I work my ass off trying to get you guys trained, but every once in a while, an asshole still makes it through."

"I might not always like you, Stone, but I damned sure respect you. Anyone who doesn't is too stupid for the teams."

"I can't be everyone's friend," she said, keeping her tone level. "I have to be a bitch and push people to their limits in training or they'll never discover just how much they can do or how far they'll go. Hell, even Max knows that and he's not a Snake Eater, he's Medical."

Hunt was silent as they quickly slid around the back of the hospital and up the mountain. Where they were going offered no good views of the valley or easy trail to leave the area, but it was full of gullies and wash-out ravines, the perfect area to drop a small bundle of supplies.

"If you did sleep with him, it would be career suicide for both of you."

Ali looked sidelong at the other soldier. "Really? After the conversation I just had with the moron, you're going to say that to me?"

"I have eyes in my head, you know, and they work too."

"So what?"

"So, you two have your own...language."

"What the fuck does that mean?"

"When a man and a woman really give a shit about each other, they have a way of looking at each other. Expressions and gestures that mean something more. Code words and phrases. They talk with their eyes."

"I had no idea you were such a romantic."

"I'm not, but my parents are like that."

"You think the colonel and I have...that?"

"Yeah. You both try to act professional, but to anyone who knows you, it's obvious. You defer to him like I've only ever seen you do with your father. Actually, it's more. And he, shit, he eats you up with his eyes, and when you see it, you smile. If you saw that expression on anyone else, you'd tear their face off." Hunt chuckled. "It's been kind of cute watching the two of you."

Cute? It was *cute* watching them? It was lucky she hadn't eaten anything much in the past couple of hours or she would have thrown it all up right on Hunt's boots.

It was her worst nightmare, and now it was a reality.

All the men she'd trained, all the respect she'd gained, gone.

Poof.

They could all see it. They all knew. Sergeant Stone was fucking a man who was her superior officer and the man she was assigned to protect. She'd lost her objectivity, broken regulations and crossed a line she'd sworn never to cross.

"Say the word *cute* again in reference to me and I will punch you in the face." She said the sentence absolutely deadpan.

Hunt chuckled again, unaware of how close to death he was skating, because right now she really, really wanted to choke him.

They left the village behind and she forced herself to walk ahead of Hunt so she'd have time to calm down before they stopped and she had to look at him.

If he wore a smug expression of any kind, she wasn't sure she'd be able to stop herself from…what? Taking her stupidity out on the first handy person who came within reach? She was the one who turned her relationship with Max into one that violated every promise she'd ever made to herself when she joined the army.

It wasn't Hunt who deserved a beating.

She deserved every smirk and joke that came her way. Every one.

"I see it," Hunt said behind her.

She stopped and looked in the direction he indicated. There it was, a camo-green package.

They scrambled down an embankment to reach it. Bigger than she'd expected. Four feet by four feet and covered in green cargo netting, it might be hard to sneak through the village without attracting attention.

Then again, people might still be interested in the drone they'd shot down.

It didn't require conversation for Hunt to grab one side of the package while she nabbed the other. It didn't require conversation to start heading up the hill either.

Hunt kept glancing at her, though, actual concern on his face.

"What?" she asked as they reached the goat track. "Worried I'll break a nail?"

"Uh, no." He cleared his throat. "I should have kept my mouth shut."

"Probably, but you didn't."

He'd done her a favor, really. At least now, she had time to figure out some kind of exit route before shit got embarrassing.

"Look," Hunt said, sounding nervous. "I'm sorry. It was unprofessional of me to bring it up while we're out on a mission."

"It's fine."

"It's none of my business and, hell, you haven't even admitted it, so maybe I'm wrong and there's nothing going on between you and Max."

"Just drop it, okay?"

"On one hand, I'm happy for you, you know," Hunt continued, seemingly unaware of her deteriorating temper. "You've got this iron maiden reputation, but it's good to know you—"

Ali cut him off. "Shut. The. Fuck. Up."

He shut up.

So did she.

They reached the edge of the village and took a moment to make sure they were unobserved before slipping in through the outermost houses. The smell of death and decay from inside told Ali that their occupants were no threat.

As they made their way to the old hospital, the odd gunshot was audible in the distance, but nothing close by. The locals, or whoever was around, must still be picking through the crash debris, looking for useful bits to sell or trade.

A small herd of goats and two cows trotted past them, on their way to the grassy hillside surrounding the village.

Either the farmer had let them out, or their owners were dead and they'd found an escape. One of those goats would make a decent meal for the people who were now under their protection.

She glanced over her shoulder and noted the direction the animals took. She could go after one once the package was delivered.

The hospital finally came into view and they walked through the doorway without incident.

Why did that feel way too easy?

Max came rushing toward them. "Everything okay? No one followed you?"

Hunt was right. Max treated him like he was invisible. All of the colonel's attention was on her.

# TWENTY-SIX

ALI LOOKED MAD enough to tear a man apart with her bare hands.

Something had gone wrong, but he could see no injury on her, no evidence she was any less healthy now than when she left. He glanced at Hunt and saw nothing there either.

"What happened?"

"We picked up your package." Ali sounded like she was angry with him. Furious with him. She dropped her end of it and walked around him, going into the building without a backward glance.

Max watched her for a second, then leveled his gaze on Hunt. "What happened? And don't tell me nothing went on, because she doesn't get angry like that without cause."

Hunt winced. "It was something I said."

When the other man didn't add any details, Max's *moron* radar went off. "What is wrong with you people?" he demanded. "Have you seen us doing anything we shouldn't? Like holding hands or kissing? Or even disappearing together for unexplained periods of time?"

"Um, no."

"Do we call each other pet names?"

"No."

"Why does every soldier who spends more than five

minutes with us think we're behaving unprofession-
ally?"

"You have your own language."

"What?"

"You know, married couples develop their own code
words and body language. When you're in a room together, you each know where the other is all the time.
You're careful to keep each other in sight and if she's
in a room, you always look at her first."

Fuck. *Shit*. Their relationship was already harming
her. If he didn't do something right now to explain both
their behavior, the harm would be irreparable.

"You," Max said in what he hoped came across as
the voice of doom, "have watched one too many Dis-
covery Channel shows on human sexuality."

"But—"

"General Stone assigned Sergeant Stone as my personal bodyguard. Threats have been made against my
life. She's not just teaching me how to shoot and defend
myself. It's her responsibility to keep me alive and safe.
I wasn't all that pleased to have someone hovering over
my shoulder, and she wasn't happy about having to do
the hovering. But we both got over ourselves, worked
out our differences and developed a working relationship that actually might leave me alive long enough to
retire. I had to learn to trust her and she had to learn to
trust me. I will never do anything to damage that trust,
do you understand me? I had to deal with Nolan, Jessup
and now you suspecting I was doing things or behaving in a disrespectful way toward the one person I do
*not* want to piss off."

Hunt closed his eyes, his wince taking over his entire face. "Bodyguard."

"Bodyguard," Max confirmed.

"I wasn't trying to be an asshole," Hunt said. "I was trying to protect her. She's been limited in what she's allowed to do. None of us want to see that continue."

"Sergeant Stone is more capable of protecting herself than almost any other person alive," Max told him.

"So, you're not having sex?" Jessup asked.

When had he joined the conversation? Did Ali have to put up with this crap all the time? How on earth did she manage to not kill anyone?

"Just to be clear, so there's no misunderstanding," Max said carefully, "your question disrespects Sergeant Stone. I will never do anything to disrespect her, including answering your question, because the moment I do, I infer that the question is acceptable, when it's not."

He waited for Hunt or Jessup to respond.

Finally, after a few seconds, Hunt said, "I get it."

"Me too," Jessup said, glancing away. "She'll probably kick the shit out of me during our next training session."

"Probably," Max agreed. "Set up rotating watches with whoever is healthy and inform Sergeant Stone. She won't be on watch, but I'm putting her in charge of security in our new home until I get this damned vaccine finished."

"Yes, sir," they said in unison, saluting as one.

"Dismissed."

The men left and Max went into his lab.

Ali was leaning against the wall with her arms crossed over her chest. "Nice pep talk."

"Pep talk?" Max asked. "I was trying to save yet another moron's life."

"It's hard to be you, obviously." She hadn't moved,

hadn't changed her tone one iota, but he suddenly realized she was laughing at him.

"I damned near strangled the two of them," he confessed. "And you know how anti-violence I am."

"You're not anti-violence, Max," she said. "You're anti-murder."

He glanced at the eggs he had incubating in his makeshift incubator consisting of an ancient lamp with an intact light bulb and some thin metal sheeting he'd shaped to direct the heat generated by the bulb at the eggs. "I'm most definitely anti-mass murder."

She pushed away from the wall. "How long until you have a vaccine you can test?"

"Another eight hours. The kids came back with more eggs, so I can start a second batch now."

"How many people can you vaccinate with the first one?"

"Maybe three or four, but I'll need to test it before I give it to anyone."

"Test it?"

"Normally I'd use mice, but…" He gestured at the shabby interior of the hospital. "I'm going to have to improvise."

"Improvise how?"

There was no point in hiding it. "I'm going to test it on myself."

"What's the worst-case scenario if the test goes wrong?"

"I die of the flu."

She snorted. "Don't be ridiculous. You're the only doctor we've got. You can't test it on you."

"I'm not expecting anyone else to do something I won't."

"I can guarantee you'll have volunteers." The determined expression on her face told him she was going to be first in line.

He had to head that off right now, but he knew Ali, knew she wasn't going to let this go. She'd fight him tooth and nail. "If I can't be the test subject, neither can you."

She rolled her eyes. "Fine."

"The test subject has to be healthy, no sign of the flu."

She frowned. "That doesn't leave a lot of people."

"I guess you'll have to cross your fingers and your toes that someone volunteers who's not already sick."

She didn't answer, just watched him with a frown.

"I'm going to get these eggs cooking. After you've approved the watch schedule, could you try to sleep?"

"I will, if you'll do the same when you're done playing mad scientist."

"Deal."

Ali left the room and Max got to work.

He opened the package and was pleased to see all the supplies he'd asked for inside and unbroken during its landing. Syringes, needles, gloves, masks, saline and a number of small but vital things needed to prepare his homemade vaccine.

He candled the eggs the boys had brought and discovered fourteen that were at the right stage to use to grow the virus. He put four eggs that were too far along in their growth to chickens aside. The remaining ten unfertilized eggs, he gave to Fatima. She was soon happily transforming them into some kind of scramble with potatoes and a root vegetable he didn't recognize.

The smell of food, real food, was so out of place in his stressed brain that it made him feel a bit nauseated.

Or it could be the lack of sleep.

Or the insane desire to choke Akbar, if he ever caught up to the slippery bugger, with his bare hands. For some reason, he didn't think he'd have trouble killing Akbar, hand-to-hand or with a gun. Akbar was sick in a way no medicine or treatment could cure.

Predicting his next move was like trying to see through muddy flood water. Too much, too fast, no obvious path.

Max carefully inoculated each egg. What was Akbar going to do next?

Making an accurate prediction was difficult. There were so many variables.

There were also a lot of militant and extremist groups who would welcome Akbar into their fold, supply him with a place to work and medical equipment on the promise that he was creating a massive weapon to use against the Western powers. None of those militants would suspect that he was willing to kill them along with their enemies.

All Max could do was imagine the worst-case scenario and assume that was what Akbar would attempt to engineer.

A worldwide pandemic that killed hundreds of millions. Was this flu capable of doing that?

Possibly.

And that possibility was enough to ensure that Max would break rules to try to stop it, including testing the vaccine on himself. Not a fact he was going to share with Ali.

He finished with the last egg and set them up to incubate alongside the first batch. He checked his watch—a few more hours and he'd be ready to harvest the virus growing and multiplying inside the first set of eggs, mix it with a stabilizing agent, screen out impurities and inject it into his body.

He turned from his work, stripped off his gloves and found a plate of scrambled eggs covered with a cloth on a backless chair just inside the door of his makeshift lab.

Ali was asleep on the floor, her feet almost resting against the chair legs.

He ate, drank a full bottle of water, returned the plate to the woman he was thinking of in his head as their house mother, and lay down a few feet from Ali.

He wanted to spoon up behind her, but that, after all the posturing and lecturing he'd done to the team, would have been stupid in the extreme.

At least she was only a few feet away.

MAX WOKE TO the sound of his alarm going off. No, not his alarm, it was his timer. For the eggs. The virus was done cooking.

He rolled to his feet and noted that Ali was gone from her spot on the floor. As he glanced up, she walked through the doorway and looked at the eggs. "Is it done?"

"Done enough for the next step in the process." He gave her a once-over. "You got enough sleep? Had something to eat?"

"Yes, thank you. I got four hours and some scrambled eggs that tasted so much better than an MRE."

"Good. On to the next step of the process." He took a couple of steps, then turned back to her. "Who is healthy and who isn't?"

She blew out a breath. "No one is one hundred percent. Almost everyone in the building is coughing. Thompson and Hunt have fevers."

"The kids?"

"Berez has a fever and a cough, but he seems okay. Coban got sick already and recovered. At least, that's what his dad says. Ferhat's cough is getting bad."

Max ground his teeth, but there wasn't anything more he could do for anyone other than creating a vaccine that worked.

"I'm going to see what's going on in the village."

Max frowned. "Why? Has there been more fighting?"

"No. It's been eerily quiet for a couple of hours now. I don't know if people are hiding out or if they're all dead, and I think we need to know which one it is."

"It's the middle of night now, isn't it?"

She glanced at her watch and shook her head. "Yeah, zero three twelve." She gave him a wry smile. "No wonder it's quiet. Sorry."

"No apologies necessary," he told her. There was a flicker in the shadows behind her. Someone was either waiting to talk to one of them or listening in on their conversation. "Assuming our vaccine is a success, can you see what's left for furniture in the building? Or anything that could be jerry-rigged into a gurney or cot?"

"Yes, sir."

Had she figured out someone was behind her?

"Thank you, dismissed."

Ali turned and walked away, but she wasn't gone five seconds before he heard the murmur of her voice out in the hallway.

Someone had been there. Interesting.

Not interesting enough to pull him away from his work, however. He removed the first batch of eggs from the incubation area and began the painstaking process of removing their contents. This virus, rendered less virulent than its parent, was his vaccine. He carefully added each bit to a test tube of stabilizing agent and then, when he'd harvested everything he could, put the tubes into the centrifuge to separate out any particulates or impurities.

After spinning the tubes, he removed the vaccine from them and put it into one test tube. Altogether, the resulting vaccine measured approximately twenty-five milliliters. Enough for just over two doses.

He prepared two hypodermic needles and, before anyone could walk in and stop him, injected himself with one of them.

There. He'd done it, and no one was the wiser.

He laid the used needle on the counter and looked around for the sharps container he'd seen not five minutes ago.

One of the kids came running into the room. "My father won't wake up."

Oh no.

Max followed the boy into the room they'd been using for sleeping and found Ferhat unconscious and burning up. At this point there wasn't a whole lot anyone could do, but Max started an IV anyway and had Holland watch over him.

He headed back to his lab.

Ali stood next to the tray he'd left on the counter, the used hypodermic in her hands. "You injected yourself already, didn't you?"

# TWENTY-SEVEN

"Yes."

"And if you die?" How dare he do this? They couldn't afford to lose him. *She* couldn't afford to lose him.

"The response to that would be no different than if I died of a bullet wound or an IED." His tone was even and his words rational, but she couldn't reconcile how it sounded with what it meant.

He'd just given himself an injection of an untested homemade vaccine, one that would kill him, protect him or not do a damn thing.

Frustration clawed at her insides until she wanted to knock him onto his back and tie him down so he couldn't put himself in more danger.

"You're not replaceable, Max."

"Bullshit."

Now she just wanted to smack him. "How many doses do you have left?"

"One and a third."

"How can you have a third of a dose?"

"I didn't have enough eggs for a complete third dose."

"One test subject isn't very many."

"No, I need to choose another."

She pointed a finger at him. "Me."

When he just looked at her she rolled her eyes. "Why not?"

He didn't say anything for a while, busying himself

with tidying his work space. Finally, he said, "I don't have a good reason."

"What you have is an overdeveloped sense of chivalry."

"I suppose." He picked up a hypodermic, and walked to the doorway.

"Where are you going?"

"To dispose of this in the fire." He disappeared.

She strode over to the counter and glanced at the hypodermic with the one full dose. She was only going to get one chance at this.

Ali picked up the syringe, opened her coat and pushed her clothing aside so she could inject the vaccine into the triceps muscle of her upper arm. She hesitated only a moment before sinking the needle in and depressing the plunger.

She pulled it out, put the cap back on and put it back where she found it.

No, she couldn't leave it there. She grabbed it and made her way to the room where everyone was sleeping and threw it in the metal fire pit with its glowing embers.

Max was talking to someone in the next room, his voice a low rumble. He calmed a part of her that normally never relaxed.

She left the sleepers and stood outside the room where Max spoke to Tom, Hunt, Holland and Thompson. The other two relatively healthy soldiers, Jessup and Warren, were on watch.

"We've received the package of flu vaccine that I requested and I need anyone not sick to be vaccinated as soon as possible. I'm going to need a team of two to go into the village and identify the healthy and ask them to come here so I can give them a shot. If it works, it could mean ending this pandemic before it can begin."

"You want us to go?" Hunt asked.

"I want Sergeant Stone to go with one of you." There was an edge to his voice that set off Ali's radar.

"And you're afraid we might say something to piss her off?" Hunt asked. "Colonel, I've pressed my luck as far as it will go on that front already."

"I'm not going to go there at all," Thompson said.

"Good."

Footsteps approached the doorway, then Max stepped through it. "Sergeant Stone," he said. "Eavesdropping?"

"I heard my name mentioned. I'm going into the village?"

"Yes, you're less of a stressor to the locals."

"Sir," she said. "Instead of another soldier, I'd like to take Fatima with me. These people have been under an attack of one kind or another for at least two days. I think they'll respond better to a woman and a young man than to soldiers with guns."

"Taking your weapons is not optional. You will be armed."

"I understand that, sir. I don't have to wave it in anyone's face, though."

He thought about it for a moment, but nodded after a few seconds. "Your reasoning is sound. Proceed, Sergeant." He stepped backward a couple of steps and said to the four men he'd just left, "Did you guys catch that?"

"Yes, sir," Hunt said. "We're staying home."

Ali stuck her head around the doorway. "Sorry, fellas, none of you looks good in a skirt."

"Thank God," Hunt muttered.

"I think I would rock a skirt," Thompson said. "I've got a great ass."

"Who told you that?" Hunt demanded.

"My last girlfriend."

Ali sighed dramatically. "Dude, she lied."

"Fuck off."

Grinning, Ali went into the room and woke Fatima. It only took a couple of minutes for Ali to explain what she wanted and Fatima agreed to help without hesitation.

The two women walked the short distance to Max's lab and found him looking for something on the floor on his hands and knees.

"Max, we're going to head out now. Are you okay?"

He glanced at them briefly. "I'm fine." He stopped and looked at her again, but this time his face was accusatory. "Stone, did you do what I think you did?"

She cleared her throat. "If it involved an injection, I did. I dropped the plastic into the fire in the sleeping room."

He got to his feet, his lips tightly pressed together. "I should be angry with you. You disobeyed orders."

"Special circumstances."

"We'll talk later." That might have been what he said, but he meant she was getting yelled at.

"Yes, we will."

She led Fatima to the exit and the two women headed out into the village. It was still dark and very few homes had a light of any kind, so they stopped at the ones that did, and found more sickness and death than anyone should ever have to see.

So FAR, SHE and Fatima had only found a dozen people in the village who hadn't gotten sick yet.

That, more than the lack of sleep or fear of a militant attack, made her stomach clench into a hard knot that threatened to make her throw up the eggs she'd eaten.

A dozen people out of hundreds.

Not everyone had died of the flu. Some had been killed by bullets and bad men, and others had survived the flu.

Max was going to be very worried by everything she'd seen. The sickness, murders and abandoned homes. Twice, she'd walked into a home to find everyone dead of the flu except the woman of the house, who hung from a ceiling rafter.

Not everyone could survive the destruction of their family.

She came out of the house she was in, having found two teenage boys trying to bury their parents in their backyard garden. She sent them up to the old hospital, telling them that there were children there that would need help.

She walked to the next house, rounded a corner and came face to face with eight men armed with semi-automatic rifles, all of them pointed at her.

She put her hands up in the air and began babbling in Arabic. "Don't shoot, don't shoot. I'm not sick."

No one moved for several seconds and the silence had begun to get uncomfortable, when movement behind the line of armed men signalled the arrival of someone new.

A man made his way to stand in front of her.

*Akbar.*

He looked different than the photos she'd seen. Then, he'd been an average-looking man in his late thirties, someone she wouldn't look twice at if she'd met him on the street. Now, he sported a puckered scar along the left side of his face that went from his ear up into his hairline. He wore a hat, but she couldn't see any evidence of hair on his head at all.

He stared at her like a reptile does when sizing up prey.

A shiver went through her and she held herself very, very still.

"Sergeant Stone, daughter of General Stone," he said to her in barely accented English. "When I heard they sent a woman to protect Colonel Maximillian I was skeptical, yet here you are." He looked around the village. "And gathering the, as yet, uninfected."

He asked no question, so she remained silent.

"My men tell me you're responsible for the deaths of some of our fighters." She watched, but he didn't sound or look angry.

Fear rolled over her in an icy wave that made the world spin and threatened to suck her under.

She forced herself to breathe through a throat constricted until it felt no larger than a straw.

Despite his accusation that she'd killed his men, he didn't seem to care. His face remained impassive, cold and unmoved by any emotion. He didn't care one bit that she'd killed people, *his* people.

From the shuffling of feet and hands tightening on their rifles, it seemed like his men cared. She couldn't predict what Akbar would do next. Kill her? Disarm her and give her to his men? Use her as a hostage to get Max under his control?

Wait, Max was the important person in Akbar's eyes. Perhaps the only person he saw as a potential threat to his plan to wipe out the world with a lethal plague. Her value as a hostage was probably the only thing keeping her alive.

Movement and cries of fear from behind her grabbed Ali's attention.

Armed men shoved forward Fatima and most of the people the two of them had sent to the old hospital.

Fatima stumbled and fell, and when Ali would have offered her hand to help the other woman up, a gunman pointed his weapon at her and shouted at her to stop and get back in Arabic.

Fatima got to her feet and spat at Akbar, calling him a murderer of children. She was too far away to hit him with it, but that didn't seem to matter.

Akbar finally did something other than stand there and stare.

He strode over to Fatima and punched her in the face, knocking her to the ground. Then he did it again, and again, and again.

Numb disbelief held Ali immobile for two entire seconds before the heat of anger and a desire to protect got her moving. She didn't get far. Two goons with guns got in the way and ordered her to stay back. The people she and Fatima had gathered cried out in shock and horror as Akbar continued to beat the woman until she stopped making sounds and her body flopped unresponsive on the ground.

When Akbar stepped back he was covered in blood spatter, his right fist and arm coated in gleaming red.

One look at Fatima told Ali that she was dead, her skull cracked and eyes open and sightless.

The other people held at gunpoint cried, or made sounds of horror and fear. When Akbar looked at them, all sound stopped.

Because he had no expression on his face. None. No disgust or victory or satisfaction. It was as if he'd stepped on an ant and was continuing on.

"Put these people in front," Akbar said, gesturing at the local survivors. He looked at Ali and smiled. "She will walk with me."

She didn't resist when one man pushed her to a spot next to Akbar as they started walking toward the old hospital.

When they were about twenty feet from the front entrance to the hospital, one of the other men with Akbar yelled out for Max to come and negotiate or he would kill all the hostages.

All was silent until Max shouted at them from inside the building. "What do you want?"

"Your surrender," Akbar yelled, bringing Ali along with one hand wrapped vicelike around her right biceps, until they stood where Max could see her. Akbar hid mostly behind her, denying a clear shot to anyone inside the building who might have a sniper rifle handy.

For a moment, Max said nothing, then he shouted, "Are you behind this flu outbreak?"

"I'm the wrath of God. I made it lethal. I made it a weapon to kill my enemies in large numbers. That's how I sign my work, through the number of bodies it leaves behind."

"Killing people isn't an art project, it's murder. The scale you seem to be seeking is called extermination."

Akbar smiled again and this time it wasn't just cold, it was coldly satisfied. "I knew you would understand my message, Max."

"So, why haven't you blown me up with that grenade launcher I see behind you?"

*Grenade launcher?*

She whipped her head around and saw the weapon, times two. Shit, he had two of the fucking things.

Max's question jerked her mind out of the deep freeze it had been in and made her think. Did Akbar need Max alive for a reason beyond someone to taunt?

"Put on a pot of tea and let's talk about that."

*Tea?*

Akbar was crazy.

That didn't make him any less dangerous. *Think, Stone, think.* What would a nutcase like Akbar want with Max?

"I have your special friend, Sergeant Stone." He gave her a shake, as if she were a doll he could throw around. She didn't resist. If he thought being female made her weak and not a threat, good. It was a mistake she'd ensure he'd regret.

"I promise, if you cooperate, no harm will come to her."

That's what Akbar wanted. Max's cooperation, but for what?

# TWENTY-EIGHT

"SON OF A BITCH," Max said under his breath, his hands wrapped around the butt of his Beretta just like they were supposed to be. Just like Ali had taught him.

Akbar had her, was jerking her around like she was a *thing* he could use to bring Max to heel.

"He wants to come in here and drink tea?" Hunt asked, incredulous. "He's fucking nuts."

"Yes, he is," Max agreed. "That makes him even more dangerous."

Hunt turned to stare at him. "You're not considering it, are you? Letting him in here, I mean?"

"Yes, I am."

"We need to find out what the nutcase wants," Thompson said. "We're small fry in the scheme of things."

*"Jesus,"* Hunt whispered.

"Is that a complaint?" Max asked him.

"It's a prayer, because I know you're going to say yes."

"Feel free to hide a weapon or two around the building," Max said. "I'm going to keep him talking for another minute."

Hunt blinked, then nodded and disappeared into the rubble behind them.

"What about the people in here with me?" Max

shouted. "Some of them are civilians, children. Will they be unharmed?"

"Why do you have children in there?" Akbar seemed genuinely curious.

"Their parents died or were killed. There wasn't anywhere else for them to go."

Max couldn't see Akbar's face, Ali's was the one he could see clearly, but Akbar's hesitation was the only sign so far that the man had any empathy left in him at all.

"Keep them out of the way and they won't be harmed," Akbar said after a few seconds. "Any soldiers with you must disarm now or they will be killed. If they try to fight, they'll be killed, but not before one of the children is killed in front of them first."

So much for empathy.

The ultimatum was enough to make Max sick. His fists clenched so tight the joints were white against his skin.

The soldiers around him swore, turning the air blue.

"He's not sane," Max said to the men around him. "He's exhibiting psychopathic behavior, which means he'll have no hesitation in hurting or killing anyone, and no guilt afterward. If you provoke him, he will kill you first and not bother with questions."

"Sounds like he'll kill us anyway," Hunt said.

"No." Max thought about it. "He wants something or he wouldn't be here looking for my surrender."

"What does he want?"

"I have no idea, though…" He thought back to Dr. Sophia Perry's clash with Akbar. "He might want my professional expertise in some way. He tried to force one of my doctors to genetically alter a rabies virus into a superbug."

"Did she?" Hunt asked.

"No, she blew up her lab instead. Nearly blew up Akbar too."

Hunt grunted. "Too bad she missed."

"So, as soon as you're of no use to him, we'll all die—is that what you're saying?" Thompson asked.

"In this plan-for-the-worst-hope-for-anything-better situation, yes."

*"Fuck."*

"What is your decision, Max?" Akbar called out.

"I agree to surrender. My men, as well," Max shouted at the madman. "How do you want to do this?"

"You come out first, walk ten feet, then disarm. After you've been searched by my men, you may join me and your men may come out one at a time."

"Fine. I'm coming out." Max followed his words with actions, leaving the safety of the building. He stopped approximately ten feet out and set his Beretta on the ground. He put his survival knife there too. Then he stood and walked toward Akbar with his hands in the air.

A militant came toward him, searched him thoroughly, then frog-marched him to stand by Akbar, not quite close enough to touch.

Akbar had his right hand wrapped around Ali's arm and a handgun in his left.

Max looked her over, but didn't see any new evidence of abuse or mistreatment.

"I have not hurt the woman," Akbar said. "Nor will I, unless you provoke it." He smiled. "Thank you for surrendering. You've saved me a great deal of money."

"You put the bounty on me?"

"Of course. I had to keep you busy while I created my masterpiece."

Whatever sanity Akbar had retained after the death of his family, it was all gone now.

Hunt came out of the building and was searched, followed by Thompson, Jessup, Tom, Warren and Holland.

"I had heard she was a fierce fighter."

Max watched Akbar tighten his grip on Ali's arm. The bastard was going to leave bruises.

"She's the best shot I've ever seen," Max said softly. "And she teaches some hand-to-hand to soldiers in training, but this..." He looked around. "This isn't training."

"Women," Akbar said, disdain coating every word, "are better suited to intellectual and family pursuits." He smiled faintly. "Dr. Perry surprised me when she blew up her lab. I hadn't expected that."

There was an underlying tone of curiosity in Akbar's voice that finally gave Max something to work with, something to distract him from Ali's deadly threat. "I was furious when I found out what she had done," he said, shaking his head. "Her reason for doing it only made me madder."

Akbar tilted his head to one side and leaned slightly toward Max. "What was the reason?"

*Oh, yes, he really wanted to know.*

"You attempted to use emotional blackmail to get what you wanted from her. Fear isn't a good motivator to someone who's as pragmatic as she is. She has little patience for that sort of emotional outburst."

Akbar stared at Max, unblinking for several seconds before saying, "I almost wish she was here rather than you."

Max shrugged. "She'd just blow something else up."

Akbar's stare finally left him and the terrorist glanced at the line of Special Forces soldiers kneeling with their hands behind their heads.

"There are only six of them," Akbar said. "There should be more."

"One of the men died of the flu last night," Mac explained. "Others died of injuries sustained in a fire-fight."

"Where are their bodies?"

"Inside, wrapped up."

Akbar's dead eyes didn't flicker or flinch. "Show me."

Max led the way into the old hospital. Akbar followed, his grip on Ali's arm unchanged. Several armed militants came with them, and the rest stayed outside to guard the Special Forces soldiers.

Max took them to the room with the bodies. Akbar's men unwrapped the dead with little care.

Akbar ignored Nolan's bloody cadaver and leaned down to examine Bull. "Symptoms before death?"

"Cough and fever. He complained of shortness of breath, took a couple of cold pills and went to sleep. He never woke up."

Akbar looked down Bull's shirt. "You didn't autopsy him?"

"I didn't deem it necessary. We'd already seen enough dead bodies to know what killed him."

"And that is?"

"A cytokine storm. An overreaction of the body's own immune system to the presence of the virus in the lung tissue."

Akbar stepped away from the body and faced Max. "How infectious is the disease?"

"Why are you asking me questions to which you already know the answers?"

"One never knows how an infection is going to behave once it's out in the world. Twice now, my weapons have not performed the way I would have liked. What is it you Americans say? Third time's the charm?"

"What do you want from me, other than a pathologist's report?"

"Where is your field lab?"

Max had never wanted to kill another human being, until now. Whatever had happened to Akbar when his family died had destroyed the human in him and left only an animal. A cunning animal. One he had to treat with extreme caution, because he still didn't know what Akbar really wanted from him.

"This way." Max indicated that they had to leave the room, and walked out first. His lab wasn't far, just a short walk down the hallway and into the operating room he'd taken over.

Akbar stepped through the doorway, looked around slowly, then released Ali, shoving her at one of the armed men with them.

He examined the workspace Max had set up, taking his time, but touching nothing. When he got to the package they'd received only hours before, he asked, "What's this?"

"Supplies."

Akbar glanced at Max, then walked over and calmly slapped Ali hard enough to knock her to the floor.

*Stay down, stay down.*

Akbar stood over her like he was preparing to do more harm. "Don't make me ask again."

*Shit.*

"Syringes, stabilizing agent and the current influenza vaccines for North America and Asia."

"You believe the current vaccine provides some protection?"

"I don't know. The man who died had been vaccinated, but he's the only one so far. None of the people in this village had been vaccinated, so I felt it was worth trying."

"You wanted to vaccinate the local people?"

"Yes."

"When did you do this?"

"I haven't yet. I'd sent out Stone and a local woman to find healthy people who were willing to be vaccinated."

"Test subjects, Max?" Akbar asked with a raised eyebrow. "I thought you condemned such actions?"

"Not test subjects like when you tested your anthrax on that unknowing village in Afghanistan," Max said with some heat. "These people will be fully informed and I'll only vaccinate those who agree to it."

Akbar watched him as if he were a bug he wanted to step on. "They will not be vaccinated at all."

*Son of a bitch.*

"What do you plan on doing with them?"

"Nothing." Akbar sounded like a benevolent leader. "Since so many people here have died, I'm sending some to a nearby town and others to the city."

His plan was so simple, it would probably work. "You want them to spread the disease."

Akbar's response was a sneer. "Disease has always

been part of the human condition. I'm simply allowing it to purge the weak from the strong."

"Is that what you say to the militants who've been helping you? Funding you?"

"The truth is a powerful thing."

"Your truth."

"Everyone's truth."

"No, yours is tainted by tragedy, and you won't be satisfied until the whole world suffers with you."

Akbar turned away, his hands curling into tight fists. He looked at the package again and Max could almost hear the gears in his head turning. "Tell me about this stabilizing agent."

Back to the questions and answers. He glanced at Stone, but she was looking at the floor, giving an amazing performance as a defeated female, helpless and hopeless. Akbar wouldn't hesitate to brutalize her again to get what he wanted. "I'm attempting to create a vaccine from samples of the virus. I can't do that without a stabilizing agent."

"How far into the process of creating a vaccine are you?"

"I've just begun. I injected the virus into those eggs a few hours ago, but they need another twenty-four hours to incubate before I can harvest any of it."

"Very good, Max. Very, very good. How many doses will these eggs make?"

"Two or three."

"That's all?"

"It's the same method the pharmaceutical companies have used for years to produce their yearly flu vaccine."

"Is this your first batch?"

If he was going to lie, it had to be convincing. "No.

My first batch didn't produce enough for even one dose. I didn't let them incubate long enough."

Akbar stared at the eggs for several moments before saying, "I wish to see this process. I will have more eggs collected."

"Didn't you use a process like this to produce the virus you wanted?" Max asked. How the hell had he done it otherwise?

Akbar didn't answer him. He turned to one of his men. "Collect several dozen eggs." The man left the room.

"What is your estimated fatality rate of the flu?" Akbar asked him.

A hard knot formed in the pit of Max's stomach. Akbar wasn't having a conversation with him. There was no give and take, no exchange of information.

Akbar was interrogating him, violence a vibrating threat in his posture and clenched fists.

"I don't know. People have been dying too fast for me to get any real numbers. I don't even know how many people lived here to begin with. The refugee camp shot any estimates to hell."

That wasn't the answer Akbar wanted either. "An estimate, Max."

Max scowled, uncaring if Akbar got angry with him. "My very unscientific fatality rate estimate is between thirty and forty percent." An idea occurred to him and he spoke before he could censor himself. "How did you introduce the virus to this place? And when?"

Akbar's reptilian gaze was unwavering. "You think you can discover a way to beat me, to combat this virus and save the world?" He shook his head and walked casually over until he was standing next to Stone where she still sat on the floor. "You can't stop the spread of this disease. You can't save yourself or anyone else. This virus will finally bring about justice. For me, my dead wife and children, and every man who agrees that the Western powers, the United States, need to be shown that they are as powerless as we are."

Max could feel the blood leaving his face. "Why? Killing more people won't bring your family back."

Akbar sneered. "If we aren't safe from grenades, rockets, hunger and disease, neither are you."

# TWENTY-NINE

ALI STARED AT the floor as she listened to Akbar grill Max, careful to remain motionless. Catching the attention of a man without a conscience could be deadly. She just hoped Max was aware of the tightrope he was walking in his conversation.

"But this virus won't just kill Americans—it'll kill people in every country, everywhere in the world."

"Where were those people, those countries, when my family died? No one stepped forward to stop you from interfering in the affairs of others, in countries you had no business invading." He paced away, then back again, crowding Ali, almost kicking her. "Your leaders lie to you and what do you do? Nothing. *Nothing.*"

"What happened to your family was a horrible mistake," Max told him hoarsely. "Killing a third of the world's population won't bring them back."

"The world will suffer as I have suffered, and when it's over everyone left alive will know my name and the names of my wife and children."

It was an almost unimaginably appalling legacy, and this time, it might just work.

Akbar walked over to Max until they were only a few inches apart. "You are powerless to save anyone."

"Then I have no reason to cooperate with you."

Akbar laughed, and it sent a shiver of fear down

Ali's spine. "Don't you?" He strode over to her and she braced herself for the violence to come.

Akbar grabbed her by the back of the neck and yanked her up to her feet, displaying a strength that wasn't obvious in his slight stature. He shook her hard, her teeth rattling, and squeezed her neck, cutting off the flow of blood to her head. The pain was enough to make her whimper, and she had to force herself to not fight him.

She could've gotten out of his hold a dozen ways, killed him with a dozen more, and might have been able to incapacitate one or two of his armed men before the others shot her, but that would get her and Max killed.

Max needed her alive.

So she hung, stiff but not fighting, in Akbar's grip.

"You will follow my orders or I will kill this woman, your soldiers and the civilians you've brought here under your protection, one at a time in front of you."

For a moment the only sound Ali could hear was Max's breathing, deep and fast.

"What do you want me to do?" The words came out of Max's mouth broken. She wanted to beg him to stay strong and not give in.

"Show me how you create a vaccine."

"Fine, fine," Max said, his voice cracking. "Let her go. She's helping me with the work."

Akbar dropped Ali, and she let her body flop onto the floor like she had nothing left.

"She will stay in this room, under guard. Do you require anything besides the eggs?"

Ali tilted her head so she could see Max's face out of the corner of her eye. His face was pale, his eyes dark with strain.

"I have everything else."

"Prepare the materials. I'll be back in a few minutes." Akbar paused in the doorway. "If either of you attempts something heroic, these men will kill you." He left.

Max swallowed hard and approached the counter. He stared at it unblinking for a moment, then said to her in an undertone, "Are you okay, Ali?"

"Yes, sir," she replied. "My neck is sore, but I'm able to help. What do you want me to do?"

"Could you help me unpack the supplies we just got? I need to sort through it for more syringes and stabilizing agent." He showed her what the agent looked like. A glass bottle with a blue cap, containing about half a cup of clear fluid. The syringes were small, only two milliliters in capacity.

There were other things packed into the Styrofoam package. Vials of flu vaccine, alcohol wipes, one hundred doses of an antiviral medication that was widely available in the United States but hard to get in this part of the world, a sharps container for used needles, miscellaneous first aid supplies and a few MREs.

They had a couple of goons watching them, but could they hide some of this stuff?

Akbar strode into the room again. He came over and looked at the supplies, picking up a vial of the vaccine and a box of the antiviral medication.

He grabbed all of the vaccine and left with it. A few seconds later he came back for the medication and left with that too. He was gone a lot longer this time. Long enough for Max to complete his preparations before needing the eggs.

They sat down on the floor to wait.

"What did he do with the vaccine?" she asked softly.

"I suspect he destroyed it."

"Threw it in the fire."

"The medication, he might actually keep for his own use or for some of his men."

"Max," she began. "What does he want?"

"I think he wants to understand how dangerous this flu is. Perhaps he stumbled on it and now needs to know how to reproduce it."

"How can he fool around with something this deadly and not know what he's doing?"

"He's a chemist. He knows enough to get the job done."

"But the job is done, isn't it? He's got his killer pathogen. If he's achieved his goal, why does he need to understand it better?"

Max didn't respond right away. "I don't know." And that made him look worried.

"You can't show him."

Max shook his head. "It doesn't matter if I show him or not. He's already got the virus."

"If he had control of it, he wouldn't need to know how to grow more of it. You can't show him."

"He'll kill you, those kids, our men, everyone."

"No, he won't. He needs enough people alive who have the virus or carry the virus, so he can spread it faster."

"He will kill someone." Max stared at her, his gaze heavy. "He'll kill you."

"It's a risk, but it's one I'm willing to take. You *can't* show him."

"Can't show me what?"

Akbar walked into the room with two more armed

men. He grabbed her by the neck again and pulled her away from Max. "Continue with the vaccine."

Max injected the eggs with virus and set the timer. "In about forty-eight hours the virus will have multiplied and can be extracted by syringe."

"What is the next step?"

"Mix it with the stabilizing agent."

"Excellent." Akbar told one of his men to take the inoculated eggs. "Thank you. I don't need you anymore. Any of you." His smile was grotesque in its anticipation. He dropped Ali and walked up to Max until there were just inches separating them. "You are...disposable."

He began giving orders in Arabic, telling his men to destroy everything in the building and kill everyone. He wanted Max to watch while his men raped Ali and gelded Max. Then they were to kill everyone else in front of Max, killing him last.

"It's very satisfying to know you're dead," Akbar said to Max. He nodded at his men and left.

Two of the men grabbed Ali by her arms and dragged her across the room from Max, their intentions clear from the eager expressions on their faces.

Anger swept through her, a firestorm that cleared her head of conspiracies and petty worries and dumped rocket fuel into her bloodstream.

Max bellowed, then launched himself off the floor. He'd covered more than half the distance between him and the men holding her when a gunshot reverberated through the room. Max fell to the floor, blood turning his left pant leg dark and wet.

*That's it, you're done.*

Her mind shut down everything but the warrior she was at her core.

The two men who thought they were about to have some fun had her by her arms, one on each side. They'd slung their rifles onto their backs when they took her.

Big mistake.

She threw her weight up and twisted, hitting one man in the chin with her leg while grabbing the other man by his shirt and yanking his head down so she could knee his temple.

Their grips loosened and she twisted again, thrusting out with open palms. She was free.

But not safe.

She struck the closest one with a punch to the temple and he went down. The other man was bringing around his rifle as he staggered to his feet. She moved in close, kneed him in the kidney, stepped around grabbed his head and twisted hard.

The snap of his neck seemed louder than a gunshot.

The other man yelled as his hands scrabbled for his weapon, leaving him open to a throat strike. She hit his Adam's apple with a sickening crunch and he abandoned his rifle to clutch at his throat.

She took the weapon and turned, slamming the butt of the weapon down on the back of the neck of one of the men now trying to hold down Max.

He collapsed, freeing one of Max's arms.

Max punched the other man in the face, just like she'd taught him, with the heel of his hand in an upward strike against the other man's nose.

The militant fell backward, his eyes wide and sightless.

Max stared up at her, his gaze wild. "Ali?"

"I'm okay, I'm okay." She looked at his leg. "But you're not."

His hands grasped at her shoulders. "They didn't… Didn't…"

"All they did was die," she said. "Just like these two."

Max jerked to look at the man he killed and the one she'd taken out. "I…killed him." His hands were shaking.

"Yes, and I killed three of them, so don't freak out on me." She knelt next to him and tried to find the bullet wound. "Where did you get hit?"

"What?" He glanced down at his leg, a frown on his face, and blinked. "Oh."

"Not feeling it yet?"

He shook his head, his frown deepening.

"Adrenaline will do that sometimes. Don't worry about it—it'll start hurting soon."

"How reassuring."

Now *that* was her Max.

She grabbed a rifle and put it in his hands. "Watch the door while I bandage you up."

He didn't say anything—he didn't have to—his hands putting the rifle into position as competently as hers would have done.

*Hot damn that was sexy.*

She found wound pads and bandages in the pile of supplies Akbar wanted to destroy. "Now, where are you?" she muttered as she found the hole in his pants and tore open the fabric.

The wound was in his thigh and was bleeding freely, but not so fast as to make her suspect an artery had been hit. She slapped the pads on the entry and exit wounds, then wound the bandage around them to keep them in place and add pressure to stop the bleeding.

He was okay. He'd been shot, but he was focused and

ready to go. There was no reason to panic, yet all she
wanted to do was hold him.

Max grunted once, but didn't take his attention off
the doorway.

When she was done, she picked up one of the other
rifles, inhaled a calming breath and asked Max, "Got
a plan?"

"Wait for the next bunch of militants to show up with
people they're going to shoot?" It sounded sarcastic, but
she gave it serious thought.

"I don't think we have that kind of time," she said
after considering it. "We need to get our guys out of
jail and armed if we hope to stop that bag of dicks."

"Suggestions?"

"Walk up like we're in charge and kill the bad guys."

"How refreshingly direct."

"Got a better idea?"

"No."

"Then let's go. I'll take point."

"If I argue you're going to complain, right?"

"No, I'm just not going to follow that order."

He looked like he was going to argue anyway, so
she added, "By the way, I loved how you kicked ass
just now."

"You…approve?"

"Approve? You delivered a textbook punch that killed
your assailant. Boom. I'm so proud it's disgusting."

Max shook his head. "I don't understand you, not
even a little."

"That's okay, you don't have to." She loved him, but
it was obvious he was having trouble with her rational-
izing the lives they'd taken.

So, she tucked away the sadness of that realization, smiled and asked, "Ready?"

"What exactly are we going to do?"

"We're going to fake it 'til we make it."

"Oh. That."

She grinned. She didn't like his sarcasm, she loved it.

They left the room and walked the short distance to the room where the children had been sleeping. It was empty.

"They took the children?"

Max's voice was rough when he said, "They're going to use them as carriers of the flu, send them to populated areas. We have to get to them first."

# THIRTY

Max STARED AT ALI, hoping she had a plan that would end with them alive and free and Akbar dead.

"Let's get to it."

Not the answer he was looking for. "With what, pretend bullets?"

She was insufferably calm. "No, Hunt stashed a couple of weapons." She pulled a pile of debris aside in one corner and handed him a rifle. "We're going to distract and disarm."

"I thought you preferred a more permanent solution."

"We need to know where Akbar is going to send, or has sent, the infected."

"He has a lot of men. We need a big distraction."

"We could blow the place up," Ali suggested. "Isn't that what Dr. Perry did?"

"She wasn't trying to distract anyone. She was trying to deny Akbar access to her work." Max grimaced. "We'd probably kill ourselves."

She shrugged. "At least we'll go big."

"If the entrance is abandoned we'll make contact with the general and get the whole area quarantined. If there's someone guarding it…" Max looked at her. "What if you pretend you're sick, dying, and I bring you out, make a lot of noise, get you close enough to do some damage?"

"Okay, let's go take a look."

They worked their way quietly toward the front of the building and discovered several armed men talking in a group. Just past them, outside, the Special Forces soldiers still knelt on the ground with their hands behind their heads.

Ali let loose some colorful language. "How do you want to do this?"

He considered her for a moment, then said, "Me Tarzan, you Jane."

She raised a brow and stepped toward him, her arms reaching for him. "You're crazy, you know that?"

He picked her up, one arm under her knees, the other behind her back. "Cough a little, would you?"

She wilted and her coughing became hoarse and wet sounding, like she really couldn't draw in a good breath.

He purposefully allowed his own breathing to speed up, like he was barely managing to carry her weight, but she wasn't heavy at all.

How could such a tiny, curvy woman wreak the havoc that she did? Holding her like this made her seem fragile, breakable. She was nothing of the sort. She was a tornado touching ground.

It went against his every instinct to carry her into the fight like a husband carries his bride over the threshold, but she'd have his hide if he didn't respect her skills and use her like the weapon she was.

He was in love, not an idiot.

His stride faltered as the word registered.

The situation was even worse than he'd thought.

No time to change anything, he'd been spotted by an armed man, so he staggered into the dirtiest reception area on the planet, huffing and puffing.

"She's got the flu," he moaned in Arabic. "She's

dying." Max made sure to cough deep in his chest where it would sound like he was sick too. "Where's Akbar?"

The men pointed their weapons at them and took at least one step backward.

"I need the medicine he took. She'll die without it."

There were six. Four of them stared at him with growing horror, but two glanced at each other.

So, not all of them knew Akbar's plans. He took a step forward.

One of the men said in Arabic, "Stay back. Take her away."

"She needs medicine," he moaned again.

"Take her away or we'll shoot you both," the same man said again. He was a little bigger than the rest, but not one of the two who'd reacted to his mention of medicine.

One of those two stepped forward and whispered something in the self-appointed leader's ear.

He froze for a moment, then his expression changed to one of practiced indifference. "Go. Take her back there." He pointed into the hospital.

Max turned slightly, as if complying with the order, then let the arm under Ali's knees drop as he pretended to stumble on some unseen thing on the floor.

Ali slipped out of his hold and lunged at the leader.

She had him down in the next three seconds and was working on taking down two more when Max joined her. He didn't try to make it fancy or even fair. They would kill his Ali if they could, so he wouldn't let them.

He crashed through them like a linebacker, using his body to knock them off their feet. Shots went off, but he didn't feel anything hit him, so he elbowed and kneed his way out of the tangle of limbs.

A rifle muzzle was pointed at him. Before it could go off, he grabbed the barrel, pulled it hard past his ear, then shoved the butt into the face of the man holding it. That stunned the militant long enough for Max to twist the weapon out of his enemy's hands and into his own.

The boom of another shot rang hard on the other side of his head. Instinct had him ducking away, just in time for another one. Who was doing the shooting? He couldn't tell who'd taken the shots.

A woman screamed and everything inside Max came to an abrupt halt.

Ali?

Where was she? He searched, stumbling over the legs of a man who lay unmoving on the floor, but she wasn't anywhere he looked.

More shots rang through the room, each one seeming to come from farther and farther away. There was a confusing mass of bodies, limbs and weapons filling his vision, but he couldn't see Alicia anywhere.

More men suddenly piled into the room through the windows. They looked familiar, but hazy, as if someone had put a pane of warped glass between him and the rest of the world.

He couldn't get that scream out of his head.

A surge of gunfire rocketed through the room and seemed to echo inside his head for minutes, hours.

His sight narrowed and went dark, and for a moment, all he knew was the sound of his own breathing, then…nothing at all.

THE WORLD CAME back in a hazy gray. At first Max thought he was dreaming, but his head and body hurt so bad it couldn't be a dream.

Things came into better focus after a few seconds, but what he saw made no sense.

Bodies, several of them. Adult men covered in blood were piled around him. Local people, from their dress. Smoke curled around the room. A room with windows empty of glass.

A crash from deeper inside the building fractured the eerie silence, then more smoke billowed out in a dark wave and threatened to suck everything in.

Memory returned in bursts.

Ali, the children, a confusing fight.

Up, he needed to get *up*.

Max put his hand down on the dirty floor to push into a sitting position and looked down at himself. He was covered in blood. His left side hurt and he had a horrible headache.

He wiped his face with one hand and it came away smeared with blood. His injuries would have to wait. The smoke was becoming denser with every second.

He struggled to his feet, but was immediately driven back to his knees by an intense wave of dizziness. He'd suffered some kind of head wound, and between that and the smoke, walking was out. He crawled toward the door leading outside.

When he crossed the threshold, he found more bodies. He recognized three of them as Special Forces soldiers. The rest were part of the group of men Akbar brought with him.

The madman's name triggered a rush of memory. Akbar holding Alicia's arm and pointing a gun at her head. Akbar demanding information on the flu virus. Akbar ordering Ali to be raped and Max gelded.

Where was Akbar now?

Where was Alicia?

He turned and scanned the bodies inside the building, but she wasn't there. She wasn't one of the bodies in front of the building either.

He attempted to get to his feet again, but was forced down by extreme dizziness. He wasn't going to find her crawling on the ground. He needed to get *up*.

Movement at the corner of his vision grabbed his attention and he lifted his head to see the two little boys Alicia had saved running toward him.

They reached him and their small hands tugged on his clothing.

"Hurry, hurry," they said in Arabic. "We must run!"

He glanced at the building behind him. Flames had burned a hole in the roof and were dancing in the empty windows.

All his equipment…gone.

His people…gone.

"Where is Ali?" he asked the boys, holding on to them like they were his lifelines.

"The bad man took her and the others away. We snuck out." Coban put his hand on Max's head. It came away bloody. "You're bleeding."

Max looked at the bodies on the ground. He shuffled over to grab a rifle from one and a scarf from another.

"I need a mirror," Max told the boys. "Help me find one in one of these houses."

Coban stayed with Max, helping him to stand, while Berez ran ahead to the nearest house and went inside.

Max's head hurt so much he had to breathe through his mouth to keep from vomiting. He had acquired a concussion at some point he couldn't remember.

As he reached the house, the younger boy came out

and waved at them to go in. There was a mirror hung on the wall a few feet inside the door.

His reflection wasn't reassuring.

His head, face and neck were coated in blood, though it was concentrated on the left side. He turned to get a better look at that side and realized there was a furrow carved out of the skin down the side of his skull.

That explained the blood on his head and his dizziness.

One of the boys tugged at his hand and held out a cup of water.

"Thank you," Max said to him then took the cup, dipped one corner of the scarf in it and began to clean some of the blood off his face. Then he used the scarf as a bandage and wrapped it around his head, tying it into place to keep fresh blood from obscuring his vision.

He checked his side next and found a hole in his clothing. Another bullet had hit him just below his hip, but it had gone through clean, leaving an exit wound that was only bleeding sluggishly.

"Can you get me another one of these?" Max asked Coban, pointing at the scarf around his head.

The boy nodded and dashed out the door.

Max went into the kitchen and found a bottle of homemade wine on the table. He drank a couple of long swigs, then took the scarf the boy brought him, folded it and tucked it into his pants so it covered the bullet wound, front and back, and applied enough pressure to hopefully stop the bleeding.

He glanced at his two junior team members. "Which direction did the bad man go?"

The boys led him back outside and they walked cautiously down the street. Behind them, the building on

fire was collapsing in on itself. The air was cool enough
that it didn't look like the flames would spread to other
houses.

There weren't many people visible, though the
sounds of crying and gunshots echoed across the valley as if the dead were fighting to stay with the living.

A familiar shout caught Max's attention. It came
from inside the village, not outside it. He turned to follow the noise and found himself on a narrow street that
led to the center of the village.

He pushed the two boys behind him as he hugged
houses to keep out of sight. When they got to the last
house between them and the spot all the noise was coming from, Max crouched down to talk to his guides.

"I want you two to find a house to hide in. Far away
from here."

They looked at each other, then at him and shook
their heads.

"I need your help," he told them very seriously. "I
need bandages and food for the sick and wounded. Can
you find some for me?"

Coban studied him with narrowed eyes, then slowly
nodded. "When I am older," he said to Max, "I will
come with you to kill the bad men."

Max smiled sadly. "When you are older, I won't stop
you."

He nodded, then grabbed his brother's hand and trotted away down the street.

Max took in a deep breath and inched his way around
the house until he could see what was happening in the
center square of the village. The home he was using as
cover had a low fenced-in area for chickens. He was

able to lie prone on the ground and peek through the wood slats.

Akbar paced in front of four people kneeling with their hands behind their heads, yelling in English at another man with what looked like a smartphone. There were seven, no…eight armed men with Akbar, including the one with the phone.

"These four soldiers have been found guilty of attacking innocent civilians and will be executed for their crimes. We will not allow others to come into our land to tell us what to do, attack us or kill us. The time for diplomacy is over. The time for action is now."

Max could see Alicia, the shortest of the four kneeling, Thompson, Hunt and Jessup, but he couldn't tell how badly they were injured. Thompson leaned increasingly to one side, as if losing a battle with consciousness.

If he didn't get them out of there in the next couple of minutes, they might not stay alive at all.

How was he going to get them out?

He wasn't a good enough shot to use the rifle he'd picked up with any hope of success. He'd either get shot himself if he broke cover, or get captured, if he didn't hurt himself while attempting to rush Akbar.

How was he going to save Ali and the men of his team?

Max thunked his head on the ground. *Idiot*.

*He* didn't have to do the saving. Alicia and the three Special Forces soldiers were more than able to save themselves. Well, maybe not Thompson who was falling over, but…all he had to do was provide them with the opportunity.

That was a job he could do.

So, what was the biggest distraction he could come up with? Something that would keep eight or nine enemy fighters busy…

He needed more than one, and he'd start with something easy.

Nolan had discovered that the bad guys were listening in on the radio. Turnabout was fair play, wasn't it?

Max worked his way back until he was behind the house, near the back door, then using a gravelly voice, proceeded to inform the medical team—himself—via a radio he'd pick up off a body that a supply drop of medical supplies and food was imminent. He repeated the radio call, then shut off his radio and slid into the house.

Not thirty seconds later three of the armed men ran past the house, heading for the valley. Thanks to all the fighting and subsequent fires, visibility outside the village wasn't that great. They'd be gone for a while.

That left five goons and Akbar.

He'd need to do something dramatic, loud and noisy this time. Should he follow in Dr. Perry's footsteps and blow something up?

No, there were too many civilians, plus his own people. He was going to have to think of something quickly, before Akbar killed the hostages he'd taken.

Ali's words came back to him.

*"Think of it like this:*

*you're not attacking anyone, you're getting them out of the way, removing them from the possibility of coming to harm."*

If he didn't remove the danger to Ali and his men, the armed men Akbar commanded were going to kill them.

He couldn't allow that to happen.

He wouldn't allow that to happen.

Swallowing hard, Max forced himself to sneak back into the fenced chicken coop. The rifle he'd picked up wasn't a great weapon, but it was all he had.

Akbar was still ranting and pacing in front of his prisoners, but each kneeling soldier had one of Akbar's men standing behind them with weapons trained on the back of their heads.

Hands shaking, Max sighted down the barrel of the rifle at the man standing behind Ali.

*Fuck.* If he didn't control the shaking, he was going to shoot her instead.

He pulled in a deep breath and focused on her. She was splattered with blood, dirt and soot, her scarf and mask had been torn away, and he could see bruises on her face.

*Bruises on her face.*

Memory punched through his brain. His mother, bruises and blood on her face, yelling at him to run. But he hadn't run. He'd tried to fight his father, tried to stop him from hurting his mother. His father punched him so many times he lost count. This was where his memory fragmented. The smell of iron and gunpowder. Disjointed flashes of pain, screaming, gunshots and blood.

His father had shot every member of the family, then himself. Max had survived. The shot to his chest had gone wide enough that it cracked two of his ribs, but did little other damage.

Handling a gun or rifle had been impossible after that. Just the metallic smell of one made his hands shake.

He hadn't been able to save his mother and sisters.

He was going to do everything necessary to give

Ali and the rest of the team the opportunity to help themselves.

He'd gone through the worst kind of trauma a child could go through, but he wasn't going to let it define him anymore, not even a little bit.

Ali's voice echoed through his head. "*Focus on your target, compensate for distance and wind, breathe in, then out and...shoot.*"

Max pulled in a breath, sighted down the barrel of his weapon at the man whose rifle was pointed at Ali's head, and let the breath out. He fired one shot. Without hesitation, he turned the weapon toward the cameraman recording Akbar and fired again.

The extremist went down.

Chaos erupted.

Ali and two of the American soldiers were on their feet and moving.

Akbar was yelling and running around, his arms flailing around like a windmill.

Two of the remaining militants began firing their weapons, but one of them was tackled by an American soldier and they went down in a tangle of arms and legs.

Max had to search for Alicia, and finally found her as she flipped a militant over onto his back, ripping his weapon out of his grasp at the same time. She turned the weapon around and shot him, then searched for her next target.

She didn't see Akbar moving toward her at a dead run. Not until it was too late.

Max fired, but the shot missed.

Akbar plowed into her, knocking her off her feet and sending her flying. She lay on the ground, stunned.

Max got to his feet and sprinted toward them, but

Akbar was up and striding toward her, menace written in every muscle of his body.

Max was going to be too late.

Just as Akbar reached for Ali, she threw something at him and he froze.

Max ran into him from the side in a move that would have looked right at home in a professional hockey game. The chemist crumpled to the ground and didn't get up.

Ali rolled to her feet and began shooting past Max's shoulder.

He got out of the way, letting her help Hunt and Jessup subdue the last of the armed militants.

As quickly as it started, the fight was over.

As he looked at the carnage he'd instigated, he shook his head. No, his fight was really just beginning.

"Max?" Ali said carefully. "Are you okay?"

"Probably not, but since I'm conscious and on my feet, I'm okay enough." He looked her over, but saw no injuries that would require his attention. "What about you?"

"I'm all right. Thompson needs medical attention, though."

"I'll take care of him," Max said. He should move, get right to that, but he found he couldn't take a single step away from her. He needed... *Fuck it*.

He closed the distance between them and pulled her into his arms for a tight, fast hug. "Are you hurt?"

"Only a few bruises, I promise."

He nodded and released her. "Okay, now I can go to work." He released her and moved to examine Thompson. "The three guys who went to watch for the airdrop will be back at some point," he said, tossing the words over his shoulder. "Someone is going to have to disarm them, and I don't know if there are any other armed militants wandering around. I had trouble focusing…before."

"That wound on your head—" Ali began.

"Is a surface wound, nothing more," he interrupted. "I need some first aid supplies and a radio." He stopped and looked around for two seconds. "We need…" He stared at Alicia.

*Wait a minute.*

His head and side hurt, his whole body felt like a giant bruise, but no cough. No fever.

She wasn't coughing either.

"How do you feel?"

# THIRTY-ONE

ALICIA WASN'T SURE if Max was having an epiphany or an aneurysm.

"How do you feel?" he asked again.

She'd been trying not to think about how she felt.

"You're not coughing."

She frowned. "No, I'm not. I don't think I have a fever either. I hurt everywhere, but I'm not sick."

They stared at each other until Thompson groaned.

Max looked at the soldier, who was slowly regaining consciousness.

"It's too soon to know," Max said, answering the unasked question hanging between them. He turned back to Thompson, his voice low as he asked the soldier about his injuries.

Ali made eye contact with the other two men, Hunt and Jessup. "We need to clear the area, hunt down those three that took off after Max's distraction and get in touch with our brass. I think Max is going to want more supplies dropped ASAP."

"There are dead bodies all over the place, Stone," Hunt said. "We need a fucking brigade in here to clean this shit up."

"Yeah, we aren't getting any sleep anytime soon. I'll stay with Max. Can you two take care of our rabbit problem?"

"Yeah, we're on it." They waved and moved off at a walk rather than a run.

Ali didn't blame them. She moved over to begin checking the bodies for weapons and made a pile near where Max was helping Thompson get his clothes out of the way so he could check the man for broken bones.

"Max, we need help," Ali said to him.

"I heard and agree. I used a radio I picked up off one of the dead extremists, but it's no good for contacting our people. My sat phone got destroyed."

"Akbar took mine." Along with most of her weapons, knives and guns. "I'll get it."

"Is he still alive?" Max asked.

"No, I sort of killed him with a knife through the eye."

"Sort of?"

She walked over to the chemist. "Fine. He's all the way dead." She rolled the body over, pulled out her knife and began patting him down. She'd seen him stick her satellite phone inside his jacket.

She opened his coat, began patting and searching pockets. A puff of powder hit her in the face. It shocked her enough that she sucked in a breath.

She immediately began to cough convulsively.

"Ali?" Max called to her, his voice rising. "Alicia?" He got to his feet.

She put her hand out to stop him from coming closer. "Don't." She continued to cough convulsively. "Whatever it is, it's still in the air."

Max swore long and loudly as she reached back into the pocket, pulled out her sat phone and punched in some numbers.

"I'm calling my dad," she told Max, then had to yell, "Stop!" when he took a few steps toward her.

He halted, his hands clenched into fists.

"Ali?" Her father's voice barked at her from the phone.

"Dad?" she said. "We need…help."

"Report, soldier!" Her father's disciplined bark offered a comfort she'd never expected.

"Akbar is dead," she said, coughing and wheezing into the phone. "There are still armed militants not in custody. This place is ground zero for a deadly flu, so we've got sick and dead bodies all over the place." She had to stop to try to catch her breath.

"What else?"

How did he know there was more to her report?

"When I searched Akbar's body, I triggered a booby trap and got hit in the face with some kind of powdery substance."

The silence from the phone was louder than a death knell. Finally, General Stone asked, "What do you need?"

She almost laughed. Nothing could help her now. "A full brigade of soldiers, a combat support hospital and a fucking miracle."

"Tell him," Max yelled as he helped Thompson to his feet and began guiding the man farther away from Ali and Akbar's body, "to put all personnel into biohazard suits. We'll need that antibiotic cocktail I developed for Akbar's anthrax strain and enough medical and food supplies to support several hundred."

She relayed all that.

"Tell him to get the antibiotics here as fast as he can." Max's voice broke and he fell silent.

She relayed that too.

There was some noise coming over the phone, voices, yelling and a door slamming shut.

"Ali, everything is on its way. The antibiotics are going to be dropped first via drone."

"Thanks, Dad. I don't think it's going to get here in time, though."

"Are you sure the powder was anthrax?" her father asked in a subdued tone she rarely heard from him.

"Don't know," she said, coughing. "Whatever it was is making it hard to…" She stopped talking to cough and cough and cough. "Breathe," she finally got out.

"Support is on its way. Hang on, soldier."

"I will, sir." She ended the call, not wanting to make her father listen while she slowly died.

"Ali, move so you're sitting up against the well," Max ordered, his voice still broken.

"Yes, sir, Colonel, sir," she said, crawling over to the stone-and-wood well housing. "Any other orders?"

"Yes, an extra-large pepperoni with mushrooms."

"Ha, ha."

She heard footsteps. When had she closed her eyes?

Max was walking toward her, a determined expression on his face.

"Oh no you don't, Doctor," she said, pointing at him. "One of us dying of this shit is enough."

"I can't just stand by and watch you—"

"You're not standing and watching at all," she said between coughs. They weren't as body racking as they'd been a couple of minutes ago. Or maybe it was because she was so damned tired. "You need to make sure those armed men are secure and then prepare for that air drop." She smiled at him and patted the ground beneath her. "I'll be right here if you need me."

Gunfire in the distance helped to emphasize her point.

"Give me a weapon," Thompson said from where he was sitting on the ground in front of a house. "I'll keep an eye on things here."

Max rolled his eyes. She could almost hear what he was thinking... *Goddamned Special Forces soldiers.*

"Fine. Stay here and don't get up, either of you."

"It's just cracked ribs," Thompson complained.

"It's not just anything," Max snapped. "You have a concussion and several deep tissue bruises." He whipped around to stare at her. "And you," he said in a tone that allowed for no argument. "No dying while I'm gone."

"I wouldn't dream of it, sir."

He stared at her, his face a mask of anger, frustration and hopelessness. Seeing him this way hurt worse than the pain in her body. "Good," he said, but the word was almost unintelligible.

That's when she saw the tears on his face.

Her ultra-competent doctor was coming apart at his emotional seams. Before she could think of something comforting to say, he nodded at her, turned, then marched toward the valley.

"He's totally in love with you," Thompson said to her after about ten seconds.

"Don't make me shoot you, asshole," she replied. "I don't have time to hide your body before someone comes back."

"Just sayin'."

"Don't. Don't say it. He's doing a job no one else

can do and he doesn't need schoolyard gossip fucking him over."

Thompson was silent for all of two seconds. "Does he know you're in love with him too?"

She sighed, which led to a nasty coughing fit. "I'm going to find my gun, load it and fucking murder you if you don't shut up."

"No worries, Stone. I think you two are kind of cute."

"Asshole," she said, running out of energy all of a sudden. Her chest was so tight, and she'd hit her wall. Her eyes slid shut and all she heard was white noise.

SHE HAD TO fight her way back to consciousness.

At first, all she knew was Max's voice. She couldn't understand what he was saying, but she'd know his timbre and tone anywhere. She blinked heavy eyelids open, but nothing seemed familiar.

A flurry of movement at the edges of her vision caught her attention and pulled her further into the world.

There were people, lots of them, all in biohazard suits, rushing around with body bags on gurneys. A hand crossed her vision and she followed it back to her own left hand. An IV had been inserted and a tube led up to a bag of fluid, dripping its contents into her vein. Two other, smaller bags were connected to the IV tubing, also contributing to whatever was being administered to her.

A shadow crossed overhead. A tent, tall enough for a man to walk upright in, passed over her and settled around her. She wasn't sitting up against the well anymore. She was lying down on a gurney. She tried to talk, but all that came out was a painful cough that wouldn't

let go of her lungs. She rolled to the right in an attempt
find a position that would allow her to breathe easier.

Hands supported her shoulder and back until the fit
passed, then gently helped her to lie down again. Max's
face, distorted by the faceplate of a biohazard suit, hovered over her.

"Sergeant Stone, how do you feel?"

So, they weren't alone.

"I haven't really taken stock, sir." She did an internal audit, but had no good news to report. "Breathing
is difficult, chest is tight." She coughed and something
wet splattered across her face. She wiped it away with
her free hand, and it came away bloody. "And this isn't
a good sign."

"What did I say about dying?" Max demanded.
"You're not allowed to die. *Ever.*"

God, she loved him. "Honey," she said conversationally, "I don't know where you got them, but you can take
the crazy pants off now."

Instead of rolling with the joke, he paled and looked
like she'd knifed him in the heart.

"Max? I'm sorry," she said, shocked at his response.
"I promise not to die."

"She's delirious?" asked a female voice.

"No," Max replied. "She thinks she's a damn comedian."

The woman approached and nodded. "The tough
ones are like that. It's a coping mechanism for when
shit hits the fan."

"Hey, Dr. Samuels," Ali tried to say between coughs.
"Tough ones what?"

"People, soldiers, heroes," the doctor replied with a
tight smile. "Like you."

"Give her a break, Grace," Max ordered. "She's had to put up with me and my lack of soldiering skills."

"Ha," Ali managed to say clearly. "You shot at two enemy targets and hit both."

Max shook his head. "No, you're right, Grace. She is delirious."

Now who was the comedian? She wanted to ask the question out loud, but another coughing fit hijacked her body. Who knew how much longer she'd be breathing, let alone talking.

"Colonel," she said, finally able to speak after several seconds of concerted effort. "Could I speak to you privately for a moment?"

Dr. Samuels looked surprised, but she quickly moved out of view.

Max looked at her questioningly.

"I don't know how long I have, so I figured I'd better say this while I still can."

"Ali, it's okay. There's no need to give me your report."

Report? Either they weren't alone or he was trying to put off the bad news. "You are the bravest man I've ever met."

He stared at her like she'd just spoken gibberish. "What?"

"Didn't you know? Brave doesn't mean aggressive. It means putting other people before yourself, putting their safety before your own. You've never once hesitated to do that."

His mouth opened and closed a couple of times before he managed to say, "Well, some might just call me...slow."

"Tell them to talk to me. I'll set them straight." She

smiled at him, tasting far too much iron on her tongue. "I love you. I wish we could have had more time together."

His mouth did another excellent fish-out-of-water impression before he gathered his wits and growled at her. "Don't you dare give up now, you stubborn, hard-headed woman."

She almost laughed. "I'm not giving up, I'm strategically retreating."

"All retreats, surrenders and capitulations have been canceled." He leaned down and pointed a finger at her. "No exceptions."

The weight on her chest had gotten a lot heavier, pressing down, making her fight to breathe. "Promise me you'll follow your own orders, sir," she managed to say just before the heavy blanket of night closed over her head.

# THIRTY-TWO

MAX WATCHED ALICIA lose her battle with consciousness. She wasn't responding well to the antibiotic cocktail. Her labored breathing and bloody discharge worried him the most, but she'd also been badly beaten.

"I want her on a plane and back to the base as soon as possible. She may have broken bones or have a small internal bleed," he said to Dr. Samuels and the two nurses who'd entered the tent.

"Sir," one of the nurses said, "it'll take some time to get an isolation medevac prepped and here."

"As soon as possible," he said, not caring that he sounded like an inflexible asshole.

"Yes, sir." The nurse saluted and left the tent.

"Sir," Dr. Samuels said to him in a careful tone. "I took a closer look at the powder Stone breathed in under the microscope. There are anthrax spores in it, but also flour and cinnamon."

"Cinnamon?"

"It's quite irritating if you inhale it."

There could be only one conclusion. "He used it to facilitate the spores getting deeper into tissue."

"That's my fear as well," Dr. Samuels said softly. She put her hand on Max's shoulder and squeezed.

"Increase the dosage of the antibiotics and shorten the time between doses." Unconscious, Ali looked far too small to be the lethal physical threat she was. Her size and bruises made her look vulnerable and beaten.

A small hand tugged at his.

"How did you get in here?" he asked in Arabic to the boy standing next to him.

Coban stared at Ali, a huge frown on his face. "Is she going to die?"

"I'm doing everything I can to prevent that," Max told him. "Where is your brother?"

"The soldiers gave us food and he fell asleep." Coban looked up at Max. Calm, much too calm. "Father is dead. What will happen to us now?"

Max crouched in front of the boy and met his gaze. "A doctor is going to make sure you're not sick. You will have to leave this place, but we will make sure you are safe. Do you have family in another village or town?"

Dr. Samuels came back into the tent with more IV antibiotic bags. When had she left? Max shook his head. He needed to sleep too.

"I don't know," Coban said, his chin quivering.

Max pulled the boy into a hug, though the biohazard suit made it awkward. "You and Berez are going to be safe, I promise." He stood and took Coban's hand. "Let's get you back to your brother so you can sleep too."

The village looked very different than it had only an hour ago. The first air drop had happened only an hour after Max made the desperate call for antibiotics. He'd spent that hour guarding Ali and triaging the sick who'd ventured out of their homes after the gunfire stopped.

He estimated that 90 percent of the occupants of the village had become infected with the flu. A dangerously high rate. Any virus that could infect that many people in only a few days was alarmingly infectious. Any virus this contagious, with a death rate of 35 percent, could only be described as an infectious nuclear bomb.

As a result, he'd ordered the entire village and the region around it quarantined.

Four hours after his call for help, medical and security personnel began arriving. The fires were put out and a house-to-house search for survivors was undertaken. Anyone with symptoms was separated from those who appeared healthy and taken to a hastily erected tent where a combat support hospital had been set up.

Healthy survivors were taken to another tent with hot food, clean water, cots and heaters, so they could eat and sleep.

Blood samples had been taken from everyone, including Max, Alicia and the surviving members of their team. Only Max and Ali had tested negative for the flu.

Dr. Grace Samuels and Dr. Sophia Perry arrived with the medical team. Grace was overseeing the assessment and treatment of the disease, while Sophia took over the investigative side of the mission, confirming Max's determination of the virus and restarting the production of onsite vaccine. It wouldn't help Ali, but it had to be done.

As Sophia put it, why fuck with a method that's working?

His biggest concern now was Alicia and her worsening condition. They'd gotten antibiotics running into her within an hour and a half of exposure. She shouldn't be getting worse.

He and Coban reached the tent where the relatively healthy citizens of the village were being cared for. He got the boy into a cot next to his brother and tucked him in. He should tell Alicia that the boys were safe. She'd want to know.

Before he left the tent, he let himself watch the staff and villagers interact, ensuring all that needed to be done was being done.

Max nodded to the staff and returned to Ali's tent. She wasn't alone.

Sitting next to her was someone in a biohazard suit. Max recognized the man by his posture.

General Stone.

Max stood in the doorway of the tent, his stomach dropping into the very bottom of his steel-toed combat boots.

"Come in, Max." The general's voice sounded tired.

"Sir." Max hesitated, then moved to stand on the other side of the cot. "I… There's no excuse for…"

"Max," General Stone said, "I know. It's not your fault."

"Sir, with respect, bullshit."

General Stone smiled. "I see she's been a positive influence on your attitude."

"As the ranking officer, the responsibility for this clusterfuck is mine."

"Max, you came into this situation with a team of four. We sent in another dozen to help. Do you know how many militants were here?"

"Uh, no, sir."

"There were two different groups with over eighty fighters. You had bad intel, facing an insane adversary deploying an out of control biological weapon. There is only so much you can control, and my daughter has never played anything safe in her entire life."

"I appreciate that sir, but I should have anticipated that he'd booby-trap his own body."

"She'll argue she should have thought of it." General Stone cleared his throat. "What's the prognosis?"

"I wish I could say it's good, but to be honest, I don't know. She's not responding to the antibiotics as well as I'd like."

"She's a fighter."

"Yes, sir, she is."

"So are you." The general stood. "You're dead on your feet, Max. I order you to get some sleep."

He didn't want to leave Alicia, wanted to monitor her progress. But his brain just couldn't come up with a believable excuse for the general.

"Before you can protest, you can sleep here."

On cue, a biohazard-suited nurse brought in a cot and set it on the ground on the other side of the small tent.

This he could do. "Thank you, sir."

Max was so tired, there was no point in putting off. He lay down facing Alicia and closed his eyes.

MAX WOKE TO a flurry of activity.

There were several people inside the tent surrounding Alicia's cot shouting at each other.

He blinked the last of sleep away and the realization that they were performing CPR on her smashed into him.

His first reaction was to get to his feet and charge in to take over, but there were too many bodies between him and Ali. No, they didn't need him barging in when they were already doing as good a job as he could. What he could do was get out of their way.

He could see Ali's face in gaps between the first responders. Her pale skin, dark, dark circles under her eyes and the ventilator tube down her throat told him she'd gotten a lot worse very quickly.

They'd barely had any time together, but he already knew she was the best partner he could have ever asked for, professionally as well as personally. He couldn't lose her now. He *couldn't*.

Grace shouted, "Clear!" Everyone stepped back and Grace hit Ali with a jolt of electricity.

For a moment there wasn't a sound, not a cry or cough, total silence. Then a beep echoed through the tent. And another. And another.

"She's back!" Grace cried. "Let's get her ready for transport."

"Grace," Max called out.

"Max, good. You're awake. General Stone wants you on the same transport as Sergeant Stone. The base has an isolation room ready for her and you'll be decontaminated when you arrive."

He hesitated, torn by dual responsibilities. This had been his mission, his situation to resolve. He didn't want to leave the job half-finished, but he didn't want to let Ali out of his sight either. "What happened while I slept?"

"We had to put her on a respirator with one hundred percent oxygen. Her oxygen saturation got as low as sixty-two percent, but it's back up to seventy-one now."

Max glanced at the monitor and confirmed that number. "Has she coded before now?"

"No, that was the first one."

"Can you manage here without me?"

Grace's eyes smiled. "Yes. Besides, the general issued an order not a suggestion. You're supposed to stay with Ali. You're the best person we have to determine what she needs." She pushed him to follow Alicia's gurney. "Go. I'll keep you updated on things here."

Duty and desire warred within him so hard his fingertips tingled with the need to do something, *anything*. "Thank you, Grace."

"Whatever you need Max."

Max followed the transport team carrying Alicia's gurney down one of the narrow roads leading from the center of the village toward the valley. Once past the last houses, he could see a waiting medevac helicopter poised to take off, its rotors creating enough wind to make the inside of his biohazard suit sound like he was taking off in a balloon.

He waited while the team strapped Ali's gurney securely onto the bulkhead, then stepped forward when one of the combat medics grabbed him by the arm and helped him into the bird.

It took more muscle power than it should have. Then again, he was sleep deprived, hadn't eaten enough food to feed a mouse and had taken a beating. The fact was, he should've been on a gurney of his own.

He hadn't even reported his own injuries yet. Oh, the head wound had gotten looked at, cleaned and rebandaged, but the bullet wound in his side hadn't. He was going to hear about that one from someone.

Max sat at Ali's feet with a clear view of her heart and ventilator monitors. She was stable for now, and her oxygen saturation was up to eighty-eight.

He'd take any good sign there was.

He put his head back, intending to rest for just a few minutes, but when he opened his eyes, they were coming in for a landing at the base in Bahrain.

He glanced at Ali's monitors, but nothing had changed.

He got out first, then waited to one side while the team off-loaded Ali and ran her into the base. They didn't go very far. She was taken into one tent, while he was guided into another next to it.

Three people in biohazard suits were waiting for him, as was a portable decontamination shower. They literally hosed him, his biohazard suit and clothing down as he removed it. After he got his pants off, he had to peel the dirty scarf away from his side carefully to avoid causing unnecessary bleeding. One of the decontamination team looked at the wound, then made a radio call.

By the time he was declared clean there were a couple of nurses waiting to take a look.

"How old is this?" one of them asked.

"I don't know." He shrugged. "Maybe seven hours."

The nurses took him by the arms and led him toward a wheelchair.

"What is Sergeant Stone's current condition?" he asked.

"We're still evaluating her, but she's stable."

He looked at the tent she'd gone into and balked at sitting in the chair. He wanted to stay with her. "Have you moved her to the hospital already?"

"Yes, sir. The on-duty physicians want to consult as soon as you're ready."

"They'll consult now. My being ready has no bearing on Stone's treatment." He gave the two nurses his best hard-line look.

"Yes, sir."

He began giving the nurse a history of Ali's injuries and how the anthrax was introduced into her system.

They entered the hospital a minute later and Max insisted on seeing Alicia before he allowed the medical staff to put him in a treatment room so his wound could be cleaned and sewn up. They also insisted on antibiotics, which he agreed with, and at least eight hours of rest, which he completely ignored.

His head wound was actually worse than he'd thought. The bullet that grazed him hadn't just cut a furrow through his skin, but scraped off a layer of bone as well. They did an X-ray and decided there wasn't much more they could do about it than bandage it up.

They'd given Ali an MRI and thankfully she'd sustained no internal bleeding. It did reveal two broken ribs, and the extent of the damage to her lungs.

Whatever Akbar had put in the powder she breathed in caused a great deal of irritation and swelling, which meant less oxygen was reaching her bloodstream.

Max went to explain it to General Stone. "It's out of our hands now and in hers. If she can survive long enough for the antibiotics to kill off the anthrax, she's got a good chance. But her lungs aren't in good shape. The spores she inhaled along with the other ingredients of Akbar's poison have irritated the tissue enough to cause significant swelling. Fluid in the lungs. We have to give the lungs time to recover and allow the swelling to go down."

"But if her lungs are full of fluid, is she drowning?"

"As long as some oxygen is making it into her bloodstream, she'll survive. We can do some things to help. Put her on one hundred percent oxygen, medically paralyze her so her muscles don't use up any oxygen, and even give her a unit or two of packed cells to increase the number of red blood cells available—"

"You're babbling, Max," the general interrupted. "You know your job. You don't need to explain it all to me, just do it."

"I will, sir." Max paused, then squared his shoulders and said, "I'd like to formally apologize for the mission going so wrong. I'll have a report for you in a few hours and will present myself for any disciplinary action you'd like to take."

"No."

"Sir?"

"And don't mention it again, Max," General Stone said, pointing a finger at him. "Get your head back in the game. Got it?"

He didn't agree, but he wasn't the general in the room. "Yes, sir."

"Keep me informed, but don't wait for my permission if she needs some kind of medical procedure. You're the expert. I trust your judgment."

His judgment had gotten them into the situation they were in now. His judgment had failed. Max opened his mouth, but General Stone turned on his heel and left before he could make a sound.

That was just as well. What could he say that he hadn't already? General Stone had made it clear he didn't want to hear any more explanations, excuses or apologies.

Max was able to set up a sort of mobile office right outside Ali's intensive care room. Mostly a laptop computer, a cell phone and a small rolling desk. His proximity allowed him to maintain a constant watch on her condition while still writing his mission report, communicating with Dr. Samuels and Dr. Perry at the village and reviewing the mini-flu outbreak at the base in Bahrain.

The flu that had spread through the supply department like wildfire was very nearly the same virus that caused all the death and destruction at the village. Max wondered if Akbar had tried to release it first via person to person contact between the receiving staff and local suppliers of fresh fruit and vegetables. Its lack of virulence must have spurred Akbar into tinkering with it further, creating a more deadly version which he'd loosed on the refugees at the village.

Dr. Perry had done some backtracking on Akbar's movements, thanks to a couple of the militants they captured. The chemist had released his flu among his supporters, and their families had become infected. For a chance at receiving the vaccine, they were willing to confess all.

Akbar hadn't just cooked up a few deadly pathogens, he'd taught other people how to do it too. Most had caught the flu and died, but not all. Some survived and left the training camp Akbar ran in northern Syria for who knew where.

Not only was Max going to need his team of medical specialists and their Special Forces partners working harder than ever, he could see a need for soldiers who could be trained to find the people actively creating biological weapons.

There was just no other way to find all the militants Akbar had trained.

He was going to have to request more people, more supplies, more everything.

He just didn't know if he could do any of it.

He listened to Ali's ventilator thunk and hiss in its steady pattern. If she died…would he want to?

She'd given no sign of improvement. No change at all.

The current nurse on duty came out of the room and stopped in front of him. "Sir, would you mind going in and talking to her? I'd like to see if she's aware."

Max nodded and went inside. He stood next to her bed and for the first time in his career as a doctor, his ability to separate himself emotionally from a patient failed. "Ali?" he asked, his voice cracking. "The nurses want to know if you're awake. Personally, I'd pretend to be sleeping if I were you."

Next to his head the beep of her heart monitor sped up as her heartrate rose by ten, then fifteen beats per minute.

"Excellent," the nurse said. "She's reacting well to the sound of your voice. Thank you, sir."

Max nodded, but didn't follow the woman out of the room, didn't say anything at all. He couldn't. His throat was totally blocked by a lake of tears.

All because the bravest person he'd ever met in his life recognized his voice. Despite the half a dozen machines she was hooked up to, with all their beeping and white noise. Despite the drugs keeping her from losing her mind while medically paralyzed. Despite the crushing weight she had to feel sitting on her chest, preventing her from getting the air she needed, she knew him. Reacted to him. Showed him how much he mattered to her with just her heartbeat.

He stood there for a solid minute, not even breathing.

Stood there and prayed for that miracle again, because he knew only one thing.

He couldn't live without her.

He swayed and realized his knees were shaking so bad he wasn't going to be able to stand up much longer.

Fuck it. He was going sit down right here next to her bed and pray.

He sank down to his knees and leaned his forehead against the rail of the bed. "I love you," he told her. Her heartbeat sped up once more and tears rolled down his face. "I love you," he said again. "You've shown me every moment since the day I met you what courage was. I thought it meant keeping your word and causing no harm to anyone, but you've shown me real courage has to be ready to fight for what's right. I've been so afraid of fighting, afraid I wouldn't be able to think through the rage. You showed me how to stay me and still fight. I want to wake up next to you every morning for the next forty or fifty years. I want to be your partner, your friend and your lover."

He wiped the wetness away, but there was no stopping the waterfall of grief. "Fight for me, Ali. Fight for us. Don't go."

He hadn't cried since his father had destroyed their family.

Now he did.

# THIRTY-THREE

MAX WOKE TO someone shaking his arm.

"Sir? Colonel Maximillian, sir?"

He looked up into the masked face of a nurse he didn't recognize. "Yes? What is it?" He sat up and realized he'd fallen asleep on the floor in Alicia's intensive care room. "How is Ali?"

"Her oxygen saturation started to go up about twenty minutes ago. It's at ninety right now… Wait, it went up again to ninety-one."

Max got to his feet and looked at all the monitors. He put his stethoscope in his ears and listened to her lungs. They sounded less congested. "Can we get X-ray in here to do some chest pictures? I want to see if her lungs have cleared at all."

"Yes, sir."

They'd done a chest X-ray only eight hours ago. It was probably going to look the same, white lungs instead of ghostly, but increasing oxygen saturation was a good sign.

The tech came, took the chest X-rays then came back with the films. Max stared at them, shock holding him frozen for several seconds.

Her lungs were clear.

They'd been completely congested, a solid white on the films only eight hours ago. "How is this possible?" he whispered to himself.

"She's a fighter," one of the nurses said behind him.

Exactly what General Stone said ten minutes later when Max gave him the news.

"She's a stubborn thing, my daughter." The general patted Max on the shoulder. "I told you she'd pull through."

"She's remarkable." Max didn't care that he sounded as far from detached as a man could get.

The general grunted, shook his head and left.

The miracle of Ali's recovery didn't stop. The swelling in her lungs disappeared so fast they were able to take her off the ventilator for good two days later. She had trouble talking due to the tube that had been down her throat. It had irritated her vocal cords, but she was able to make her needs known.

She slept a lot, sometimes falling asleep in the middle of trying to explain what she wanted. But her recovery continued to amaze everyone.

Max found himself in the role of her doctor with little time for more.

Finally, a week after she'd killed Akbar, Max went into her room to find her sitting up, alert and waiting for him.

He stopped cold in the doorway. He had so much to tell her, but had no idea where to start.

"Hey," she whispered. "Don't rush off. I want to talk to you."

"Okay." He could do this, had been waiting for this chance to tell her how he felt.

Damn if he could even open his mouth.

She stared at him for a long time before saying, "I seem to be missing a few days." She tapped her temple with one finger. "I remember dreaming, though."

"That's not uncommon with patients who've been as sick as you have been."

"Do you know what I dreamed?"

Max waited. This was important for her recovery. Important for her to make sense of what had happened to her, and what hadn't.

"You told me you loved me. I dreamed a wedding and a baby girl."

"Oh," he said. His throat closed up.

"I'm not sure it was all a dream," she told him. "Do you know anything about that?"

He cleared his throat. "How would I know anything about your dreams?" When her brows went up he hastily added, "Though they sound very nice."

"Nice," she repeated, then rolled her eyes. "Did I dream you saying you love me?"

He swallowed, then took all of his courage in both hands and answered with the truth. "No. You didn't dream it. I love you."

"Was that so hard to say?" She didn't wait for an answer. "Idiot. I love you too." She paused. "What about the wedding?"

"That never got mentioned, but do you..." He hesitated, then decided that since he was being courageous he might as well go all the way. "Want one? With me?"

She shook her head and smiled. "Only ever with you." She held out her hand to him and he strode over to take it, kissing her palm.

Relief coursed through him like a river bursting a dam. "I never talked about a little girl, but it just so happens that there are two little boys who need a family, a home. Two little boys who are determined to take care of you the way you took care of them."

"Berez and Coban? They're okay?" Joy dawned on her face. "Could we…?"

"There's a lot of red tape to adopting, but given the circumstances, I think we could make it happen. It's a lot to take on. We'd be going from single to a family with two kids."

Her mouth opened and closed a couple of times before she managed to say, "It sounds wonderful. I thought I knew what courage was until I saw you come to my rescue," she said, her smile so deep and happy he felt ten feet taller.

"You showed me what it was," he countered. "You had faith in me even when I was certain I couldn't do it."

"That's because you're the best man I know. I knew you could do it. So…" She tilted her head to one side. "What's a girl got to do to get out of this place?"

"Hmm, would you agree to some very private nursing by a relieved and grateful doctor?"

"If he's as sexy as you, I think I could see my way to allowing it."

"Then I'm happy to break you out of here," Max said as he leaned over and kissed her. He pulled back after a couple of moments and cupped her face with one hand. "I thought I'd lost you, just when I figured out how much I loved you, needed you, wanted to be with you."

"That's how I felt when Akbar pulled me out of that broken building and left you to die inside. It took three of them to drag me away, and they had to beat the shit out of me to do it."

"I'll talk to your father about resigning my commission," Max began, but she put a quivering finger over his mouth.

"No, it's time for me to make a change. There are

many people who can take my place in training the teams. I'm going to go private and be your very, *very*, personal bodyguard."

"Are you sure? Your job has been important to you for a long time."

"*We're* more important. Besides, I think your job is only going to get more interesting, and someone has to keep you out of trouble."

That sounded perfect. Max smiled at her. "Yes, ma'am."

# EPILOGUE

GENERAL STONE STOOD outside his daughter's hospital room listening to her and his soon-to-be son-in-law fuss over each other.

One less thing to worry about.

He'd seen this coming long before either of them had. Max was already a friend, and now he was family.

He was going to be a grandfather to two little boys. Bonus.

The future looked a lot brighter now than it had an hour ago when he got the latest report from Dr. Perry and her Special Forces partner, and fiancé, Weapons Sergeant Connor Button. As near as they could figure, Akbar had trained no less than a dozen people in his low-tech version of biological weapons creation.

Seven of them were dead, most from the flu.

That left five very dangerous extremists loose in the world. Madmen who had the capability of creating bioweapons that could wipe out entire towns or even countries. A cell phone found on Akbar's body provided enough details to make two things clear. A traitor, someone inside the American military, had managed to warn Akbar's surviving apprentices in enough time for them to get away. And the next attack would be on American soil.

\* \* \* \* \*

# ABOUT THE AUTHOR

JULIE ROWE'S FIRST career as a medical lab technologist in Canada took her to the Northwest Territories and northern Alberta, where she still resides. She loves to include medical details in her romance novels, but admits she'll never be able to write about all her medical experiences because "Fiction has to be believable." Julie writes contemporary and historical medical romance, fun romantic suspense and military romance. Her most recent titles are *Deadly Strain*, *Lethal Game* and *Viral Justice* in the Biological Response Team series. You can find her at julieroweauthor.com, on Twitter @julieroweauthor, or at her Facebook page, Facebook.com/julieroweauthor.

# REQUEST YOUR
# FREE BOOKS!

## 2 FREE NOVELS
## FROM THE ROMANCE COLLECTION,
## PLUS 2 FREE GIFTS!

**YES!** Please send me 2 FREE novels from the Romance Collection and my 2 FREE gifts (gifts are worth about $10). After receiving them, if I don't wish to receive any more books, I can return the shipping statement marked "cancel." If I don't cancel, I will receive 4 brand-new novels every month and be billed just $6.49 per book in the U.S. or $6.99 per book in Canada. That's a savings of at least 18% off the cover price. It's quite a bargain! Shipping and handling is just 50¢ per book in the U.S. and 75¢ per book in Canada.* I understand that accepting the 2 free books and gifts places me under no obligation to buy anything. I can always return a shipment and cancel at any time. Even if I never buy another book, the two free books and gifts are mine to keep forever.

194/394 MDN GH4D

Name _____ (PLEASE PRINT) _____

Address _____ Apt. # _____

City _____ State/Prov. _____ Zip/Postal Code _____

Signature (if under 18, a parent or guardian must sign)

Mail to the **Reader Service:**
**IN U.S.A.:** P.O. Box 1867, Buffalo, NY 14240-1867
**IN CANADA:** P.O. Box 609, Fort Erie, Ontario L2A 5X3

**Want to try 2 free books from another line?**
Call 1-800-873-8635 or visit www.ReaderService.com.

*Terms and prices subject to change without notice. Prices do not include applicable taxes. Sales tax applicable in N.Y. Canadian residents will be charged applicable taxes. Offer not valid in Quebec. This offer is limited to one order per household. Not valid for current subscribers to the Romance Collection or the Romance/Suspense Collection. All orders subject to credit approval. Credit or debit balances in a customer's account(s) may be offset by any other outstanding balance owed by or to the customer. Please allow 4 to 6 weeks for delivery. Offer available while quantities last.

**Your Privacy**—The Reader Service is committed to protecting your privacy. Our Privacy Policy is available online at www.ReaderService.com or upon request from the Reader Service.

We make a portion of our mailing list available to reputable third parties that offer products we believe may interest you. If you prefer that we not exchange your name with third parties, or if you wish to clarify or modify your communication preferences, please visit us at www.ReaderService.com/consumerchoice or write to us at Reader Service Preference Service, P.O. Box 9062, Buffalo, NY 14240-9062. Include your complete name and address.

ROM15R

# REQUEST YOUR
# FREE BOOKS!

## 2 FREE NOVELS
## FROM THE SUSPENSE COLLECTION,
## PLUS 2 FREE GIFTS!

**YES!** Please send me 2 FREE novels from the Suspense Collection and my 2 FREE gifts (gifts are worth about $10). After receiving them, if I don't wish to receive any more books, I can return the shipping statement marked "cancel." If I don't cancel, I will receive 4 brand-new novels every month and be billed just $6.49 per book in the U.S. or $6.99 per book in Canada. That's a savings of at least 18% off the cover price. It's quite a bargain! Shipping and handling is just 50¢ per book in the U.S. and 75¢ per book in Canada.* I understand that accepting the 2 free books and gifts places me under no obligation to buy anything. I can always return a shipment and cancel at any time. Even if I never buy another book, the two free books and gifts are mine to keep forever.

191/391 MDN GH4Z

Name _____
(PLEASE PRINT)

Address _____ Apt. # _____

City _____ State/Prov. _____ Zip/Postal Code _____

Signature (if under 18, a parent or guardian must sign) _____

### Mail to the **Reader Service**:
**IN U.S.A.:** P.O. Box 1867, Buffalo, NY 14240-1867
**IN CANADA:** P.O. Box 609, Fort Erie, Ontario L2A 5X3

**Want to try 2 free books from another line?**
**Call 1-800-873-8635 or visit www.ReaderService.com.**

* Terms and prices subject to change without notice. Prices do not include applicable taxes. Sales tax applicable in NY. Canadian residents will be charged applicable taxes. Offer not valid in Quebec. This offer is limited to one order per household. Not valid for current subscribers to the Suspense Collection or the Romance/Suspense Collection. All orders subject to credit approval. Credit or debit balances in a customer's account(s) may be offset by any other outstanding balance owed by or to the customer. Please allow 4 to 6 weeks for delivery. Offer available while quantities last.

**Your Privacy**—The Reader Service is committed to protecting your privacy. Our Privacy Policy is available online at www.ReaderService.com or upon request from the Reader Service.

We make a portion of our mailing list available to reputable third parties that offer products we believe may interest you. If you prefer that we not exchange your name with third parties, or if you wish to clarify or modify your communication preferences, please visit us at www.ReaderService.com/consumerschoice or write to us at Reader Service Preference Service, P.O. Box 9062, Buffalo, NY 14240-9062. Include your complete name and address.

# REQUEST YOUR FREE BOOKS!
## 2 FREE NOVELS PLUS 2 FREE GIFTS!

**✦HARLEQUIN®**

# INTRIGUE

## BREATHTAKING ROMANTIC SUSPENSE

**YES!** Please send me 2 FREE Harlequin® Intrigue novels and my 2 FREE gifts (gifts are worth about $10). After receiving them, if I don't wish to receive any more books, I can return the shipping statement marked "cancel." If I don't cancel, I will receive 6 brand-new novels every month and be billed just $4.74 per book in the U.S. or $5.49 per book in Canada. That's a savings of at least 12% off the cover price! It's quite a bargain! Shipping and handling is just 50¢ per book in the U.S. and 75¢ per book in Canada.* I understand that accepting the 2 free books and gifts places me under no obligation to buy anything. I can always return a shipment and cancel at any time. Even if I never buy another book, the two free books and gifts are mine to keep forever.

182/382 HDN GH3D

Name _____ (PLEASE PRINT)

Address _____ Apt. #

City _____ State/Prov. _____ Zip/Postal Code

Signature (if under 18, a parent or guardian must sign)

Mail to the **Reader Service:**
**IN U.S.A.:** P.O. Box 1867, Buffalo, NY 14240-1867
**IN CANADA:** P.O. Box 609, Fort Erie, Ontario L2A 5X3

**Are you a subscriber to Harlequin® Intrigue books
and want to receive the larger-print edition?
Call 1-800-873-8635 or visit www.ReaderService.com.**

* Terms and prices subject to change without notice. Prices do not include applicable taxes. Sales tax applicable in N.Y. Canadian residents will be charged applicable taxes. Offer not valid in Quebec. This offer is limited to one order per household. Not valid for current subscribers to Harlequin Intrigue books. All orders subject to credit approval. Credit or debit balances in a customer's account(s) may be offset by any other outstanding balance owed by or to the customer. Please allow 4 to 6 weeks for delivery. Offer available while quantities last.

**Your Privacy**—The Reader Service is committed to protecting your privacy. Our Privacy Policy is available online at www.ReaderService.com or upon request from the Reader Service.

We make a portion of our mailing list available to reputable third parties that offer products we believe may interest you. If you prefer that we not exchange your name with third parties, or if you wish to clarify or modify your communication preferences, please visit us at www.ReaderService.com/consumerschoice or write to us at Reader Service Preference Service, P.O. Box 9062, Buffalo, NY 14240-9062. Include your complete name and address.

HII5

# REQUEST YOUR FREE BOOKS!
## 2 FREE NOVELS PLUS 2 FREE GIFTS!

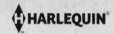

## ROMANTIC suspense

*Sparked by danger, fueled by passion*

---

**YES!** Please send me 2 FREE Harlequin® Romantic Suspense novels and my 2 FREE gifts (gifts are worth about $10). After receiving them, if I don't wish to receive any more books, I can return the shipping statement marked "cancel." If I don't cancel, I will receive 4 brand-new novels every month and be billed just $4.74 per book in the U.S. or $5.49 per book in Canada. That's a savings of at least 12% off the cover price! It's quite a bargain! Shipping and handling is just 50¢ per book in the U.S. and 75¢ per book in Canada.* I understand that accepting the 2 free books and gifts places me under no obligation to buy anything. I can always return a shipment and cancel at any time. Even if I never buy another book, the two free books and gifts are mine to keep forever.

240/340 HDN GH3P

| | |
|---|---|
| Name | (PLEASE PRINT) |

| | |
|---|---|
| Address | Apt. # |

| | | |
|---|---|---|
| City | State/Prov. | Zip/Postal Code |

Signature (if under 18, a parent or guardian must sign)

### Mail to the **Reader Service:**
**IN U.S.A.:** P.O. Box 1867, Buffalo, NY 14240-1867
**IN CANADA:** P.O. Box 609, Fort Erie, Ontario L2A 5X3

**Want to try two free books from another line?**
**Call 1-800-873-8635 or visit www.ReaderService.com.**

\* Terms and prices subject to change without notice. Prices do not include applicable taxes. Sales tax applicable in N.Y. Canadian residents will be charged applicable taxes. Offer not valid in Quebec. This offer is limited to one order per household. Not valid for current subscribers to Harlequin Romantic Suspense books. All orders subject to credit approval. Credit or debit balances in a customer's account(s) may be offset by any other outstanding balance owed by or to the customer. Please allow 4 to 6 weeks for delivery. Offer available while quantities last.

**Your Privacy**—The Reader Service is committed to protecting your privacy. Our Privacy Policy is available online at www.ReaderService.com or upon request from the Reader Service.

We make a portion of our mailing list available to reputable third parties that offer products we believe may interest you. If you prefer that we not exchange your name with third parties, or if you wish to clarify or modify your communication preferences, please visit us at www.ReaderService.com/consumerschoice or write to us at Reader Service Preference Service, P.O. Box 9062, Buffalo, NY 14240-9062. Include your complete name and address.

---

# READERSERVICE.COM

## Manage your account online!

- Review your order history
- Manage your payments
- Update your address

> ***We've designed the
> Reader Service website
> just for you.***

## Enjoy all the features!

- Discover new series available to you, and read excerpts from any series.
- Respond to mailings and special monthly offers.
- Connect with favorite authors at the blog.
- Browse the Bonus Bucks catalog and online-only exculsives.
- Share your feedback.

*Visit us at:*

# ReaderService.com